TOOTH AND NAIL

A SHIFTER'S CLAIM NOVEL

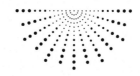

L.B. GILBERT

DISCLAIMER

This book is a work of fiction. All of the characters, names, and events portrayed in this novel are products of the author's imagination. Any resemblance to actual events or persons, living or dead, is entirely coincidental.

This eBook is licensed for your personal enjoyment only and may not be re-sold or given away to other people. If you would like to share this book with someone else, please send them to the author's website, where they can find out where to purchase a copy for themselves. Free content can be downloaded at the author's free reads page.

Thank you for respecting the author's work. Enjoy!

TITLES BY L.B. GILBERT

Discordia, A Free Elementals Prequel Short,
Available Now
Fire: The Elementals Book One
Available Now
Air: The Elementals Book Two
Available Now
Water: The Elementals Book Three
Available Now
Earth: The Elementals Book Four
Available Now

Kin Selection, Shifter's Claim, Book One
Available now
Eat You Up, A Shifter's Claim, Book Two
Available now
Tooth and Nail, A Shifter's Claim, Book Three
November 2020

Writing as Lucy Leroux

INTRODUCTION

PROLOGUE

J ust put it in.

Jackson Buchanan fiddled with the thumb drive in his hand. The LED surrounding the empty USB socket of his tower mocked him.

All the answers you've ever had about your old pals might be on that drive. That—or he'd just be scanning lab reports detailing illegal animal experimentation. Either way, he was in for a fun night. The kind that required vodka.

The data on the drive had come from an animal research facility in Wisconsin. He'd been hired by Douglas Maitland to steal it. Actually, the exact terms of his agreement with Douglas had been to break into the Reliance Research with one of his people. They were to copy all the data on their servers before planting a virus that would corrupt all their systems. Not a single byte of data was to remain.

His agreement had stipulated that he make a single copy of the Reliance data and then turn it over to the Maitlands. But Jack had made two.

Douglas had hired him directly instead of going through Cassandra, the woman who booked his jobs and handled payments from his clients. Normally, Jack didn't do jobs where the clients could identify him, but the Maitlands were a special case. Jack had served with several of them, and he considered Connell Maitland one of his closest friends. When Connell's father, Douglas, had contacted Jack about a job requiring he work with one of his people, Jack had immediately agreed.

Admit it, it's because you were hoping your partner on the job would be Mara Maitland. Jack had only met Connell's sister once, but she had made an impression.

But his partner hadn't been Mara. Instead, Jack had infiltrated with Yogi Kane and the man's girlfriend, Denise.

Denise Hammond was an animal activist with a vested interest in taking Reliance down. It was the kind of job he could do with one hand tied behind his back, and the paycheck had been substantial. He should have had no complaints.

He fingered the thumb drive, turning it over in his hand. *The Maitlands will have my ass if they find out I looked.*

His client had been clear. Looking at the data was a violation of his unspoken working agreement, one the Maitland family expected him to uphold despite the fact they hadn't signed a contract.

Jack never wrote any. Leaving a paper trail was verboten in his line of work.

He'd wanted to ask what was so important about a single animal research lab. After all, Jack had broken into more secure places and been privy to some highly sensitive data in his day, the kind that toppled governments. But when Jack agreed to a job, he did it, no questions asked.

The mission had gone off without a hitch. Well, almost none. There had been the matter of the chimpanzee, but he'd resolved that this morning.

Jack pursed his lips and slipped the drive into the computer port. What the hell? It was only his reputation and livelihood on the line...

CHAPTER ONE

TEN MONTHS LATER

J
ack held his breath, crawling on his belly through the underbrush. He suppressed a gag as the wind changed, and the scent of old skunk urine hit him full in the face.

Maybe covering myself in it wasn't my best idea, he silently acknowledged.

He hadn't been excessive, applying just a few diluted drops of it to his carbon clothing—the best scent-eliminating hunting outfit money could buy. But a little bit of skunk piss went a *long* way.

His longing for a shower was visceral, something he craved on a cellular level, but there was no going back now.

Jack had spent over a week planning this surveillance op. He had intended to do at least as much research as he normally did for a six-figure corporate job.

Unfortunately, he'd soon learned there were few public resources he could use to determine the Maitland family compound's layout. No building plans had ever been filed with the local government. Despite their modern look, the buildings dated from the turn of the century. There were no architectural blueprints to be had for love or money.

He'd hit a wall searching for power or sewage line schematics. Even Google Earth had failed him. Whenever he'd input the address, the image redirected to an unbroken canopy of virgin forest as if the dozen or so buildings simply weren't there.

Jack had been forced to rely on his memory of his single visit to the Maitlands to make his plans. That long-ago visit had lasted two days. It had been smack dab in the middle of his last deployment with Connell Maitland's Ranger unit, shortly before the group had been disbanded.

The entire squad had taken honorable discharges within months of each other. Jack couldn't understand why the hell such a crack team —and they were seriously the best he'd ever worked with—would take themselves out of the game in their prime. Despite the fact he called most of them friends, they had been tight-lipped about their post-army life plans.

Not quite done having his fun, Jack had continued as a black-ops specialist. When he finally called it quits a few years ago, he'd been inundated with offers from the private sector. But he turned them all down. After a decade of taking orders, he'd chafed at the idea of doing it again.

At loose ends, Jack tried his hand at various jobs where he could apply the skills he'd learned at Uncle Sam's knee. His favorite had been skip tracing, but he eventually settled into what he affectionately termed 'professional problem solver,' which meant he did a bit of everything. He'd been a bodyguard, a security consultant, an extraction specialist, dabbled in corporate espionage, etc.... The fun was endless, and he got to work for himself.

He snapped back into the present when a leather boot crunched the dry pine needles about a foot in front of his face. Jack held his breath, hoping he was adequately concealed by the shrubbery and the carefully selected camo pattern of his clothing.

A strong and slim arm grabbed him by the collar, then hauled him out of the bushes. On his knees, Jack blinked in the cold sunlight, his eyes devouring the woman he'd been fantasizing about on and off for the last four years.

"Well, hello, Miss Daisy," he drawled, hoping she wasn't about to bash him over the head with a rock or the nearest fallen tree branch.

Mara Maitland towered over him, her leaf-green eyes glaring down at him.

He sat up, taking advantage of the movement to check her out. She was, as always, flawless. Peaches-and-cream skin with red lips was combined with a wealth of dark mahogany that set off those amazing eyes.

Above the hiking boots, she wore skin-tight black leggings. Those were paired with a turtleneck sweater made from one of those impossibly soft-looking wool blends that made it look as if she'd dressed in candy floss. However, judging from her expression, there was little chance he was going to get to touch it to confirm.

He didn't hear the other person behind him until the air whistled, presumably from their fist flying through the air toward the back of his head. His last impression before the world went dark was Mara shaking her head.

"What the hell is *he* doing here?" Derrick hissed, standing over the unconscious human he used to believe was his friend.

"I don't know, but you better call Kiera," Mara replied, naming the pack medic. "We need to make sure you didn't fracture his skull."

"He's fine," Derrick snapped. "I pulled it. Besides, I know for a fact the fucker has a pretty hard head."

Mara raised an eyebrow. As the pack's third, Derrick didn't usually show any mercy. Like all the other pack soldiers, he was ruthless when it came to protecting their territory.

"This idiot saved my life once." Derrick glowered down at the unconscious man. "But if he thinks that entitles him—"

He broke off, his jaw tight. "If Jack Buchanan is here, it means someone paid him to be. The fact he took the fucking job is a betrayal on a level I can't even address. Connell is going to be pissed."

Mara crossed her arms over her chest, nudging the muscled body with her foot. "I don't think that's it."

She didn't pretend to know Jack Buchanan the way Derrick did, but she was her father's daughter. That meant Mara was more than a soldier. She could read people, and she'd been around Jack Buchanan long enough to get a feel for him. He was annoying as hell, but he wouldn't betray them.

Connell and Derrick had trusted Jack to have their backs on the battlefield, and he, in turn, had trusted them. Instinct told her the man wouldn't have breached the trust. Jack was more like them than his own species. Loyalty was in his blood.

Lamentably, he also possessed a wolf cub's natural curiosity.

"No," she said, rubbing her face. "If I'm right, this has to do with more recent events."

Confusion flicked across Derrick's face. "Are you talking about the Reliance job?"

She nodded, barely resisting the urge to say, 'I told you so'. "We should have never brought him in."

Jack had been an armed forces specialist, a no-rank black ops floater who had done work with her brother's ranger unit on and off for years. He was a hacker who could infiltrate secure facilities in his sleep.

Six months ago, her father had decided to hire Jack to break into a research facility run by an outfit known as Reliance. He'd done it with Yogi Kane, one of their people, and the woman Yogi now called his mate. Denise Hammond was an animal activist who had liberated one of their wolf cubs from Reliance's laboratory, only to learn the cub was a shifter.

When the pack learned their secret was threatened, they decided to go back in and ensure Reliance kept nothing that could lead the organization back to them. Their pack maintained the secret of their existence by putting down any threats to the pack and its anonymity.

Jack had been hired to accompany Yogi and Denise back into the facility to hack and wipe the computers, after making a copy for the Maitland pack so they could assess how much Denon knew about their kind. They needed to know if the pack had been exposed.

That was supposed to have been the end of the human's involvement.

Derrick scowled. "Reliance was a straight smash and grab. Jack handed over the data, and he got paid—a lot. He has no reason to come sniffing around here."

Suppressing an urge to roll her eyes, Mara nudged the man with her foot again. A waft of foul odor assaulted her sensitive nose. Good God, what had he covered himself in?

"He had a mystery to solve," she said in a cold voice when Derrick threw up his hands, clearly expecting an answer.

That was what her father and the other men hadn't understood. This one wasn't the kind of man who would let sleeping dogs lie.

This is why you didn't bring in an outsider to protect the pack's interests. Especially a man like Jackson Buchanan. He was too much of a wild card.

"Get him up," she ordered.

"Are we taking him to the main house?" Derrick frowned, gesturing down the hill to the complex of buildings they called home.

"Hell no," she answered. "I don't want him anywhere near the place."

Judging from all the surveillance equipment on him, that was exactly what the human wanted.

Derrick reached down, hauling up the prone man and throwing him over his shoulder. Given they were close to the same size—Jack was large for a human—Derrick should have had some trouble. But Weres had denser, more powerful muscles than humans. It meant they were heavier and substantially stronger than humans.

"Then where do we take him?"

Mara narrowed her eyes at Jack's face. In repose, his was an arresting combination of strength and prettiness, with more of the latter than was good for him. It tempted her to forgot what he was—a scoundrel through and through.

Mara thought about it, then a hint of a smile lifted the corners of her lips. "I know the perfect place."

Jack's head was throbbing, his neck hanging down sharply enough for him to get a literal pain in it. But he was careful not to move. Schooling his breath, he made sure his breathing pattern didn't change.

"Oh, good. You're awake."

Damn. Cracking one eye open, he squinted at his captors. Mara stood six feet away, leaning against a wooden wall, one foot crooked to brace behind her. Her arms were crossed. She watched him with an amused smile. "Are you going to fake amnesia now?"

Twisting his head to stretch his sore neck, he attempted a charming smile. "Would it do any good?"

The smile fell flat. Mara's gorgeous face could have been carved from stone. "No."

He nodded. "It was worth a shot..."

His voice trailed off as he took in his surroundings. *Well, hell.* He was in *his* cabin, the tiny hunting lodge he kept in Colorado. It was several hours from the Maitland compound.

The sound of a booted foot scraping on wood alerted him to the presence behind him.

"Connell?" he asked hopefully, trying to turn enough to see if the other person was her brother.

Slowly, Mara shook her head. Tensing, Jack waited until the other party came into his line of sight.

"Derrick," he called with genuine affection. "It's been forever, man."

Since he'd been hired remotely for the Reliance job, the only man he'd seen from the old unit had been the one assigned to accompany him, Yogi Kane. But he and Derrick went back longer. They'd bonded in a way people only did with those they served with. Except his former brother-in-arms was glowering at him.

"What?" Jack pouted. "No hug?"

Derrick took the space next on the other side of the door, mirroring Mara's posture. He did stony silence better than her.

Jack turned to Mara. "And you? Don't suppose I can interest you in a hug?" he asked, deciding it was in his best interests not to mention his preference would be post-coital snuggling.

Her gaze was flinty. "You watched the video, didn't you?"

"I did," he confirmed softly.

The surveillance footage file in question had been part of the data he'd stolen from Reliance before injecting a destructive virus of his own concoction. It had wiped all data from their computers, corrupting the drives so badly that any recovery was impossible.

His job had been to hand over a copy of the data without looking at it. But his curiosity about the Maitlands had overwhelmed his good sense and usual sense of professionalism.

For years, he'd watched Connell, Derrick, Leland, and the others in that team do things that should have been impossible. The physicality—their strength, sharp senses, even their sense of balance, was too good.

There was that one time, with the bomb in Bahrain. They should have all been blown to smithereens. It had been almost as if Derrick had smelled the damn device. Jack had disarmed it with minutes to spare.

Mara cocked her head to the side. "I really wish you hadn't said that."

His mouth tightened. "And I really wish you all had invited me to Leland's funeral."

Derrick winced. "Sorry, man, but it was just family."

"Don't you mean it was just your wolf pack?" Bitterness crept into Jack's tone.

He hadn't found out about Leland's death until weeks after the fact, long after his friend had been buried. Connell had called him and apologized for the late notice, explaining he'd been laid up in the hospital himself at the time.

But this wasn't about that. This was about learning their secrets.

"Pack is family," Mara replied coldly.

The ropes binding him were too tight for him to shrug, so Jack did it with his face.

Derrick rubbed his temples. "Well, that does it. The chief is going to kill us."

"Why?" Jack and Mara asked at the same time. That got him another jade glare.

"The chief decided to hire Mr. Buchanan here," Mara pointed out.

She didn't have to add she had been against it. He knew that without having to ask.

"Hey," he protested. "The last time I saw you, it was *Jack*. Not Mr. Buchanan."

The register of her voice had flattened, but it still so damn throaty and sexy he wanted to lick it.

"You've lost some standing here," she said in a cold voice. "Get over it."

He leaned back in the chair, unable to keep from staring. Even when angry, she was magnificent.

Tall and lean with curves that were stamped in his brain like a brand, Mara Maitland was hands down the most arresting woman he'd ever seen. Being so close to her did things to him, things he couldn't and shouldn't admit aloud.

And why the hell does she smell so good? Despite his ode de skunk, he could still pick up her distinctive perfume, a mix of tropical flowers with a hint of Tahitian vanilla.

"So, how does it work?"

"How does what work?" Derrick sniffed.

"Lycanthropy," he said in a '*well, duh*' tone.

"You turn into wolves. That much, I know. Does it only happen at the full moon? And what do you look like? Are the grown-ups like the classic horror movie wolf-man—bipedal with a snout and claws—or is it more like the kid in the video—like a normal wolf only bigger. And are normal wolves *normal*? Or do they all secretly turn into people when your back is turned?"

Derrick swore under his breath, but Mara continued to watch him, unsurprised, or at least resigned, to his long list of questions.

"So, what do we do now?" Derrick muttered. "Can we ask Logan to take a look at him? Maybe she can do something about this?"

It was his turn to frown. "Connell's girlfriend? What could she do?"

He'd only met the woman Connell called his mate—again, how had Jack ever thought they were human?—one time. Logan was an adorable Asian girl, fun-loving, and petite. Connell looked monstrously tall next to her, but Logan didn't seem to mind the size disparity. He'd seen Connell toss her up a flight of stairs once. Logan had taken it in stride, putting one little foot out and stepping on the landing like she hadn't just skipped eight steps.

"Logan could whip over to the island and get something to wipe his brain, erase all knowledge of what we are," Derrick suggested.

For the first time, Jack drew his head back, uncertain. That werewolves existed was a fact. Somehow, after being around Connell and the others, accepting that wasn't difficult. But if what they were saying were true, then there was a hell of a lot more to this world than werewolves.

"Don't do that," he said. "Whatever *that* is."

Jack didn't want his memory wiped. Maybe a lesser man wouldn't have minded. He could go back to his old life without having these questions clamoring for answers in the back of his mind.

He could go to bars, pick up women, and take the jobs Cass booked, fattening up his wallet until he could afford to retire on an island paradise, the way he'd always planned.

But that wasn't an option now. He didn't ever want to forget what Mara was.

"We can't do that," she said after an uncomfortable stretch.

"Why not?" Derrick scowled.

Yes, why not?

"Because it wouldn't be a simple matter of erasing the last few months. Jackie boy here has been wondering what we are for a long time. Years, in fact." She turned to him. "Isn't that right?"

"It's Jackson or Jack if you please. Never Jackie," he said with a shudder.

Mara twisted to face Derrick. "If we wanted to remove his knowledge of us, we would have to take *years*. That would destroy him."

And Mara and the Maitlands were good people. They wouldn't do that to him. Something tight in Jack's gut relaxed, being overtaken by a lighter, almost frothy feeling of giddiness.

"So, it's settled? I get to learn the secret werewolf handshake now, right?" A grin split Jack's face.

"Yes," Mara murmured. "But we're not all cuddly puppies like you saw in that video. Soon enough, I think you're going to find the old adage is true…"

"Which one?"

She leaned down, getting close enough for him to get a whiff of Tahiti. "Be careful what you wish for."

CHAPTER TWO

Jack was hiding something. Mara could tell by the secretive gleam in his eye. The merc thought he had something.

"Are you going to untie me?" His voice had gone drawly, the vocal equivalent of melted butter.

Belatedly, she remembered he was from somewhere down South—Alabama or Tennessee. She'd never been an accent person, and this one had been softened by years of California beaches, so there wasn't much hope of her deciphering it. Not that she cared to. The only thing she needed to know about Jack was what the hell had brought him here because the Colorado Basin Pack did not tolerate any incursions into their territory.

She didn't want to have to make an example of him, but she would if she had to.

"Is there a reason you waited until Derrick left the room to ask?" Mara batted her eyelashes.

Her packmate had stepped out to call her father. Douglas Maitland was out of town—a damn near miracle in itself. But now she had an actual security situation to handle, another miracle. Unfortunately, it involved Jack fucking Buchanan.

"Well, I would love to jump in the shower," he said, gesturing with his head to the tiny cabin's bathroom door. "And as fond as I am of Derrick, I don't relish the idea of stripping down in front of him."

The gleam in his eye became distinctly wicked. "You, on the other hand, are more than welcome to stay."

Mara pretended ignorance. "Why do you want to shower?"

He threw her an incredulous glance. "To wash the skunk piss off," he said slowly as if speaking to an idiot.

"You mean this isn't how you normally smell?" she asked, face appropriately deadpan.

Face lighting with genuine amusement, Jack threw back his head and laughed. It transformed him from handsome to ungodly beautiful. Not the well-behaved kind of god, either, but one of those naughty pagans who drew you away from the crowds to have their wicked way with mortals in the woods.

Mara had to remind herself she was no simpering maiden. She was a soldier who also happened to be the chief's daughter, and now one of the pack's protectors. Alpha wolves had been throwing their best game at her since she came of age.

That and Jack was a player, a highly successful one by all accounts. Even the other pack females had thought he was 'perfectly edible'—a direct quote. But she was immune.

Jack straightened in his bonds. He cleared his throat. "In all seriousness, I didn't come here to flirt with you. Well—I didn't *just* come here for that," he amended.

Mara raised a brow. "I know."

"How?"

"Because as infantile as you can be, you are not an idiot," she said sharply. Mara waved down at herself. "And you know there's nothing for you here."

His mouth twitched, but it wasn't a smile. If anything, his features had sharpened.

Mara paused, suddenly aware she had miscalculated. To a man like Jack, she'd just issued a challenge.

Doesn't matter. He was no different from the wolves she dealt with. Like them, he'd discover the truth, and he'd move on to easier prey.

Her jaw tightened, uncertain why that truth hurt. It made her less charitable toward him.

"Untie me so I can shower. And then we'll talk," he said, his demeanor transforming like quicksilver in response. The charming rogue was gone. In his place was the human warrior who'd held his own against a special-ops team comprised entirely of shifters.

Mara considered him in silence. Then she raised her leg, whipping out her knife from her boot. She opened the butterfly blade with a flick of her wrist.

"Holy shit," Jack breathed, his face reddening. "That is fucking sexy."

Rolling her eyes, she moved behind him, cutting the ropes.

He stood, rubbing his wrists. "I'll be right back, kitten."

Mara grimaced as he moved to the back of the cabin. He shrugged the megawatt smile back in full force. "What? Calling you puppy won't work. That's not even a little sexy."

She waited until he had locked himself in the bathroom to retch.

"What was that all about?" Derrick asked when she stepped outside.

As a Were, he had superior hearing. Mara shrugged. "Nothing serious. I got tired of the smell. I'm letting him shower off the skunk piss."

"Good. He was making my stomach turn in there."

Bad smells, even faint ones, were always worse in enclosed spaces. But she and Derrick were soldiers at the top of the pack structure. They didn't let their discomfort show in front of their adversaries.

"So, are we ripping out his throat, or what?"

Mara scowled. "Stop. You know you'd never touch a hair on his head. He's your *buddy*." Her emphasis made that last sound like a dirty word.

"If he sold us out, I would," Derrick grumbled, then shrugged. "But since you let him go, I'm going to assume you think he's in the clear."

"He has something, or he wouldn't be here," she said. "What did the chief say?"

"Couldn't reach him. I guess there is no cell service where he is."

"We know where he is—San Diego, not fucking Siberia. And if the chief isn't answering, it's because he's busy."

Or getting busy. Mara suppressed a shudder.

Her father was visiting Hope Li, Logan's mother, a witch from a powerful Elemental line. Hope was doing a special lecture series at the local naval base on the evolution of battle tactics through the ages. War was her specialty. Douglas had angled for an invitation, the topic being of particular interest to him. Or at least that was the excuse he had used.

Derrick shrugged. "Well, I didn't want to be the one to bring it up, what with it being your dad and all. But if anyone is entitled to a second chance at love—"

She held up her hand. "Stop, I'm already that close to hurling because of Skunky MacSkunkerson back there. Don't make it worse."

He leaned against the door of the cabin. "I've meant to ask—what do you think of Hope?"

Mara trained her hearing on the cabin interior. The shower was still going. "I prefer Mai. She's more straightforward." Not that Hope was shifty or anything. Both were badass witches firmly on the side of the light. She simply clicked more with Mai.

"You like Mai more because she's a ballbuster, just like you."

"Nothing wrong with being a strong woman," Mara observed.

"But you don't have anything against Hope specifically, right?" Derrick persisted.

Mara considered that. "No, but even if I did, it wouldn't matter, and you know it. It's not like she's going be my new mommy or some shit like that. It's barely even a fling."

And Douglas Maitland's one and only had been her mother, Ellen. It didn't matter that Ellen had been gone for almost a decade. Wolves only mated once.

Derrick muttered something under his breath, but Mara didn't pay it any mind. She knew what the pack had been whispering about—that as Canus Primus, the chief of all the North American packs, her father was different, the exception to the rule. The fact he'd survived the death of his mate was evidence. Many of their kind didn't. They weren't capable of going on after being ripped in half. But Douglas had because his children and the pack needed him. Hell, the world needed him.

Mara wasn't a complete bitch. She didn't want her father to spend the rest of his life alone. But she was close enough to Logan to know stuff about Hope...and it might take someone stronger than the Canus Primus of the North American coalition to break down Hope's walls.

"I think he's done," Derrick said, knocking on the wall behind him before going to the door to walk inside.

Mara had heard the shower go off as well, but she waited, having no desire to walk in on a buck-naked Jack Buchanan. He would enjoy that far too much.

W hen Mara entered the cabin a few minutes later, Jack was pouring Derrick a whiskey.

Her mouth compressed. Not five minutes alone and her packmate went from suspicion to treating the human like a trusted friend. And she didn't think it had anything to do with her decision to hear him out.

But this was Jack's way. He could disarm people as easily as breathing. It was second nature.

Connell had told her stories of them being trapped behind enemy lines, among armed hostiles, and the human had somehow gotten them out, winning over local after local until he'd secured their route out.

"His skill at manipulation and negotiation is almost preternatural. I swear he's a sorcerer," Connell had said more than once.

Derrick leaned back in his seat. "So, Mara thinks you have something," he said after downing the whiskey.

Jack sipped his glass, his startlingly light blue eyes never leaving her as she took a seat opposite him at the crowded little table.

"After I watched the surveillance footage and realized what you all have been hiding, I dug through the experimental records done on the wolf cub."

"As did we," she said. "But the cub was fortunate. Denise Hammond and her animal liberation crew got him out before the tests became invasive. The Reliance scientists were still trying to establish baseline measurements. However, there was no evidence in those records to indicate they knew what he was, aside from that video."

"There is now," he said, leaning back in his chair.

Derrick straightened up. "What did you find?"

Jack stood, reaching under his bed for his laptop.

"Stellar hiding place," Mara observed, unable to help herself. "For a security specialist."

He didn't react to her taunt. "This computer is encrypted with more layers than an Eskimo in winter. There are only five hackers in the world who can break them...and I'm one of them."

One of the others was Cass, his booker, but Jack preferred to do his own hacking. If he were pressed for time, he delegated some research to her, but that was it.

Jack typed in a password and several commands. He brought up a new window on the screen.

"This isn't going to be pretty," he warned them before turning the computer to face them.

Derrick sucked in a sharp breath, but Mara didn't flinch. She had expected this.

The image on the screen was horrifying. There was a body on a slab with the chest cavity cracked, the skin flayed and pinned open as if it were a dissection in progress. The victim was a female.

The woman's features were contorted, a death rictus that transmitted her pain and anguish. It was a scream caught on camera despite the fact the female had been dead long enough for her eyes to cloud over with a film of white. But the worst part was her hands.

They were clawed.

"Fuck," Derrick swore, passing a hand over his eyes.

"Do you recognize her?" Jack asked softly.

"No," Mara said. "Those are cat claws."

"A were-cat?"

"We usually just say shifter. She's either a leopard or a cougar of some kind," Mara informed him. "There's a good-sized colony in the pacific northwest. It's the biggest in our territory, but there are many smaller ones. While we're on speaking terms with only some of them, they all talk to each other."

She turned to Derrick. "Reach out to all the feline packs we're friendly with. Find out which one is missing a middle-aged female."

Jack raised a brow, tucking away that tidbit for future reference. "Know any in Spain? Because that's where I took this."

Mara leaned forward, studying the picture intently. "And you're sure this is Reliance?"

"They call themselves Inovatum now, but the players have stayed the same. They closed up shop, then moved most of their operations south of the border."

Derrick and Mara exchanged a look.

"I thought you said you took this in Spain."

He nodded. "Denon, their parent company, splintered the staff. Some went to Mexico, but the former operation heads went to Europe. My guess is they kicked up a fuss at being moved to the middle of nowhere, so they insisted on being relocated to a more cosmopolitan area. This facility is outside Barcelona."

Jack pronounced it the Castilian way with a 'th' instead of an 's' sound, Bar-*the*-lona.

Mara suppressed an eye roll. There were more important things going on than one human's pretentiousness.

"How did they get her to freeze mid-shift?" Derrick asked, his face curdled. He hadn't torn his eyes from the unfortunate on the screen the entire time.

"I don't know."

Jack straightened. "You mean that isn't normal?"

"No," Mara said. "At death, a shifter reverts to the state we were born in—human. We don't shift at birth. It takes a few months to gain our second form."

"And do all the kids born of shifter parents shift? Or are there some, um, nulls?"

Apparently, he caught their bemused expressions because he drew his head back. "Sorry, was that rude? Is the topic a sensitive one?"

Suddenly, he gazed at Mara with pity in his eyes. *Good lord. He thinks I can't shift.* Would the indignities never cease?

Keeping her eyes on him, Mara slashed out the claws on her right hand. Digging her nails into the wooden surface, she carved in a nice new design. Though crude, it was a clear enough rendering of a fist with a raised middle finger.

"Okay, so you can shift. Nice, very nice." Jack's tone said it was anything but. He took a moment to sip his whiskey.

"So how much of that intel did you all get without me?"

"A few of the Mexican facilities," Derrick admitted grudgingly. "Not the Spanish ones."

Mara could tell Jack was trying not to gloat, but the man didn't have a humble bone in his body. His smug satisfaction was like a cologne.

"So, what are we going to have to pay for the details?" Derrick asked, a bite in his voice.

Jack closed the computer screen. "That's an interesting question. And I'm afraid I can't tell you the answer yet."

"What the bloody hell does that mean?" Derrick's face hardened. "We need that information. Or are you okay with them butchering the dual-natured?"

"Of course I'm not," Jack snapped. "What do you take me for?"

The men glared at each other.

Mara, however, wasn't offended. Despite Derrick's longer acquaintance with the soldier of fortune, she understood the man's nature better, having gleaned it from the many stories about him. Meeting him in the flesh had confirmed her conclusions about him.

Although it didn't quite prepare you for the impact of his smile.

A flash of that first meeting ran through her mind. Mara had been out for a run. She had come in to find her brother, and the rest of his team had come home unexpectedly. It had only been a few days, which was probably why they had let Jack come home with them. He'd been attached to the unit at the time.

He'd made me so angry. It wasn't anything he'd done exactly. Aware her brother and extended family were watching him like a hawk, he'd behaved himself—at least when he knew the others were watching. But the way he'd watched her when her brother and the others had been busy…it had been almost indecent.

The man had trouble written all over him. It was a good thing a pretty face didn't sway Mara.

"Relax," she told the other wolf. "It's not money he wants."

Jack beamed at her as if she'd just won a prize.

"Then what the hell does he want?" Derrick whipped his head back and forth between her and the mercenary.

"I suspect we'll learn that after we burn this facility to the ground," she said, tapping the top of the closed laptop.

Derrick scowled, catching on. "With him tagging along?"

"Nothing so reasonable. He wants to lead the mission. What was it you said to my father when he hired you to break into the Reliance lab?" she asked, imitating his southern drawl. "'My op, my rules'?"

"See, this is why I like you so much, Mara." Jack flashed bright white teeth against his California tan. "You get me."

CHAPTER THREE

"He's going to try to wear you down," Derrick growled as he pulled their SUV off the highway.

"What?" Mara asked absently. Her mind was a thousand miles away in Spain, with a woman on a cold slab.

When their cub had gone missing, there had been room for doubt. They hadn't been sure if they had been intentionally targeted or if Reliance had stumbled on one of theirs by happenstance. But the cat's death had been no accident.

Now they knew for certain. They were being hunted. *Denon is going to burn,* Mara promised herself.

"I said Jack is going to try to get into your pants."

Jarred out of her plans for fiery revenge, she turned to scowl. "Tell me something I don't know."

The scent of lust had been there in his scent, along with a dozen other emotions. Despite his flirtatiousness, Jack probably believed he'd hidden it. Mara had to admit he had a hell of a poker face, but there was no hiding emotions from wolves.

Derrick gripped the steering wheel. "You have to be ready. Don't get me wrong... I like the guy. It was funny at the time, but I have seen Jack talk a *nun* into going home with him. The man is lethal."

Mara threw up her hand. "And how is he any different from the long line of Weres trying the exact same thing?"

Sometimes it felt as if Mara had been hit on by every dominant wolf west of the Mississippi. Since her eighteenth birthday, it had been an endless stream. But the only man who had come close had been Malcolm, who'd been her father's third for a time. He'd spurned her for easier prey...and then he'd died.

"That's different, and you know it." Derrick sniffed. "Those wolves were courting you. But Jack's an operator with more notches on his bedpost than there are grains of sand on a beach."

Mara wrinkled her nose. "Which is exactly why he'll get nowhere —like all the wolves looking to further their positions by bedding me."

Derrick threw her a commiserating glance. Like her brother Connell, he'd done his fair share of running off those suitors, including the few she wouldn't have minded getting to know better.

What was the opposite of beggars couldn't be choosers? Women being pursued by wolves couldn't stop to find the needle in the haystack?

"You have to admit that kind of thing has tapered off since the chief made you acting second in Connell's absence," Derrick pointed out.

That was only because she'd finally had a chance to show her true strength...except the dominance challenges she'd put down since were less about overtaking her in the pack structure and more like auditions. Mate auditions.

Mara checked their location out the window. "I want point on this one."

"I think you're going to get your wish."

Surprised, she turned back to face him.

"When we were leaving, Jack said he'd rather go it alone, but he understands that won't be possible, so he wants a liaison with as few steps between him and the chief as possible. That means either you or Connell—and who the hell knows when your brother is going to get home from his latest attempt to save the world?"

That last was said without irony. Connell and his Elemental mate *were* off saving the world. The only problem was it never stayed saved.

"Father will have to cut his trip short," she said.

Derrick nodded. "This is more important."

J ack tried not to swallow as Douglas Maitland paced a short circuit in front of him. His black eyes bored into Jack's soul.

In his line of work, Jack had been in the same rooms as Army generals and heads of state as well as the shadow powers behind them. His skin had itched a little while in proximity to those authorities, but it was nothing compared to this sensation.

This was like being flayed alive.

And you've met him before! But that time, Douglas had been playing the genial host. Apparently, he could throttle down some of his natural energy. He had to. Otherwise, it would give him away anytime he moved among normal people.

"Your instructions were specific. You were told to make a single copy of the data and hand it over," Douglas said with a voice that rumbled with distant thunder. "Under no circumstances were you to keep a copy for yourself."

Jack tried to smile, but instinct told him that his charm would be about as useful as a lead life preserver. "If I hadn't, I wouldn't have known where to find out where Reliance, excuse me, Inovatum, has relocated—the real facilities. Not the dummies set up in Mexico."

He leaned forward. "Reliance's footprint in the States vanished almost overnight. Yogi, Denise, and I went back to wipe their computers. But that wasn't unexpected, not given the size and resources of their parent company. I did get a little whiplash when I realized how quickly they moved their operation."

Douglas watched Jack with what he could only call a *growly* expression. "They had a contingency plan in place."

"Yes," Jack agreed. "All of it smacks of premeditation, doesn't it?

That they were surveying your people, waiting for the opportunity to snatch someone, preferably one of your young and vulnerable."

Douglas crossed his arms. "We long suspected as much. When they didn't chance upon such an opportunity, we believe they got impatient and created one."

Jack straightened, waiting for the story, but it was not forthcoming. Instead, he got more distinctively hostile scowls.

"Have you identified the woman in the picture yet?" Jack had tried, but had no luck. She could have been from anywhere in the world.

"No," Derrick answered. "But we've reached out to our allies, shared her picture—well, her face," he amended. "We thought it best not to show the rest."

"Yeah," Jack agreed, but he took careful note of the mention of allies. The politics of shifter life promised to be as complicated as humanity's.

"Look, kudos to you for finding the Mexican facilities. Denon Corp did a hell of a job setting those up. You'd have to get inside to know they're fake because the paperwork and traffic in and out were perfect." He bunched his fingers, kissing them to emphasize the professional caliber of the work.

"It looks so real down there," he continued. "But they're scattering and regrouping. If you want to find them all, you're going to need me."

Douglas turned to meet Mara's eyes. "Well?" he asked.

She lifted one shoulder. "If we say no, we'll just end up tripping over him when we go after them ourselves."

Douglas turned to Jack, raising a questioning brow.

"Oh, hell yeah," he confirmed. "I'm going back."

Jack had gone into the Spanish facility with two basic goals in mind—prove Reliance still existed and that they were experimenting on Werewolves. In the back of his mind, he'd continued to doubt his mission, that he'd imagined the footage, or it had been doctored for someone's amusement.

And then he'd found the body. Faced with indisputable proof of the supernatural, he'd taken pictures as evidence and left, neglecting his due diligence. He hadn't hunted down the computers they stored their research in. But he was going to rectify that mistake now, whether the Maitlands liked it or not.

He checked Douglas and Mara's expressions. Yeah, they didn't like it at all.

"We haven't agreed to pay you yet," Douglas pointed out in a deceptively gentle voice.

"Don't worry about that," Jack said.

"You're not interested in payment?" Derrick was skeptical.

Jack took a deep breath, his eyes gravitating to Mara as he suspected they always would. "Oh, I'll get paid. Don't worry."

Jack would short the Denon stock if he had to. He'd done that sort of thing before.

"Then why are you going back?" Mara asked.

"Honestly?" Jack tipped his head up, her deep green eyes momentarily making him forget the fact some of the world's most dangerous men—her father included—were in the same room.

He searched for the right words. Jack had been blindsided when he learned the woman he'd found wasn't a wolf. The knowledge the hidden world he'd been trying to enter was much bigger than he realized had shaken him.

"I didn't expect to find what I did. I should have after the video, but I didn't," he said, drumming his fingers on the table. "And then there she was, real. That woman wasn't human, but she wasn't an animal. She had been a sentient, *feeling* being. And she died in agony."

Jack met Douglas' fathomless dark eyes with resolve. "I had to leave her behind. Taking her would have tipped them off that they'd been found. And they'd pull up stakes and move again. So, she's still there, waiting for me to come back...to bring her home."

Douglas nodded slowly. He twisted to Mara. "You leave in the morning. Derrick will be your on-call backup. Go pack."

"I can't believe your dad is letting you go off with juicy Jack," Salome said, throwing herself on Mara's bed.

"He doesn't have much choice," Mara replied, wrinkling her nose at that particularly horrible nickname. She tugged her sweater out from beneath Sal's legs with a hard yank, then folded it neatly and stowing it in her bag.

A not-so-secret part of her was glad Jack had backed her father into a corner, insisting on having someone senior in the pack involved.

It's only fair. Her brother got to fly around the world with his perfect partner, doing great and important things. Mara was sick of being sidelined.

Not two months ago, during the biggest battle of their lives, her pack had aided Connell's mate Logan and her sisters against a band of black witches allied with rogue wolves and dark Fae. It was one for the history books…and Mara had stayed home.

Her father, the chief, had assigned her to guard their den. Mara knew it wasn't a comment on her abilities. Protecting their vulnerable, the old who were too frail to fight, and the young who would be their next generation of alphas and betas were as important as the fight itself. It was an honor bestowed on her. But it hadn't felt like one.

"Where is your golden god, anyway?" Sal curled her long legs under her.

Mara's lips compressed, but she didn't correct Salome about Jack being 'hers'. The more she denied it, the more she would tease, as would all the others. They were werewolves. It was their way. *And heaven forbid I ever claim him.* All hell would break loose.

Sal didn't understand that. The younger female could afford to consort with humans if she wanted to. She wasn't the chief's daughter.

"Derrick took Jack to the cemetery to visit Leland's grave," Mara told her.

"Oh," Sal murmured. Her face was sober, but then her eyes

narrowed. "Do you think his grief for Leland is real? Or is Jack Buchanan trying to manipulate us?"

It sounded cold, especially coming out of the mouth of a teenager who appeared young and soft. But Sal had been tempered in fire. She was a lot harder than people knew, something Mara counseled her to hide. That kind of advantage worked best when people didn't tip their hand.

As for her question—their pack was notoriously insular. They had been taught from an early age to be suspicious of all outsiders. Pack meant family. Everyone else was Otherkind, even other kinds of shifters.

However, that xenophobia sometimes meant the people on the outside suffered. Mara knew Jack wasn't trying to play them.

"No, I saw him with Leland and the others on his earlier visit to the compound. He wasn't faking their camaraderie then, and he's not faking it now."

It had been a bit weird seeing him with her pack mates. Though Jack had been the only human, it had been hard to tell him apart from the others. Some humans were like that, though—natural dominants.

Jack might make his living as a mercenary, but his loyalty to that brotherhood of soldiers went bone deep.

Unless he has succeeded in fooling me. But Mara couldn't leave on this mission believing the worst of him. They were going to be working together for a while. She had to give him the benefit of the doubt, but that was all she'd give him—sexy grin or not.

Jack frowned down at the boulder inscribed with Leland's name and his birth and death dates.

"He's not here," Derrick said, the setting sun making the bristles on his chin glow red.

"You said he was cremated?"

Derrick nodded. "It's our way. We scattered his ashes in the woods so his soul could roam the wild, but I made sure to brush some under the stone so he could always have the option to come home."

Jack blinked rapidly. Fuck, that was way more touching than he'd thought it was going to be. Squinting as if against the wind, he gestured at the other stones around them. "Is using rocks a werewolf thing, too?"

"It's a pack thing."

Some of the stones were big, some were small, but all looked natural as if they just happened to be on this random windswept hill. There was no fence, no markers other than the stones. It fit the area's wildness and what he knew about the Maitlands and their extended clan.

Derrick cleared his throat. "I'm sorry we couldn't bring you out for the funeral."

"It's okay," Jack mumbled, trying to mean it.

Derrick had explained the circumstances of Leland's death on the way here. His friend had died saving Connell from something Derrick called 'an internal betrayal'. Connell had been shot in the incident. They had held Leland's funeral back long enough for him to get out of the hospital.

"It's not really. But it didn't even occur to us to let you know until way after the fact. But things were…really messed up at the time. The entire pack was hurting."

Jack sighed. "I get it, man. If it matters, I went to the nearest liquor store when I heard. I bought a bottle of that French stuff he used to like, and I had a shot in his honor."

"Chartreuse? The green liquor made of herbs?" Derrick's face curdled. "How was it?"

"Pretty gross," Jack admitted with a chuckle. "But if I ever get a cold, I may have some more. Clears the sinuses right up."

Derrick smiled, but it faded as he kicked a big rock—one that didn't have a name. It didn't budge. "This one will be mine when the time comes."

Jack winced. "Way to be morbid."

The big man shrugged. "I would have done the same as Leland, by the way, throwing myself over Connell. He is too important to lose. Mara…she's the same—and not because she's the chief's daughter, or at least not only because of it. There are some people the world needs to keep spinning."

He paused, a corner of his mouth turning down as he eyeballed Jack. "And if you let anything happen to her on this fact-finding mission, I'm afraid I'll have no choice but to gut you and jump rope with your entrails, old friend."

That sounded about right. Jack clapped him on the back. "I would expect no less."

CHAPTER FOUR

Dinner in the Maitland house had been…interesting. They ate communally, at a huge, long table straight out of a Viking hall. It didn't help Jack's equilibrium that all the people around it could have easily passed for marauding warriors, the women included. Only the presence of his former teammates made him feel comfortable.

That and the food had been excellent— a lot of high-quality steaks served rare, just how he liked them.

Now it was close to midnight. He and Mara had an early flight to Barcelona, but he couldn't sleep. His brain was buzzing with so many details he couldn't settle down for the night, which was odd. Usually, Jack could drop off wherever he lay his head. It was a habit from his time working for Uncle Sam, a gift he didn't take for granted.

Except that gift had failed him a couple of times in the last few months, ever since he found out about werewolves. Wait, they preferred shifters. Or the wolves did, at least. The same might not be true in other groups.

Damn, this was complicated. Well, he was going to have to ask what the polite term was each time. It would be like asking people what their preferred pronouns were. If he thought of it that way, it was easy enough.

Jack got out of bed, giving up on sleep. He intended to go outside and get a breath of fresh air, but then he remembered the second floor had a long balcony at the back of the house, one accessible from the hallway.

Making his way with practiced stealth, he found the exit to the balcony. The moon was full, illuminating the cleared area around the house more effectively than floodlights.

And not a single furry wolf to be seen. Clearly, the movies had gotten some things wrong.

Skin prickling, he turned around, his eyes narrowing at the sloping shingles of the multilevel gabled roof. Someone was up there. His selective spidey-sense was tingling, the one that only worked around her.

Climbing, he found Mara lying flat on the shingles, her face tilted up to the stars. Disappointingly, she still had on the same clothes from dinner, not the sexy satin baby-doll nightgown he had been fantasizing about her sleeping in.

"Are you going to say something or just stand there like a creeper?"

"How did you know it was me?"

Mara hadn't turned her head, and she faced the wrong way. The obvious answer came to him.

"You can smell me, can't you?" Sniffing under his pits, he grinned, happy he had showered.

"You use too much aftershave," she told him.

"Oh," he said, sniffing again for a different reason. It wasn't as if he wore it during active missions. But he'd been on autopilot, acting as if he'd been getting ready for a date.

Lying next to her, he resolved to toss the bottle of aftershave before they left. "I should have realized. Perfumes and cologne are probably not a good idea."

"Most commercially produced scents are too strong," she agreed. "We don't use them unless we water them down, but even that is unwise. Scent is one of the ways we take stock of our surroundings. It helps us identify threats."

"Makes sense. No point in handicapping yourself when you have that kind of advantage. I should have realized, but no one mentioned it at dinner."

It certainly hadn't put anyone off their food. Shifters could *eat.*

"They were being polite. You stink."

"Ah." He shrugged. "Sorry."

"Obviously not that sorry, " she said, pointing out how close he was to her by digging her elbow in his side.

He decided to ignore that. "I've looked at your file."

Mara raised her head, a question in her glare.

Jack lifted one shoulder. "I always check out the people I'm going to have to rely on. Nothing personal."

"And?" Her voice had an edge.

"You served as a UN peacekeeper."

"What about it?"

"Nothing. It's simply that nothing about you seems…peaceful." His voice died out with the sharpening of the chill in the air.

Jack had just enough time to concede how stupid that comment was before Mara reached over and pushed him off the roof.

"What is your problem?" Mara asked as Jack gave her another look from under his long blond lashes.

I swear he uses mascara. Clear mascara existed, right?

Mouth compressing, Jack tapped his ear. "Can't hear you!" he said in a loud voice. "Engine's too loud."

"Really?" Mara put her hands on her hips. The engine of the private plane they had chartered was noisy, but it wasn't *that* bad. She hadn't even needed to put in earplugs, which was frequently the case in older models like this one given her sensitive ears.

They could hear each other fine. "I wouldn't have shoved you if I'd known you were going to hold a grudge," she said, unable to conceal a tiny smirk.

Jack rose from the bench, shooting her a glare that blistered. "Off a roof, Mara. A *roof.*"

"You landed on the balcony. You're *fine*," she said dismissively, clapping him on the side.

Mara resisted the urge to suck on her smarting fingers. Jack's body was a lot harder than the average human. She would have pegged him as one of her kind had it not been for his human scent.

Jack ignored that, whipped out his tablet. He pulled up the schematics for the Spanish Inovatum facility, laying out their game plan.

Their strategy was simple on paper. He and Mara would break in, copy and wipe the computers, and document whatever experiments Innovatum was conducting. His goal was to take the shifter's body out of there or destroy the lab to make the body unusable, but they would have to play that by ear.

Everything would change if they found any live experimental subjects. Their objective would have to shift. Extracting the captives would become the priority.

Jack laid out their plan of action in no-nonsense terms. When she had a question, he answered it professionally. Mara assumed that meant he wasn't holding a grudge, but he disabused her of that notion when she asked him when they were landing.

"'I'm afraid we're not, darlin'," he said, pulling out the trunk under their feet.

"What the hell does that mean?" Mara scowled. "I thought we were landing at a private airfield."

"Yeah, no," he said, using a particularly annoying California-ism where the last word was the real answer. "There's been a change of plans."

"How big a change?" The reins on her temper began to slip.

With a shit-eating grin, Jack crouched, pulling out two packs from underneath the bench. He rose, extending one to her. "We're parachuting in."

"*Fuck.*" She counted to a beat of ten. "What about our gear?" They wouldn't be taking much to the Barcelona lab, but they had other equipment, not to mention their clothes.

"The pilot is a friend of mine," he explained. "He'll hold our gear at the airport. He's sending it on to a little inn I know. But you and I are getting off here."

Jack checked his watch. "Well, in five minutes—when we'll be over the drop zone. Our window is pretty tight, so I'd put this on."

Mara slapped a hand over her eyes before snatching the pack and checking it over for the make and model. "Perfect," she muttered. "Just perfect."

"What's wrong?" Jack's smug little smile made her want to deck him.

"This is the wrong size chute," she said, trying her hardest to be patient. She handed the pack to him, slapping it against his chest hard enough to make him rock back. "Can we swap?"

"Uh, no," he said, a touch condescendingly. "I got his and hers. The chutes are perfectly sized for both of us. Trust me, I'm an expert."

Flashing those baby blues, he gave her form a lingering appraisal.

"You're an expert in human bodies, jackass. But shifters have denser muscles. I am *heavier* than you," she said, snatching the pack back. Setting it at her feet, she began to strip.

"What are you doing?" Jack jerked back on the bench so far that his head banged on the wall behind him.

"If these are all the parachutes you have, then I don't have a choice. I have to shift to my second form."

Some shifters bulked up in their animal form, but Mara's wolf was compact and lean. She was about twenty pounds lighter. But what she lost in muscle mass, she made up in speed. The strength of her jaws was nothing to sneeze at either.

By this point, she stood in her bra, her shirt on the plane's floor. Jack's scent spiked, a mixture of shock with more than a tinge of arousal. But when she started to unfasten her pants, he squeezed his eyes shut.

"Are you serious about this?" he asked incredulously. "You can't weigh that much more than a normal woman."

"Are you trying to be an insulting ass, or does it just come natural-ly?" Mara yanked off her pants and rolled them into a ball. "Do you seriously believe I would be stripping if I had a choice?"

35

"I, um, I hope you treat this weight miscalculation as part of the learning curve," Jack said slowly. "Please take it as a compliment, sort of like how people enjoy being mistaken for being younger than they are..."

Mara harrumphed, stepping out of panties.

I will not lose another bra, she vowed, unclipping and stuffing it in the small handheld bag she kept for occasions such as these. She would need her clothes and shoes. She could technically stay a wolf after they landed, but she doubted infiltration would go as smoothly with claws.

That and those depraved Innovatum fuckers experiment on animals as well. No sense in giving them any ideas. She clipped the smaller bag to the chute straps.

"Um, are you decent?" Jack asked. "Or should I say furry? Bark one time for yes. Two for no."

"I'm still two-legged asshat," Mara said, wondering why he wasn't peeking. She knew he was dying to. His scent was a potent mix of lust and curiosity.

Shrugging, she slipped her arms into the chute's arm straps. Jack's puritanical streak was something of a surprise. Skin was just skin, but then most humans weren't comfortable with nudity. With Jack's reputation as a lady's man, she'd expected him to take advantage and look his fill. But he didn't even peek. Deciding not to be insulted, Mara left the straps of the pack loose around her shoulders and shifted.

It wasn't the classic transformation portrayed in the movies. Weres didn't drop to the floor, writhing in agony. The most profound secret of their pack—the change into a wolf—didn't look like much to the naked eye. To her, it was a ripple that passed over her skin from head to toe. It felt like a sneeze that encompassed her entire body. Most wolves involuntarily closed their eyes during the change. Mara didn't because her older brother Connell didn't.

Connell, the pack's second strongest alpha, never knowingly allowed himself to be vulnerable. The few seconds it took to shift was too long he said, especially in a fight. Like his twin, Mara didn't blink either—although the change did smart a little when she did that.

Mara's wolf was a sleek mid-sized beast, a mostly red-brown color speckled with white feet.

With her characteristic patience, she waited all of two seconds for Jack to acknowledge her. When he continued to sit there, his lids firmly clamped shut, she barked

Oh, for fuck's sake, she thought when he started and stared at her with wide eyes. She shook herself, jostling the parachute pack to show him how loose it was.

"Oh," he said, raising his hands hesitantly. "Should I tighten it?"

She nodded, huffing as if to say, 'hurry up, moron'. If he didn't get a move on, they were going to miss their window.

With tentative movements, he secured the shoulder straps and the clips across her chest more firmly. It took him a little longer to figure out the leg straps, but after a warning yap, he finally reached underneath her and snapped them closed. He had less than a minute to pull on his pack before the red light affixed to the plane's wall lit up.

He checked his watch before killing the interior lights and opening the door.

The wind roared into the cabin, plastering her fur to her back.

Mara stepped in front of Jack, getting into position. It was a cloudy night, but there was enough light to make out the ground below.

It was extremely far away.

Her stomach twisted. No going back now. She crouched, her muscles tensing in anticipation of her leap.

"Wait!"

Twisting, Mara turned to Jack. *What now?*

"I think we should go tandem."

Tandem as in strapped to each other? Mara snorted. *Fuck that.* Turning back, she angled her head to grab the chute handle in her jaws.

This is going to suck. Crouching, she bunched her muscles and jumped. The air whistled, her dense, compact body making the descent too fast. She felt like a bullet hurtling through the air.

Wolves preferred the ground. But Mara had done this before. She had hated every single second and nearly wet her pants, but she had gritted her teeth and borne it because it made her a better soldier.

Snapping the chute open with a wide jerk of her jaw, she did her best to curl up and swing her back legs from side to side. Without human arms, she couldn't steer or maneuver with her hands, but by moving her legs this way, Mara could make minor adjustments. It was a distinctly subpar experience, but not as bad as jumping strapped to Jack's body would have been.

The ground approached at terrifying speed. Her pulse was racing, and it felt as if her heart was going to explode. *I'm going to get Jack for this,* she promised herself as she stretched. Mara wanted to land on four feet.

It didn't work. She hit the ground hard, landing on her side, rolling twice before gaining her feet.

Tugging at the straps, she shifted back, determined to regain the upper hand before Jack touched down.

He floated down like a damn butterfly, handling the chute deftly. He turned around to find her on two legs.

His lashes flickered like he was trying to send a Morse code with them. "Are—are you going to get dressed?"

She cocked a hip, holding the rolled-up chute strategically below her waist. "Why? Don't like what you see?"

Clearing his throat, he continued to stand there, stiff-necked, his eyes never drifting down from her face.

"Whatever. I'm going get dressed," she said.

She turned around. There was a strangled sound as he caught sight of the other full moon. Smirking, she ducked behind a stand of trees to change.

CHAPTER FIVE

I *may have to fuse my eyeballs shut for the rest of the mission.*

The woman was killing him. Jack pulled off the chute, putting it away with jerky movements. How could a body be that lean and hard, and still so lush at the same time?

Okay, insisting Mara be the one to accompany him may have been a mistake. But he hadn't expected her to be naked on day one.

How would he get through this mission with the girl of his dreams dropping trou every other minute? *Dear God, this is torture.* Actually, that wasn't quite true. Jack had been tortured once before when he'd pissed off a warlord in North Africa once. This was worse.

This should not be this hard—pun not intended. Jack was a man of not inconsiderable experience. He'd seen plenty of beautiful woman *in flagrante*, as it were. However, those instances had inevitably been followed by *delicto* and plenty of it.

This was different. If Mara kept this up, he wasn't going to be able to function. And if he dared slip and try to touch her with one of his suddenly itchy palms, he'd pull back a bloody stump. An image of that incredibly tanned and toned derriere walking away from him flashed through his mind.

Yeah…It might be worth it.

No, no. Stop. Mara running around naked every other minute was not going to work. He'd talk to her and ask her to keep her clothes on —and good God, when was the last time he'd told a beautiful woman that?

Was asking a werewolf to keep their clothes on offensive?

Screw it. He could deal with this. It wasn't a big deal. And Jack really believed that, or at least he did until Mara came to the clearing, knocking the wind out of him fully dressed.

"How far are we from the facility?" Her tone was cool and professional.

He'd expected some teasing, but no. Mara was all business. Damn. *All work and no play was going to give Jack blue balls.*

"About four clicks. They start monitoring the perimeter a full two kilometers out—cameras with heat sensors. Presumably, they have a program that analyzes the data, filtering out the signals corre-sponding to wildlife. Anything bigger trips the sensor and the lab goes into full lockdown."

He didn't launch into an explanation of how motion sensors wouldn't work. To someone of Mara's background, which he'd pieced together from various classified reports, that was remedial information.

"Then maybe I shouldn't have changed."

"No," he said sternly, a flash of the dissected female shifter hitting him like a slap in the face. "I mean, it's better if we go like this," he said, his gesture encompassing her human body.

"Just follow my lead," he continued. "I've infiltrated this place before."

"Yes, oh great knowledgeable one," she answered, her skepticism bleeding into her tone. "And just how sure are you that they haven't moved these cameras?"

"Mainly because I planted a few cameras of my own the first time around."

Mara raised one fine eyebrow. "So, your cameras are watching their cameras?"

"In a nutshell."

"And what if they added more?"

Jack grinned. "Then expect a team of armed security personnel to descend on our position. If that happens, we run like hell the other way."

"That's your brilliant plan?" Mara chuckled. "Retreat?"

He scowled. "And live to fight another day—that's the mercenary way."

Mara grunted, swinging her backpack on as she kept walking.

"Relax," he said. "There's no reason for them to have added more cameras. This is Southern Spain. Things are more lax here than in the States."

"I've been to Spain before," she informed him with some side-eye.

"You have?" He shouldn't have been surprised. Well, maybe he was.

Except for her time as a peacekeeper with the UN—again, he deserved a major pat on the back for hacking those records—Mara hadn't traveled much. According to the Customs and Border Patrol database, Mara Faye Maitland hadn't left the States in the last five years. Or at least she hadn't done it by using her passport. He couldn't discount that possibility.

"Good. I hope you like tapas." There were several places in nearby Barcelona that he wanted to take her to, but that was all he said for the next few minutes. When they were about to hit the invisible two-kilometer mark, he stopped her.

"This is it," he said, keeping his voice low as he pointed to a gnarled tree approximately two hundred meters away. "That's where the camera surveillance starts. The path I've laid out should let us thread the needle without setting off any alarms, but we should each carry one of these."

He opened his bag, then pulled out two handheld devices. "These are hidden camera detectors. Do you know how one works?"

The small device was government grade. He'd gotten it from a buddy who supplied the NSA with the best toys. Jack's only addition was to solder a strap handle with a ring of Velcro to the back so he could wear the device, leaving his hands free.

"Yeah," Mara fiddled with the controls, setting the device to the maximum range. That would kill the battery pretty quickly, but he didn't comment. If all went well, they wouldn't be in the facility long enough to drain them.

"I'm going to leave mine off for the time being. Give me a yank if it goes off. If positive, the light will turn red. Also, the alert will be displayed with an estimated distance on the screen. Keep the volume down."

Nodding her assent, she fastened the Velcro strap to her forearm.

"No gun?"

"I don't normally use weapons," he told her. He carried a taser at his hip, but if somebody needed a gun during a break-in, they were doing it wrong.

But Jack was a planner. He lifted the pack. "I have one in here for emergencies. Do you want it?"

Mara gave him a subtly superior look. "I don't need a gun," she said, holding up her hands. Two sets of sharp claws sprang from her fingertips. "I *am* a weapon."

Transfixed, he reached out to test the sharpness of one of those lethal-looking tips. "Like Wolverine."

Mara rolled her eyes, but he considered her annoyance justified this time. He turned his back, signaling her to follow. From that moment on, they were ghosts.

Jack was used to skulking around, moving in the shadows without tipping anyone off to his presence. Mara, however, shamed him with her skill. She practically melted into the surrounding darkness, her steps behind him soundless. He kept glancing back to make sure she was there.

What did he expect? She was a werewolf who hunted wild game regularly. A mental image of Mara chomping on a bloody rabbit leg flashed through his mind.

Oh, wow. That was an effective arousal killer. He just needed to think of that whenever she stripped naked.

A few minutes later, they were behind the Innovatum building that housed the morgue-slash-pathology lab.

Mara gave him the signal that told him the coast was clear—according to their equipment, no new cameras had been added.

Their first task was to determine the body was still there. That would tell them whether his previous break-in had been detected. If it had, then going to the body was a trap. However, there was no way to know unless they did it.

The complex had a few points of vulnerability. The first time he'd come here, he'd used a service door. But today, he'd chosen another path. Their point of entry was a dummy vent near the roof. It had never been hooked up to the ventilation system.

The pathology lab was in the center of the building, protected by locked doors fitted with electronic keypads. The code was changed daily. Instead of wasting time hacking his way to a solution, Jack had found a way to circumvent the system.

All they had to do was go down to the basement.

Jack wasn't sure what this building had originally been. He'd guessed this had been part of a biology building because the pathology lab benches and sinks were old. It was also never meant to be disconnected from the other room. The locks on the doors were new, some added quite recently. Repurposing was the European way.

On his first visit, Jack had discovered this building had an expansive basement. It encompassed more than half the ground floor. The Innovatum people hadn't been able to bar all access to it because it was where the boilers were, and fixing up the old heating and ventilation system had been cheaper than installing a new one.

The door to the basement was padlocked. It was a moment's work to open it. Picking their way through the dusty subterranean chamber was another story. He hadn't understood how sensitive Mara's nose would be until they got down there, and she started sneezing up a storm.

"We're lucky they don't have cameras down here," he murmured.

"I can control it," she snapped in between sneezes. "Just give me a minute."

Fascinated with her ever-changing facial expressions, he watched her struggle for control, fighting her body's involuntary response with rigid discipline.

"Very impressive," he said after she'd gained the upper hand. "But why don't you take this to avoid any more attacks by rabid dust bunnies."

He pulled a handkerchief out of his pocket. It was a special microfiber, capable of filtering particles if someone had to run through a burning building or got caught in a dust storm.

Mara snatched the cloth. "You could have given this to me sooner."

She tied the handkerchief around her face, her green eyes flashing like angry emeralds.

"I didn't think a little dust would bother you so much," he said. She growled something under her breath, and he grinned.

"Come on," he said. "You can take a bite out of me later. I'll even stand still for it."

He turned his back, holding his breath until he heard her footsteps behind him.

If she'd been truly angry and decided to take him out, Jack was certain he'd never hear her coming. The fact he found that arousing spoke volumes about his character.

The basement was a crowded labyrinth of refuse. Broken desks and dusty chairs were piled high—enough to block the door hidden in the middle of the load-bearing wall dividing the basement. Given the thick layer of dust, only minimally disturbed by his first visit, it had been overlooked by the Innovatum security team. The door hadn't been in any of the plans he found for the school.

He uncovered the opening he'd taken pains to conceal. Another few minutes and they were through it, taking another set of stairs up. These led to a series of wide hallways. At the end was a pair of double doors, the entrance to the pathology lab. A simple key card reader protected these. Bypassing it a second time was no trouble.

The space behind was a cross between a medical examiner's office and a chemistry lab. One side had a long bench filled with glass apparatus set up for distillation. It had probably been salvaged from one of the building's previous incarnations. Innovatum had found some use for it, but that side of the lab didn't concern him. His focus was on the other half, the morgue side.

That section of the room was clean and efficiently organized. A metal autopsy table was stationed a few meters from the wall. Behind it was a refrigerated unit with half-a-dozen cadaver drawers.

Jack pulled open the lone drawer with a sticker on it. It was the only one occupied.

Part of him was relieved it was still there. The other, more dominant part was flat-out mad. The things that had been done to this woman were inhuman. But his cold anger was nothing compared to what he saw on Mara's face.

"We burn it to the ground after we leave."

He nodded, jaw tight. "Your call."

"They kept working on her, didn't they?" Her voice was carefully controlled, but her emotions were like a Saharan wind sweeping over him. The heat was almost enough to sear his eyeballs.

Speaking of which, what had they done with the woman's eyelids?

"Yes. They did." The first time he came around, the chest cavity had been cracked open. Now the skin had been cut back from the legs as well as if they were mapping the musculature.

He didn't have to tell her there were now pieces missing as well. He could see her examining the gaps, no doubt comparing it to the picture he'd taken in her mind.

"Before we take care of this, let's look for live subjects," he suggested.

For a moment, he thought she might ignore him.

It was the way she stood there, an explosive quality to her stillness. It sent up a big-ass red flag. *I touch her at this moment, and those claws will come out.* If that happened, he might not make it out of this room alive.

But Mara was a Maitland. One thing he'd learned from serving with Connell, her brother—Douglas Maitland was a harsh taskmaster who'd taught his son patience and discipline. His daughter was no different.

Mara stepped away from the body, pushing the tray back into the fridge. Without speaking, they swept the rooms, fanning out from their central position. The regular patrol of guards presented no problem. Mara could hear them from a far greater distance than he could with his night-vision goggles.

He'd bought a pair for her, too, but she'd rolled her eyes when he offered them.

They found a lab full of rats and rabbits, but Mara had shaken her head when he'd gestured at them questioningly.

"So, there are no shifter bunny rabbits?"

Mara shrugged. "Not in this room."

They kept searching. Mara had paused for a time in front of a large cage, but she didn't say anything, and Jack didn't ask about it. He was too focused on their other problem. "There are no computers in the building."

Mara scowled, turning around. "You're right."

There were power outlets, but no ethernet jacks. No scientist in this day and age could function without the internet. And then he noticed the shelves.

The lab books and binders were either empty or brand. He picked up one of the notebooks. The label on the spine had a number filled in—seven. Books one through six were missing.

Mara huffed when he pointed that out. "They must have learned their lesson after what you and Yogi pulled at the Wyoming facility."

"Yeah." He examined the power cable plugged in at the desk of a nearby office. "They must do all the work on laptops, taking the computers and lab books with them every day when they leave."

"Now what?" she asked.

Jack straightened, his face grim. "You already know."

They couldn't burn this shit hole down. Without the data and connections he could glean from it, the major players would remain unidentified. They would have to settle in for some long-term surveillance.

"*Fuck*," Mara spat, closing her eyes. But then she rubbed her face and straightened. It was both incredibly beautiful and painful to watch.

CHAPTER SIX

"Momma?" David called tremulously, huddling in his denim jacket.

David was almost twelve. He hadn't called his mother 'momma' in years, but he was cold and scared. He needed her right now.

"Momma?" he called again, wishing he had his wool coat. But there hadn't been any time to pack. Those people had come with their guns and their lights, and his family ran with only the clothes on their backs.

As a hyena shifter, he wasn't supposed to feel the cold, but that didn't seem to matter. He'd been freezing, shivering, since he got separated from his parents and sister over an hour ago.

Staying low, he peeked around the base of a large fir tree. *Please be there, Momma.* He'd even settle for Jana, his annoying big sister. But David was alone.

The woods were dark and quiet. He couldn't smell his family.

Why did we come here?

They should have done what his mother suggested. She'd wanted to check into a hotel—the more expensive, the better.

"The hunters wouldn't dare follow us inside," she'd said.

But his father had said they had a better chance of losing the people chasing them in the woods.

Dad should have listened to Mom. He didn't do that enough, and now look at them. They were lost, and David wore only a thin denim jacket that didn't feel warm enough.

If it doesn't do you any good, lose it. Another good bit of advice from his mother.

Stripping off his jacket, his pants, and his shirt, David stripped and shifted. A small spotted hyena with a black muzzle, he nosed at his clothes until he'd concealed them in a nook between two large tree roots. Then he used his hind legs to conceal them under pine needles in an attempt to cover his scent.

What he should do was bury them, but the men he'd seen didn't appear to have dogs with them. If they were human, that probably meant they weren't tracking them by scent. Plus, David didn't want to waste time. He had to find his family now before it got too dark. He had excellent night vision. The dark didn't bother him, but Jana would be scared. When she was little, she used to sleep with a nightlight. All he'd had was those glow-in-the-dark stars on his ceiling, and those didn't light anything up at all. They were just something to look at in the dark.

Heavy clouds obscured the stars tonight. An ominous rumble sounded in the distance. The scent of approaching rain filled the air. His stomach rumbled.

Yeah, we definitely should have gone to a hotel. One with room service —not a vending machine like his dad would have chosen.

David was going to tell his dad that Mom had been right as soon as he found him again. Then they'd find a hotel. When they did, he was going to order a big cheeseburger with extra fries and double ketchup.

Putting his nose to the ground, he tried to track. Jana was better at it than him. Dad said he needed to pay more attention to his lessons and less time on video games. He was right, of course, but his parents wouldn't be trying to hide from him. No scent tricks or traps tonight.

An hour later, it had started to rain in earnest. Shivering, he circled a big tree and smelled himself faintly.

In his head, he said a word his mother would have washed his mouth out with soap for using. But he couldn't help himself. Instead of making progress, he'd come in a big circle, back to the tree where he'd hidden his clothes.

Shaking off the rain, he huddled in the shelter of the tree, whimpering. It was a low, pathetic sound. Then he saw the light. Stealthily, he padded toward it, making sure to stay in the shadows.

He must have made a noise because the light swung toward him. The concentrated beam was from a flashlight. His parents didn't have one with them, only an old camping lantern.

David crawled backward under a bush, trying to hide. He squeezed his eyes shut so the light wouldn't reflect off his hyena lenses.

There was no sound. Frozen stiff, he held his breath, afraid to breathe. When he opened them, he saw the big boots inches away from his snout. Yipping, he tried to run, but more booted men came.

The bright lights of their flashlights blinded him, and he felt a pain in his side. Then the dark came, and he fell and couldn't get back up again. The last thing he remembered was being loaded into a cage.

But he wasn't alone. Jana was in the next cage, fast asleep. Somewhere in the same van, he could smell his parents. The men had gotten them, too.

CHAPTER SEVEN

A week later

Mara stretched methodically over the yoga mat, her eyes on the two computer screens running independent streams of surveillance footage on fast forward. It required some maneuvering to make sure she always faced the screens, but Mara was determined and flexible.

That and it bothered Jack when she did Yoga. She wasn't sure why. It may have had something to do with her yoga outfit—skintight capris and a crop top with a built-in sports bra. She wasn't the most voluptuous woman, but she filled the brief top well.

In any case, it was Jack's fault. He had forbidden her to run in her animal form outside while they were here.

The human had put it much more diplomatically, of course. Jack wasn't stupid. But the result was the same—absolutely no runs as a wolf. Not even in the dead of night.

"There's no sense in giving Innovatum another shifter target," Jack had said, trying to soften the blow by offering her a glass of excellent Spanish wine. "Please don't change anywhere near this hellhole."

It had been a reasonable and civilized conversation at the time. But Mara hadn't been on a mission that lasted this long since she was with the UN. She hadn't realized how difficult it would be. Her wolf had gotten spoiled in Colorado while her human half had chaffed at the limitations of being stuck at home.

It made her wonder. Why couldn't both sides of her nature be happy at the same time? Why did it have to be one or the other with her? None of the males in the pack seemed to have this problem.

An image of herself as a wolf chewing her leg off flashed through her mind. Shifting into a headstand, Mara gritted her teeth. She wasn't there yet, but she also wasn't that far off. It didn't help that she was trapped here with Jack, his scent blanketing the room.

That was to be expected, of course. The apartment belonged to him. If it had been a rental, it wouldn't have been so bad. But because he didn't stay here that often, and he didn't rent it out during his absences, the underlying scent was never replaced by anyone else's.

Situated in the Gothic Quarter of Barcelona, the two-bedroom flat was large by European standards. But for Mara, it was a cramped, badly ventilated closet.

The summer weather was another issue. Why the hell didn't anyone on this continent believe in air conditioning? Or screens? Mara had thrown open all the windows, trying to catch every cross-wind possible, but Jack's scent was in the furniture. The mix of ocean, sun, and musk had seeped into the couches and the small hand-woven rugs. Even the sheets she slept on carried his scent.

He was everywhere, regardless of whether he was in the building. What was more, she almost missed him when he was gone.

Despite the occasional sniping, she found Jack fun, flirty, and surprisingly considerate. Most every night, they would share a glass of wine on his tiny balcony and go over their findings.

Sometimes, she forgot to guard herself and spoke openly about her life.

In some ways, working with him was so easy. But sharing his space wasn't. If only his damn scent weren't on everything.

One of the movie files ended on the right monitor. Dropping out of her *bakasana* pose, she went to the computer to start a new one.

Before they left, they had planted small cameras in and around the morgue and lab. The security team may have been lax, but they went through the motions, doing sweeps for bugs on a regular rotation. As a result, they'd had to get creative in their placement, at least on the inside. The angles inside the building were shit, which was why Mara preferred to watch the exterior feeds. They could get better resolution cameras with a wider field of view out in the parking lot.

Behind her, there was a corkboard crammed with blown-up photographs. Everyone who'd parked in the lot was on their wall of shame. Names and addresses were pinned to most of the photographs. Jack's facial recognition program was still working on the rest.

It was her task to comb through the camera footage and tag new faces. It was a shit job, menial and monotonous, but she had to admit she was better at it than Jack was.

Mara was both predator and a trained soldier. Her visual acuity wasn't just fast, it was preternatural. She could watch the films at double and triple speeds with only a fraction of her attention, pausing only when someone new drove into the lot. Familiar faces already documented were dismissed. If she noticed someone new, she'd take a series of still images for Jack.

The people he'd ID'd so far were mostly janitorial and low-level laboratory staff, people with degrees in biology but no record of publication or travel to conferences.

Mengele didn't become Mengele without going to medical school first. The men and women they were searching for had a history of academic success behind them. Otherwise, they wouldn't have been tapped by Denon for this work. So far, none of the people they'd iden-tified had that kind of resume. They hadn't found the boss yet.

Jack blew in a few minutes later. Sweaty from a run, his scent slammed into her. Mara tried not to react, but it was a beguiling fragrance. It tested and teased, setting her teeth on edge.

Mara stiffened before shifting into *kapotasana*, her body arched, arms and legs flat on the ground to form a perfect semicircle. Behind her, Jack's scent turned musky with arousal. Sharp, unsatisfied arousal.

It was petty, but it made her feel a little better.

"Are you sure you can see the entire screen in that position?" The bite in his tone told her that he knew what she was doing. "I wouldn't want you to miss anything."

"I have officially watched three days' worth of footage without a single new face," she replied, shifting into *dhanurasana* without missing a beat.

Behind her, Jack made the tiniest of whimpers. She hid a smile.

"Something tells me there isn't going to be another one. Whoever is in charge of this facility is either doing it remotely or is already on this wall. But we won't know that until your fabulous facial recognition program finds a match."

Jack considered that. "That doesn't make sense. Denon could be running the show from afar," he grumbled. "But those lab underlings don't have the experience required to keep an operation of this size going. They're taking orders from someone. And my program will find a match. It just takes time."

"Of course it does. That's why you get paid the big bucks, right?"

"I'll have you know I'm doing this pro bono—purely out of the goodness of my heart."

"Sure, you are."

Jack threw his arms out. "If I wanted money, I'd have hammered out terms before we left Colorado. Only an amateur waits until the end to ask for the cash. Your pack won't be getting a bill."

"That's not what Derrick said. He said you'd put us all over a barrel once you figured out your angle. And he considers you a friend."

"Yeah, well, Derrick doesn't know everything," Jack replied, putting his hands on his hips. "Did you talk to him today?"

"Yeah."

"I see." Jack's lips pursed. "Well, you can tell your father that he doesn't have to monitor us so closely. I'll be the first to get in touch when we have something concrete."

"Derrick didn't call for an update."

"Really? Because he does it often. Or were you video chatting with someone else yesterday?"

Mara frowned, rolling out of her pose to frown. "What's wrong?"

Jack's face blanked. "What makes you think something is wrong?"

She raised a brow, and he shrugged. "I think it's tough they keep calling to check up on you like you are some kid."

Mara cocked her head. "Nice try, but that's not it. If I didn't know any better, I'd say you were jealous."

"Of you?" Jack's laugh was a little too hearty. He waved at her scantily clad body. "Don't be, um, don't be…funny."

Mara bit her lip to keep from laughing. "Wow, you're not even trying."

Jack's face was red. He waved, "Well, what do you expect when you spend your days in outfits like that?"

Staggering to the kitchen, he opened the freezer and took out a bottle of vodka. "But I would have appreciated a heads-up from Derrick."

Confusion filled Mara. "What are you talking about now?"

Jack shrugged, pouring himself a slug. "He could have told me you were taken."

Mara stared. *Oh.* Oh no. "Derrick is my cousin. My mother's sister also married into the pack."

Jack squinted as if trying to decide if she were telling the truth. "I thought that was a front. Everyone in the pack is a 'cousin,'" he said, adding air quotes to the last word.

"Sometimes it is." Mara shrugged. "Sometimes it's not."

His head drew back. "And you're this chummy with all your cousins?"

"Derrick and I grew up together. I talk to him more than my own brother."

"So to confirm…werewolves don't believe in kissing cousins?"

Mara didn't answer. She just took off her shoe, chucking it toward him.

Jack ducked, but it hit his head anyway. He burst out laughing, rubbing his head. "Remind me not to do that when you have a real weapon. You're pretty fast on the draw."

"The trick is not to telegraph your moves like some humans I know."

Jack scowled. "I don't telegraph my punches."

Mara tried not to laugh at his expression. She hadn't ever seen Jack fight, but he must be good to hold his own alongside Derrick and her brother. Nevertheless, needing him was fun.

Hey, if she couldn't run, she had to get her kicks somehow.

Mara frowned, twisting her head to the door. A few seconds later, there was a short knock. She pressed a few keys to pause the video feeds.

"Were you expecting company?"

Jack's face lit up. "Yes!" He went to the door, taking a wrapped parcel from a man in shorts and a Panama hat. They spoke in Spanish, their tone friendly.

Mara covered her face in her hands. What part of secret surveillance did he not understand?

"What happened to no takeout?" she asked when he closed the door, the wrapped bundle under his arm.

"This is not takeout, and it's for you," he said, widening his eyes as he held up the baseball-sized object. "A gift more precious than jewels."

Mara narrowed her eyes, sniffing the air. "You bought me meat?"

"Bite your tongue," Jack scolded, cradling the package away from her as if offended. "This isn't mere meat. This is one hundred percent pure acorn-fed Iberico ham. They cure this for three *years*. This is as far from meat as you can get."

He unwrapped the packaging with a flourish, presenting an entire shoulder of pork like a game show hostess.

The aroma was incredible. Her mouth watered.

Jack put the entire joint in her hands before proceeding to dig under the kitchen counter. He popped back up, holding a cutting board with a metal stand and holder fixed to one end. Clamping the bone in the vise, he laid the shoulder meat side down, whipping out some wickedly sharp kitchen knives.

"I noticed you like the ham sandwiches from the lunch place across the street," he said, cutting through the thick skin to reveal the deep ruby flesh underneath. "And that one is okay, especially when you compare it to what passes for luncheon meat in the US. But that ham has got nothing on this."

He laid out a series of paper-thin slices on a plate. "I can make these for you in a sandwich if you want, but I recommend trying it without anything at first."

Mara stared. A male feeding a female had special connotations among shifters. It was part of the mating ritual, which was supposed to demonstrate that the male was a good provider.

But humans were unaware of those nuances, she reminded herself. Mara relaxed, taking a sliver of ham and popping it past her lips. Flavor exploded in her mouth. It watered retroactively, and she chewed with relish.

"Good, huh?"

Her lashes fluttered, and she rocked back on her heels. "You're right. That is better."

The smug gleam was back in his eyes. For a second, she wondered if he understood the symbolism of giving and accepting food, but he turned around, opening the fridge. "We have fresh bread from the bakery so I can make you a sandwich, but we could also go fully native. I picked up a nice Manchego and some ripe cantaloupe."

Next, he was going to suggest wine. Mara needed to nip this in the bud.

She took the plate and sat cross-legged in front of the screens, resuming the playback. "This is fine."

Jack opened his mouth, then snapped it shut, his expression changing like quicksilver. He pointed at one of the screens behind her.

"New or old?" he asked urgently.

Twisting, Mara saw the man crossing the parking lot on the right screen. He was well dressed, slight, about five foot seven.

"New," she confirmed as the man disappeared into the building.

Leaning forward, she rewound the video, capturing a series of stills at different angles to give Jack a variety to feed into his facial recognition software.

"Print one out for me," he told her.

After a few more taps, the series of images was spat out of the corner's high-res color printer.

Jack studied the images, squinting and holding them at different angles. "Would you describe this guy as dapper?"

Mara frowned at the still on the screen. His clothes were tailored, and his haircut was expensive. He was even wearing a tie pin, and were those cufflinks? Who wore those to work? Someone fastidious and showy. "I suppose, in a fussy-britches kind of way."

Jack's lips regained their usual smug twist. "This is our guy."

"How do you know?"

"Because I've seen him before at the Wyoming facility—just before Denise Hammond decked him. She laid him flat."

He sounded impressed. So was Mara. Denise was human. Punching out a man was an achievement for someone so petite.

Jack held up the printed photo. "He's tried to change his appearance since then. His hair is dyed a few shades lighter and he's added glasses, but I'm ninety-five percent sure this is the same man."

"Who is he?"

Jack shrugged. "I don't know."

Mara scowled. "I thought you'd seen him before."

"In person," Jack confirmed, "But he didn't show up on any internal Reliance Research documents. Unfortunately, we didn't think to take his picture at the time. We had to get out of here before reinforcements came back. Unlike a standard research lab, there wasn't a webpage with a convenient list of staff. And they went above and beyond to cover their tracks—all the research we copied was anonymized. The lab reports didn't have names, only numbers assigned per facility and the employee start date. There might be a master list somewhere that matches each numerical ID to a name, but it wasn't in the Wyoming data server. My guess is that list is squirreled away in some secret corner by the parent company."

"The Denon corporation."

"Yes. And since they're a huge conglomerate, trying to find that information by hacking them is like trying to locate a needle in a haystack. They have facilities and offices all over the world. Which is why we're doing it this way—matching faces to real-world IDs."

Mara frowned at the picture. "Is this normal behavior for top-secret labs? For a multinational, I mean?"

"Absolutely not," he said. "But we both know they're not trying to protect anything as plebeian as trade secrets. They were ready to cover up criminal activity from the very start."

"So now what?"

He waved the picture. "I figure out what the world calls this guy, then we tear his life apart, finding out who he works for as well as who that person works for. We go all the way up the chain, gathering as much dirt as we can along the way."

Mara scrubbed her hands over her face.

"What's wrong?"

"Nothing."

He frowned

Mara sighed. "Our pack is old and part of a much larger community. We've been exposed before, but all those other cases were contained, small—either a person or a nosy reporter who thought they'd stumbled on the story of the century. But this is different. Our enemy is well-funded, with a global reach. We're not going to be able to brush this one under the rug."

"And if you can't?" he asked.

"We go to war," she said. "The amount of collateral damage depends on whether we do it in secret or wage it out in the open... assuming Denon gives us the option."

CHAPTER EIGHT

"I still think I should go with you," Jack grumbled as Mara browsed the racks of the Parisian dress shop.

Mara pulled out a red gown, holding it up against her chest. Frowning at the cut of the bodice, she put it back. A plunging neckline didn't communicate mystery. More like 'come and get it'.

"You said so yourself. Our friend knows your face."

"Debatable."

Their friend's name was Felix Dubois. Jack had identified him from the video, his program matching it to a US passport using backchannels she didn't want to know about.

As suspected, Felix Dubois was an alias, but a well-established one. Dubois was listed as a doctor with degrees in genetics and biotechnology with a specialty in gene therapy. There were some big-name schools on his resume. Mara and Jack assumed the degrees were real, albeit under another name and likely from an equally prestigious university.

Dubois' current employer was a tiny think-tank. He was listed as a consultant in biomedical research. To date, Jack hadn't found a single tie to the Denon Corporation, but that didn't mean there wasn't one. It just meant it was very well-hidden.

That secretiveness was why Mara was going to meet Felix Dubois on his own turf.

"What is this charity dinner for again?" she asked, examining and discarding another possibility, a black dress with an embroidered fringe.

"Childhood leukemia."

Mara raised a brow. "Any chance it's legit?"

"On paper, but I doubt much money makes it to where it's supposed to go. Not if they're blowing the budget to rent out the big ballroom of the Caislean Paris. The ticket price will barely cover the food budget alone. But the cause certainly gives it that air of true benevolence, doesn't it?"

She scowled at her reflection in the mirror. "I hate the rich even more now."

Jack wrinkled his nose at the plum gown she selected next. "You *are* rich. At least you are according to what I've dug up about the pack's finances."

He straightened as he caught her expression.

"Excuse me?" Her look was hot enough to blister his skin.

"Relax, I only use my powers for good."

She glared until his neck grew red.

"All right, so you guys don't live rich," he conceded. "But you have the money. I haven't figured out what you use it for."

Mara grabbed an emerald-green dress, then a purple one. She shoved them into Jack's arms, making sure to dig the end of the wooden hangers in his chest.

He winced, adjusting them as she led them to the private dressing room.

But it was a fair question, under the circumstances. She had promised to treat him as an equal for the duration of this mission.

"We learned a long time ago that a predator who is stressed out about making rent or sending their kid to school sometimes does stupid things. Having money is insurance against that. If a pack member gets in trouble, they know they can rely on the pack. We also fund our own clinics, so everyone who needs it has access to medical care—for obvious reasons. We have specialists who deal with money. It's never one person, but a team, and we don't let them talk to each other much, so their moves are independent of each other. They invest with an eye to the future."

"So, if something big goes down, you have not only a cushion, but also a war chest?" Jack said, rubbing the spot on his chest. "Smart."

Mara took the dresses from him. "You know what's even smarter? Never stealing from wolves."

His hand covered his heart. "I would *never*."

She held the door of the dressing open. "Yeah, yeah. Remember, curiosity killed the cat. But in our case, we eat them."

He was wincing when she closed the door in his face.

J ack took one look at Mara in the green dress, then immediately regretted wearing his lightweight pants. Good for the heat, bad for shopping for sexy dresses with Mara. Bad for anything with Mara, really. The woman could arouse him while brushing her teeth. *I was never envious of inanimate objects before her.* First her toothbrush, now this dress...

"I like the purple one better."

Mara considered her reflection in the three-way mirror. Emerald-covered curves stretched to oblivion, which made her eyes seem even greener. "The purple one is nice, too, but I like this one better," she said, twisting to examine her backside.

He could have told her it was perfect, but he decided against it... better part of valor and all that.

"Maybe the red?" he asked optimistically.

"No." Mara shook her head. "This is the one. The charity ball is tomorrow night, and the red one would require alterations."

Jack managed a stiff smile. Or at least, he showed a lot of teeth. "Great, why don't you take it off, and I'll go pay?"

"So you can bill us later?" she scoffed. "No, thanks. The pack will pay."

Brushing it off, he straightened. "Then allow me to make myself useful. I'll go find shoes."

CHAPTER NINE

I *am going to kill Jack*, Mara thought. It was a familiar refrain. She smiled stiffly at the lecherous diplomat she was dancing with. *Preferably with the shoes he picked.* The stiletto heel would make an excellent weapon—especially if she drove it into a soft spot.

Pretending to stumble, Mara stepped on her partner's toes, crushing them hard enough to bring their skin-to-skin waltz to a close. *It's not the lambada, dude*, she thought before exploding into apologies.

"It is not a problem," the Italian man—a count of some kind—said. "Perhaps you would like to make it up to me in my suite? I have rooms here."

Eww... Mara managed a stiff smile. "I'm afraid I can't leave until my boss shows up. She's doing business with some local bigwig."

The man took her hand, pressing his wet lips to the back of it. "Perhaps after," he said, pressing a key card into her hand. He didn't wait for an answer before leaving her in a cloud of cologne.

"*Blergh.*"

Mara took a turn about the room, scanning for Dubois, and dropped the card in the bin.

Jack's voice buzzed in her earpiece. "What? It wasn't true love?"

"Very funny," she murmured, turning so the brooch pinned to her dress was facing the middle of the room. She was trying to give the camera embedded inside it the widest angle. "That dance was almost as invasive as my last gynecological exam. I no longer think the waltz is elegant."

Jack made a strangled sound that might have been a laugh, but he recovered nicely. "Any sign of Dubois?"

"Not yet."

"Well, keep looking. How's the food?"

Mara smiled. Waving over a waiter, she picked up a lobster puff, her fifth for the evening. "Worth the price of admission."

He groaned aloud. "Rub it in, why don't you? I hate being stuck in the van."

"Well, there's a simple solution to that," she said, biting the appetizer in half. "Mmmh. Delicious."

A grunt. "What's the solution?"

"Plastic surgery."

There was a rough sound, the kind a man made in the back of his throat. "Just keep your eyes peeled for the mark."

Mara spun on her heel, giving the camera a view of the corners. "Enjoy your sandwich. What is it tonight—tuna?"

"I'll have you know I'm having the finest Iberico and manchego tonight."

"I thought you left the pork shoulder in Spain."

"I may have packed a sandwich for the road."

She gave a hovering waiter a small sign, then took another hors d'oeuvre—grilled foie gras on toast this time. "You're not sick of ham and cheese yet?"

"Not this ham and not this cheese." There was the sound of rustling. "Look alive. I got eyes on a man going into the front of the hotel that matches our description."

She frowned. "But you don't know for sure?"

"He used the valet. I only saw the back of his head."

"Distracted by your Iberico?"

"If it's him, we'll know in a minute. Angle your camera to the main doors."

"I hear and obey," she said, pivoting.

The man they knew as Felix Dubois walked in shortly after.

At once, a thousand thoughts rose and clashed in her mind. Anger and hatred were right at the top, but there was also excitement. Mara was on a mission virtually important to her pack. Her—not her brother or one of her cousins.

That giddy self-importance lasted about fifteen minutes. But Felix just schmoozed, ate, and schmoozed some more while she flitted around, aiming her camera to record every interaction.

And I don't get to maim him. It was torture. *Boring* torture.

"Remind me why we didn't break into his hotel room again?" she muttered, using yet another delicious appetizer to cover her mouth when a cluster of well-heeled men and women passed by her.

"Because even if he has his work computer with him, it will probably be more of the same—work files with no IDs. He might notice, in which case he'll go to ground, which means we'll be back at square one with no idea who else is involved. We can break into his place and plant trackers once we've established who runs in his circle."

"What makes you think anyone here fits that description?"

"I don't, but we don't have a better plan. We have to keep following him until we find someone."

Mara adjusted the bodice of her gown, tugging it down a touch. "Well, I guess I should go make myself available."

"Hold up." More rustling. "We never said you were going to make contact."

Her jaw tensed under her placid expression. "Why else am I here? We want to get into his inner circle."

"And if he shoots you down, what then? He will know your face. If we need to put you in his sphere in another context, that will put you in the same boat as me. Then we couldn't use you when it might really matter."

Mara caught a glimpse of her reflection in one of the floor-to-ceiling mirrors spaced along the left wall. "Trust me, he's not going to shoot me down in this dress."

"Are you sure? Because from what I'm seeing, he's not going to bite."

Mara took a champagne flute, masking her glance at Dubois. He was exchanging a smoldering look with one of the waiters.

She snickered. "Point taken. I think the wrong one of us is in the van. It seems our friend prefers a different kind of honey in his pot."

"It's not a total loss. Keep an eye on who he mingles with."

"I think we can cross the waiters off the list. That should narrow it down."

Mara gravitated to the wall, trying to lean against it surreptitiously. *Damn shoes.*

"I didn't think tonight would be this boring," she admitted.

"Really?" a crisply accented voice said. "I could have warned you. These things are always deathly dull."

Mara turned, surprised she hadn't heard the man approach. She blamed her shoes.

"Hi," she said, turning so the camera caught the newcomer.

Tall and dark-haired, the man was in his early thirties. He was wearing a bespoke tux that fit so well it had to have been custom made. His shoes cost more than her car.

And I bet they don't pinch.

"I'm sorry to have interrupted your conversation," the man said, throwing her a charming grin. "Should I leave so you can continue?"

She laughed. "Sorry, but the voices in my head are more entertaining than most of the men I've spoken to tonight."

The stranger's smile grew wider. "I don't doubt it."

The man bowed. "Henry Carrington, Baron Ventry."

Mara blinked. "A baron, as in the red baron?"

"Yes, but not as infamous," Henry said with effortless charm.

"I'm afraid I don't have a title. I'm Mary Butler." She held out her hand, shaking, before stepping back and gesturing at their surroundings. "I take it you're not from around here."

"My tiny holding is actually in Scotland.

She tilted her head to the side. "Is that a modest way of saying you have a castle?"

"I suppose yes," he laughed. "But it sucks more capital than it generates, I'm afraid. However, having an albatross has been motivational for me—I learned international finance to fund renovations. That early effort has served me well. I've made enough to keep the torches lit for generations to come."

Her lip quirked. It was a humble brag but flawlessly executed. Besides, with that accent, she was more than willing to let him get away with it. "Your castle is lit by torchlight?"

"It's more of a fort, rather squat, and only mildly hideous. But it's been retrofit with the necessary amenities for modern life—including hot water and, more recently, WIFI."

Her laughter was genuine. "How luxurious."

"Well, I wasn't sure you'd be impressed with indoor plumbing," Henry said. "I had to pull out the big guns."

The baron waved over a waiter carrying a tray full of champagne, but when the man offered him a glass, he shook his head, asking for something else in a low murmur. The waiter returned in a few minutes with a bottle of Cognac.

Henry presented her a glass with a flourish.

Mara feigned naïveté. "Are you sure this is allowed?"

He waved her concern aside. "I know the organizer, and she always keeps a few bottles in the kitchen as a little treat for those who know to ask for them."

"How nice to be part of the in-crowd. Thank you," she said, meaning it. She'd held on to the champagne glass, but she hadn't drunk much of it. The bubbles irritated her sensitive nose.

Henry nodded amiably. "I thought it presumptuous to ask you to join me for a nightcap, especially after Mr. Dominico's performance, but then I figured if you didn't have to leave the room for it…"

She narrowed her eyes. "You are smooth."

"I like to think so." He winked and took a sip from his glass. "So, what brings you to this riveting and star-studded evening?"

"Star-studded?" she echoed.

"I'll have you know I made page eight of the Daily Mail once upon a time." His laugh was self-deprecating. "I stopped a cutpurse from running off with a nice little old lady's handbag."

She giggled. "I had no idea I was in the presence of a hero, one lauded in the tabloids no less."

"I promise not to hold it against you if you share," he said with a nudge.

"Oh yes," she said, thinking quickly. "I am here in an official capacity to represent my boss to some muckety-muck, but now I don't think they're going to show."

"And the unofficial reason?" he prodded with a conspiratorial inclination of his head.

She lifted her glass in a toast. "Very good. There is something else."

Mara made a show of glancing around them. "I can't go into too many details," she said, lowering her voice in a confidential tone.

"I am the soul of discretion," Henry promised in a low voice, his attention fixed on her.

She pursed her lips, projecting conflict. "My employer is an impor-tant woman—she's not in finance, but she has fingers in a lot of pies. She asked me to attend this, and events like it, to gather names."

"People like me? Those in finance?" Henry's eyes flared. "Who is your boss?"

"No, not folks in finance. As for my employer—I don't feel comfortable sharing her name."

Ruefully, she shook her head. "To be frank, as exciting as it is, this is all a bit cloak and dagger for my taste. I went from being a lowly executive assistant to being sent to fancy parties."

"Now, I simply have to know."

Mara lifted a shoulder. "It's a little odd, but she'd like to get a list of doctors and scientists, the players who come to glad-hand and raise money for their research."

His brow rose. "For what reason? Is she searching for investments?"

"Well, she hasn't shared her reasons with me."

He studied her face. "But you can guess. And it's a good one, isn't it?"

Still, she hesitated. Henry was practically drooling.

"She's been shuffling her schedule around quite a bit, taking long lunches."

"Affair," he guessed.

"Nope. Doctor's appointments. More than one doctor. Specialists."

"Oh," Henry said sympathetically. "She's ill."

Mara held up a finger, a warning in her tone. "You didn't hear that from me."

He nodded soberly. "Of course. I completely understand."

Mara took a much larger sip. She let her shoulders drop a centimeter, rearranging her features appropriately. "She's a pretty demanding boss, but she's fair. I want to help her out. Even if the shoes I have to do it in pinch like hell."

He laughed. "You're a very kind person, Ms. Butler."

"I'm really not. I'm quite hard and cynical."

"But fair."

"But fair," she said, draining her glass. "I don't suppose you can tell me who here does biomedical research?"

Henry frowned. "Do you think this approach is the best? Does your employer expect to stumble on a cure?"

Mara let her eyes go distant as if thinking it over. "I think she's desperate and rich. Maybe she's hoping to find someone in the field to redirect with a liberal application of cash. But it's a guess."

She ended by shrugging and sighing, simultaneously trying to express sympathy and some fatigue for the task.

Henry sipped thoughtfully, taking his time. Mara was beginning to think she had misjudged him, but, in the end, her instincts proved sound. Henry came through for the damsel in distress.

He gave her an eager I'm-about-to-solve-your-problems smile. "Well, I can't promise to find the solution to your boss's problem, but I can certainly help you compile a list."

"Not going to dangle the offer of help in exchange for something?"

she asked, considering his expression. "That's what most of the people in this room would do."

The crowd around them might be well-heeled and prosperous, but high society was full of sharks.

"I'm not most people." Henry handed her a card. Glancing at it, she saw his name and number on the embossed paper.

"And I prefer to get my dates based on merit." He leaned toward her, giving her a whiff of his expensive cologne. Pleasant hints of leather and a little ozone teased her nose. "Call me."

CHAPTER TEN

T he apartment Jack had sublet for them in Paris was only a few blocks from the Caislean Hotel, but Mara was sure her feet were bleeding by the time she got there. It didn't help that the old building had no elevator.

Jack scowled at her from the balcony when she made it inside. And he was smoking.

Her lip curled up in distaste. Mara hadn't caught so much as a whiff of cigarette smoke on him before. Cigar tobacco she could tolerate. Her father smoked Cuban cigars on occasion, but cigarette smoke? It tainted Jack's usually pleasant scent.

You mean delicious, don't you? Mara narrowed her eyes. *On second thought, light them up, jackass...*

"What is that look for?" Mara was dying to slip off the hateful shoes to flex her toes on the cold stone tiles. *An ice bath would feel even better.* But it would have to wait until after Jack shared what had crawled up his ass and died.

He crushed the cigarette out on the rail of the balcony, dropping the stub in a nearly empty glass of beer on the table at his side. "This Henry character—you went too far with your story."

Frowning, Mara stepped out on the balcony. "It was a spur-of-the-moment construction. But I think he bought it."

"Debatable," he complained. "And I don't see the list of names he promised you from tonight's event."

Cocking a hip, she fished the folded piece of paper out of her bra. She could still see the baron's intrigued and titillated expression when she'd slipped it in there in front of him.

Mara handed it to Jack. His expression was carefully neutral. Too neutral. "When he added Felix Dubois, he said, and I quote 'he's always at these things'."

Jack took the paper, scanning the list. He sniffed. "Did he point out any of Dubois' colleagues?"

"No," she said from behind clenched teeth. "He changed the subject, and there wasn't time to steer him back to it before other guests claimed him."

Why was Jack being such a jackass?

Mara wasn't some spy who was practiced at dissembling, but she'd thought she'd done rather well. Not that she'd been expecting praise from Jack Buchanan. She didn't need a pat on the back.

Good, because you're not getting one.

Shoving down her irritation, she got back to business. "We'll have to do our own homework, but at least we have a place to start. Did you get the event's official guest list?"

That had been part of the plan, for Jack to copy the list from the event coordinator's computer. *It'll take me five minutes,* he'd bragged. But she'd gotten so engrossed in her conversation with Henry Carrington that she wasn't sure if he'd done it.

Jack held up a flash drive, a hint of a smile returning to his face.

She raised her brow. "How long did it take?"

"Three minutes."

Sure it did. Mara crossed her arms. "And are you going to tell me what was bothering you when I came in?"

Jack pursed his lips. He took a breath, staring her in the eyes. "You liked him. The red baron. I could hear it in your voice."

Mara raised a brow. "So what?"

He didn't say anything. Mara scoffed. "Oh, my God. Are we in middle school? Are you seriously wondering if I like him more than I like you?"

The tension in his shoulders disappeared. Jack leaned on the balcony rail, waggling his eyebrows suggestively. "So, you *do* like me?"

Mara smacked her hand over her face. "I am not going to dignify that with an answer because I am not twelve years old. My feet hurt. I'm going to bed."

She turned around, but Jack grabbed her arm, spinning her around. He put his hands on either side of her head, lowering his mouth to hers.

The connection coursed through her the instant his lips touched down, but she reacted before the unexpectedly sweet pressure could rob her of her good sense.

Breaking off, she jerked back and ducked, spinning to kick his legs out from under him. Jack landed flat on his back with a loud grunt.

She waited until he caught his breath.

"I realize I may have been asking for that," he conceded in a clear voice, carefully enunciating each syllable.

Mara stood over him, hands on her hips. "You think?"

He squinted up at her face. "Was it the cigarette?"

"It does stink, but that isn't why I don't want you to kiss me."

Jack put his hands behind his head, crossing his ankles with exaggerated casualness. "Care to enlighten me?"

"First of all—"

"Oh, so this is a list?"

"Yes," she snapped. "Pay attention."

"First of all—"

He held up a hand and sat up, legs splayed into a V in front of him. "Before you go on, should I grab a pen and paper? I may need to take notes."

Her jaw stiffened. Mara put her hand out to the side, snapping her claws out. But she didn't rip him to shreds. Instead, she pivoted and stepped between his legs.

Jack's eyes lit up. His hand reached up to stroke her stocking-clad leg, but she pushed him back down with a heel to the chest. Then she slid the shoe down to his crotch, pressing the spiked heel hard against him in a silent warning.

Jack's Adam's apple bobbed as he swallowed.

"Why don't I sum it up?" she asked sweetly.

His scent was more aroused than concerned, but his expression was cautious, proving he wasn't stupid.

Jack cleared his throat, glancing at his family jewels as if checking to make sure they were still there. "Please do."

"You made your move from jealousy over some other guy. Not *me*." Her eyes hardened, and she pressed down harder. "Well, this is not a competition, and I am not a prize."

That last word could have cut glass, it was so sharp.

She ground her heel down a touch harder before whirling away, her anger straining at the leash. Deciding she didn't need to make her partner bleed tonight—she'd save that for tomorrow—Mara stalked off to her room.

She slammed the door behind herself for good measure.

CHAPTER ELEVEN

The boss checked his Chopard watch as the two junior team members headed to the tree line with an empty stretcher. He'd only been out here an hour, but it felt longer.

I'm going to have to speak to the Denon research leads.

There was no reason he had to come along for this part anymore. Granted, he'd wanted to at first. Being part of the hunt had been exciting, but the more he proved his worth, the less the company had been willing to risk him, which made coming out to these things quite dull now.

The wind blew, shifting the branches of the trees overhead. A thick trickle of dirty rainwater streamed down the nape of his neck.

That settled it. From now on, he would do these confirmations back at the lab. As important as this venture was, his time was too valuable to waste in this manner.

The boss rubbed his face, mentally checking his extremely long to-do list. *It's not as if I don't have a million other things to do.*

A moment later, the team reappeared, this time with a full stretcher. Acton, the team leader, gave him a salute. The boss perked up. That meant it was a small body. It frequently took all four team members to carry their captures.

They lowered the stretcher in front of him.

"Sedated or dead?" He hated it when the team killed the shapeshifters. Regrettably, many of the beast people didn't allow themselves to be taken alive. They'd lost more than two-thirds of their targets those first few years. The animals had either committed suicide or forced their captors to kill them outright when the beasts had turned on them.

But the team had learned from those experiences. They had refined their technique, moving to lightning strikes, with better sedatives and traps. With his help, they had a live capture rate of over seventy percent.

"It's sedated," Acton said. He whipped the sheet off the animal.

His eyes widened. "A bear?" This was a first. "Male or female?"

"Male."

"Oh." Deflated, he shrugged off his disappointment. After all, he was here for a reason.

His hand hovered over the head, hesitating. He'd almost lost a finger once when the beast hadn't been sedated properly, but that had been over a year ago. The scar had healed, but it had taken longer. There had been none of the fabled side effects from the bite. He was still sometimes disappointed by that.

He touched the animal, allowing himself a satisfied smile. "Confirmed."

"Good," Acton murmured, turning to signal the rest of the team. They loaded the animal into the van.

"Any chance of getting a female?" The bear had to have a mother, at least.

Acton shook his head. "There's no sign of one."

"Not even on satellite surveillance?"

The subordinate shook his head. "I wish."

The team earned a bonus when they took a fertile female alive.

Sighing, the boss waved Acton on. "Well, maybe next time. Let's get this creature on the plane."

He clapped the taller man on the shoulder genially. "By the way, I tucked a bottle of Lagavulin in your seat pocket for you. Have a toast to your success."

Acton nodded appreciably, heading to the van. At the driver's side door, he turned with a speculative glint in his eye. "What would it have been if we failed?"

"Jack Daniels."

Acton smirked. "We would have taken the Jack and been happy with it, you know."

The boss smiled. "I'm aware. But you deserve it. A bear is above and beyond, although I still have my heart set on something else."

Acton rolled his eyes. "A wolf. Yes, we know. And I will get you one —I guarantee it. We were damn close last month."

Not close enough, but with the boss's help, it *would* happen. "You're right. We'll get one." He could practically guarantee it.

The boss breathed in the scent of the woods, letting it wash away his frustration before he climbed into the van.

The wolves could run, but they couldn't hide…

CHAPTER TWELVE

"I think I fucked up."

On the video chat window, Derrick's face twisted into a scowl. Jack had called him to catch him up on their progress at the crack of dawn, Colorado time. Derrick hadn't liked that, but he'd answered.

Jack's call was redundant. Mara kept her family informed, but Jack didn't like being cut out of the loop, so he'd called Derrick. But Jack had ulterior motives. He needed advice.

"You made a pass at her." It wasn't a question.

"Maybe."

Suddenly, Derrick smirked. "How bad did she hurt you?"

"I have an ice pack on my balls...but I don't think she did any permanent damage. We'll still be able to have beautiful children together," Jack added hopefully.

Derrick burst into a loud guffaw. Jack joined in, but something about his expression must have tipped the other man off. The werewolf's laughter died.

"*Fuck.* You fucking idiot. You're serious." Derrick pulled his computer screen closer to his face. "Are you in love with her? Oh, God. You are, aren't you?"

"Of course not," Jack scoffed. Then he lifted a shoulder. "Well, maybe a little. But only since I met her."

Derrick's groan was loud. He rubbed his face. "What the hell, man? I thought you were just trying to get into her pants."

"How is that better than..." Jack racked his brain for the right words. "Than having feelings?"

Derrick snorted. "You know, after watching you clean up with so many babes, I admit, I kind of wanted to see you fall head over ass for someone and lose. I figured it couldn't hurt if you got your heartbroken."

Derrick leaned back, scrubbing his face with his hands. "I thought it might teach you a little humility. It's never happened before, right?"

Jack thought about it before turning to the screen. "Untrue. Deirdre Wilson, second grade. She crushed me *and* put glitter glue in my hair. It took a week to get it all out."

The Were rolled his eyes. "I meant real heartbreak. As an adult, by an adult."

He shrugged. "I guess not. But that's not that unusual. I mean, you haven't either."

"Of course I have," Derrick replied.

"What?" Jack sat back in his chair. "But you're a werewolf."

Derrick's scowl deepened. "I'm still a person, asshole. Except for the whole turning-into-a-wolf part, anyway. I live my life the same way you do yours. Mostly. But I get my heart broken like anyone else —except you."

"Well, there's a first time for everything," Jack said glumly, adjusting the ice pack on his crotch.

Derrick made a rough rumble deep in his throat. "You know Mara can hear everything we're saying, right? Weres have preternatural hearing."

"Relax. She went for a jog—on two legs. It's safer that way."

There was a long silence on the Colorado end of the chat. "You can't do this."

"I can try," Jack muttered.

"No, you *can't.*"

Now they were getting to it. Jack leaned forward. "Is it forbidden? Is there an interspecies interdiction?"

"No, but there is a Mara interdiction. I told you—she's the chief's daughter. She's off-limits."

There was something about the way he said it that made Jack sit up straighter. "Is there someone waiting for her back home? She's like royalty to your people, right? Does that mean there's an arranged marriage in the works for her?"

"Uh…"

Jack winced. "Fuck, there is one."

Derrick held up a hand. "No. Not anymore. And it wasn't like that —not arranged. It wasn't that formal. But given who and what Mara is, she doesn't have a whole lot of options for mates."

"Can you be a pal and explain without me having to drag it out of you?" The suspense was killing Jack.

Sighing, Derrick closed his eyes. "His name was Malcolm. He was my friend."

Jack raised a brow. "*Was?*"

"Yeah. Was." Derrick's face was stony, and his eyes were distant like he was staring deep into the past. "You never met him because he was protecting the home front while Connell and I did our tour. We trade-off that way, making sure we never leave our homes vulnerable while we go out to serve."

"Why do you serve?" Jack asked.

"It keeps us sharp, and, for the most part, the work is noble. We know people who make sure we don't compromise ourselves or our ethics."

Jack nodded. "What happened to Malcolm?"

"Some shit went down, and a traitor took him out. The same one who killed Leland and almost got Connell."

Fuck. "Sorry to hear that," Jack said. Why was nothing easy with these people? "Was Mara heartbroken?"

More importantly, was she still suffering? She didn't act as if she was pining… *How do I compete with a dead guy?*

Derrick lifted a shoulder. "I'm not sure she was in love with

Malcolm, but she was getting there. Up until he fucked it up. And then he got dead and couldn't fix it."

Jack started to regret not pouring himself a drink before making this call. "I'm guessing that's a long story."

"One that isn't mine to tell, so I'm stopping there. But if you take nothing else away, believe me when I say this. Ever since Malcolm died, the field was cleared. After the mourning period passed, it was as if open season had been declared. Since then, Mara has been courted by every ambitious male wolf shifter looking to get a leg up in the world. Rich guys, connected guys, shifters of other species offering strategic alliances—you name it, she's had the opportunity to marry it. And she's hated every minute of it."

Aw shit. The words '*I am not a prize*' rang in Jack's head louder than a jackhammer. He had stepped in it by trying to kiss her because that Scottish prick pissed him off.

"Go back to what you said about her being special and having limited options. Because what you said about being courted like a princess makes it sound as if she has too many."

"Yes and no," Derrick said. "A lot of shifters think they can stand at Mara's side, but it's not true. She has to be careful. Mara can't take just anyone as a mate. Especially not a human."

Jack threw up his hands. "Why not? Is it cause her babies won't be wolves or something?"

"No. Weres breed true. We're not exactly fertile, but when we have kids, they *are* shifters. It's a dominant gene. But…you have no status."

"So, it is because she's a princess," Jack said, picking up a pen so he could toss it at the wall.

"No. It's because she is a dominant wolf." Derrick's hand made a slashing motion. "Almost any other female wolf, and it wouldn't be a problem. Some of our females have human mates. But they're not like Mara."

I definitely should have gotten a drink. "Are you going to get to the point this year?"

Derrick lifted his hands, mimicking strangling him. "The point is that females in the pack take their status in the hierarchy from their mate. All the ones in the pack with human mates are submissives. But if Mara mated a wolf of lesser dominance than her, it wouldn't matter that she's an alpha. She would lose her status to be ranked whatever he is. That would leave her with two options."

Derrick held up two fingers. Apparently, shifters liked to count on their fingers during lectures. "Mara could accept it. That means she would live every day of her life being forced to act like something she's not by being subordinate to wolves of lesser dominance."

Well, that sounded fucked up. "What's behind door number two?"

"She can do what the other dominant females did when faced with this dilemma—she can leave the pack and live as a lone wolf with her mate."

What kind of fucked up rule was that? "That's not fair."

Derrick shrugged. "Our pack is old. This is our way. And some traditions are more problematic than others."

"What happened to wolves living the same way we do?" Jack wanted to throw his computer at Derrick's head

"Things are a little different when you're at the top of the food chain." His friend's face darkened. "And Mara *is* at the top. With her level of dominance, she'd never be able to live as anything less than an alpha wolf. And forget about leaving the fold. Douglas would never allow it, and she would never want to. She loves her father and her brother. And me. With few exceptions, wolves *need* a pack."

And living as anything but an alpha would be asking her to be less than what she was. *Forever.* Jack swore under his breath.

Derrick leaned forward. "Look, when it comes to fighting ability, Mara is tough as nails. But romance is something she doesn't know anything about. She doesn't have the experience—how could she, given who her father and brother are? They'd have torn apart any male who was interested in getting into her pants and nothing else."

Jack scowled suddenly. "But your friend Malcolm got a pass."

Derrick shrugged. "He was the pack's third, right under Connell. Malcolm was an appropriate match. The fact he would be Mara's mate was never mentioned, but the entire pack expected it to happen. Hell, Mara expected it…"

And I'm not appropriate. The fact Jack had never felt this way about a woman before didn't seem to matter. If he acted on his feelings and, by some miracle, Mara returned them, he'd be wrecking her life.

Derrick turned his head as if he heard something in the background. "I have to go. Think about what I said. You're playing with fire. But Mara is the one who will get burned."

"Yeah, yeah. I heard you." Jack sighed, rubbing his jaw.

"Good."

"Wait." He leaned forward. "I have one more question...do werewolves mate for life?"

Derrick narrowed his eyes. "We do casual sometimes, have boyfriend and girlfriends, especially when we're younger. True matings aren't as common as some of us would wish. But yes. When you do find your mate—your true mate—it's for life."

CHAPTER THIRTEEN

Henry Carrington, Baron Ventry, was an extremely busy man. He'd been working nonstop at his office since five that morning. He'd slept there on the long leather couch that turned into a king-sized bed with a touch of a button.

He'd been too tired to hit that button last night, so now he had a crick in his neck. But Henry ignored it. The deal he was working on was the biggest of his life, so he powered through like a machine. But the moment they told him Mary Butler was waiting on his second line, he took her call, despite the fact he had the oil minister of Venezuela on the first.

She couldn't talk long. After they hung up, he couldn't remember much of what she said. But the buzz of contentment stayed with him long after.

Sometime later, in the middle of his important meeting, Henry stopped stock still, realizing how seldom he'd ever felt that way.

The opposite was the norm. Henry went out of his way to make people happy. It was the secret of his success. But someone making *him* happy? That didn't happen much. Not these days. It was the reason he worked so hard. Making deals and the scads of cash that came with them had become an acceptable substitute.

Mary had shown him that it wasn't enough.

There was still a lot to be done. Henry could tell she didn't like him as much as he liked her. But that was fine with him. He enjoyed a challenge. And when it came to winning over the people he wanted, Henry Carrington had never failed.

Jack was leaning against the wall outside of the bathroom when she got out of the shower. Mara had taken her clothes into the bathroom with her, as was her habit, so he wasn't trying to catch her in a towel or anything stupidly juvenile like that.

"What?" she snapped.

He gave her that patented Jackson Buchanan grin, the one that no doubt made sorority girls drop their panties *en masse*. But Mara saw something behind his eyes. Melancholia was weaved into his scent, subtle but deep.

Straightening away from the wall, he inclined his head. "I wanted to apologize for yesterday. It won't happen again."

"Good," she said, scowling. "What happened?"

Jack had an excellent poker face, but something was wrong. "Nothing. I just feel bad. You were right. I kissed you because I was jealous, and that was a stupid reason."

Mara cocked her head. The truth of his words was there in his scent, but it was mixed in with a lot of other stuff she couldn't untangle. Was the sadness? *Damn it.* Why did he have to be so damn complicated?

He waved a rolled-up piece of paper. "Ready to get back to work?"

"Yeah," she said, following him out to the living room with narrowed eyes. Whatever was eating him would come out sooner or later. Jack wasn't one to stew, and he wasn't afraid to voice his opinion. She had to wait him out.

He unfurled the roll on the dining room table. It was a large sheet of premium paper, the kind people printed building plans on.

He'd sketched out a suspect tree. "I thought it would be better to have a larger and portable copy so we wouldn't have to keep squinting at the computer screen."

Mara traced the neatly drawn lines connecting Felix Dubois to the names of three other people. One was a name without a picture—Anders Galt. The two with images were captured stills from the camera footage she had worn the night of the benefit. The second was a woman who spoke to Dubois for a solid twenty minutes and even co-schmoozed with him at one point. Dubois had introduced her as Josie. The nickname was all they had, but Jack worked on it, and Mara had gotten a superior-to-subordinate vibe from watching the pair interact. Still, it was another link in the chain.

The one with both name and picture was familiar enough.

"You sure Carrington should be on here?" she asked. "He and Dubois are likely only passing acquaintances."

"We are turning over every stone looking for worms," Jack said. "We keep everyone on here until we know for sure. Unless you want to give Henry a pass?"

"No." She wasn't going to argue if he wanted to spend the time on Carrington. It wasn't as if they had that many leads. And who knew? Handsome Henry could be a closet serial killer. The Bishop Kane incident had taught her that sometimes monsters hid in plain sight.

She returned to the name without a picture. "Who is Anders Galt, and is it an alias?"

"I have no idea," Jack said with a grin, his habitual easy manner reasserting itself. "But his office just confirmed a dinner with Dubois via the hotel switchboard for the day after next. And my money is on an alias as well. Fifty bucks says our mysterious Mr. Galt pulled it out of a book."

"Pass, because I'd lose." Mara went to the kitchenette to pull out the bag of ground coffee. Jack drank pots of it when running down leads. "Let's figure out who this guy is."

A few hours later, they had their answer. Anders Galt was ten years old. Or, at least, that was how long the man had been operating under that name.

Jack spun around from his desk, waving two pictures at her

triumphantly. It appeared to be from the US passport database. Mara didn't ask how he had gotten it. The other was older and from a distance. It looked like a police surveillance shot.

He laid them both in front of her side by side.

"I can't find any records of an Anders Galt before a decade ago, but, after a little digging, I discovered an Androv Galyautdinov, a former enforcer for the Russian mob. This old photo is from before Galyautdinov dropped off the radar."

Except for the absence of tattoos, the similarity between the two photos was striking. "Running biometrics was kind of redundant, but I did it anyway. Ninety-eight percent certainty of a match." He held the phone closer to his face. "It must have hurt like hell to laser off all those tats."

"If they were real to begin with," she observed, coming around to squint at the younger Androv over his shoulder.

Her arm brushed his, and there was a subtle tightening around Jack's mouth.

Mara blinked, unexpectedly stung, but she didn't let it show. *What else did you expect after making a big deal about him kissing you on the balcony?*

"I doubt he could get away with fakes in his old outfit. The Russian mob doesn't do press-ons," Jack joked, a weak attempt to excuse his obvious tension.

"There is another possibility," she volunteered. "Tats tend to disappear on a shifter during the change. We have to add special compounds to make the ink last, but they are rarely permanent, not unless you do some hoodoo to make it stick. Most of us don't. If the tat matters that much, it's less hinky to have them redone."

Jack snapped his fingers, a light of vindication in his eye. "I knew something was up with that."

Mara raised a brow.

He shrugged. "I worked with Connell's team long enough to notice most of them didn't have tattoos. The few who did strangely didn't last. I asked Derrick about a black dagger he used to have on his shoulder. I saw it when it was new and, then again, a few months later, when it was barely visible. He told me he got tired of it and was having it lasered off, but it was gone before we finished that op. When I pointed it out, he shrugged and said they must have used cheap ink."

Mara's lip turned up at the corner. "That's a pretty lame excuse." No wonder he hadn't bought it.

He lifted the coffee mug in salute. "I know."

Jack tapped Galt's picture. "That being said, my gut is against him being one of you given what they are doing to shifters. Can you tell others of your kind by sight?"

"By scent, actually. It's a far more reliable sense when it comes to identifying species," she said. "But it's not foolproof."

"The only way to mask your scent involves heavy-duty magic," she clarified. "The spells to hide our essence are complicated. You have to be motivated. If he's moving in the human world, I doubt Galt would bother with them, but I could swing by his hotel to try to pass him in the street. If he's a shifter, I'll know."

Dubois was human. So was his gal-pal. She'd made sure at the event.

"I don't think that's necessary, but we'll see if the opportunity presents itself at dinner."

That would have to be good enough. "So, what is a former mobster doing in this mess?"

"Anders Galt is a respected businessman—hard, sharp, possibly corrupt—but nothing is proven. Just rumors of shady backroom deals."

She wrinkled her nose. "So, the mob enforcer moved to business because he yearned for legitimacy?"

Jack chuckled again, seemingly back to his irrepressible self. "It's good to have goals."

Mara picked up the older picture. "He removed the tattoos, but he didn't have plastic surgery?"

"Androv Galyautdinov wasn't wanted for any crimes at the time of his disappearance. Nor were there rumors of him being in trouble with his mob overlords. He was there one day, and then..." Pressing his fingertips together, he opened them. "Poof."

"That's a little weird," she observed. "Usually, necessity is the mother of reinvention."

He shrugged. "Androv was ambitious. And his criminal cohorts were a family who passed on the mantle generationally, not a crime syndicate where he could work to the top—not without a massacre. So, he walked away. Four years or so later, Anders Galt was wheeling and dealing on the international stage."

"Any of those dealings with Denon?"

Jack looked as if he wanted to pat her on the back. "Funny you should ask, a few of them are—all through subsidiaries, of course, but I had already ID'ed those before I came to your father."

Mara burst into laughter. "*Came* to my father? Don't you mean crawled through our bushes covered in skunk piss?"

Jack harrumphed, rolling up the suspect map. "Semantics."

"Think there's more to dig up?"

"On Galt?" he asked. "Probably not, but the program is still working. I'm still waiting on a facial recognition hit on Josie."

"Good. I'm starving. Let's get out of here." She grabbed him by the collar, then pulled him out the door.

"I didn't think you'd like this sort of place," Jack said, leaning over the table.

He'd had more than a pitcher of Sangria by this point, so some of the words were a bit garbled, but Mara still understood him despite the music's volume. It wasn't loud, but it was starting to skirt the edge of her tolerance.

"What's not to like?" She gestured to the club around them.

Nueva Noche was a dance club only a few blocks from Jack's apartment. Mara had passed it on her runs, usually when it was empty. But tonight, Friday night, it was starting to fill up despite the earliness of the hour.

Jack propped his arm on the table, leaning his chin on it. Thanks to an earlier spill, the tabletop was sticky, but he didn't seem to care.

"You doing okay, buddy?" she asked softly, nudging a plate of tapas toward him. Perhaps she shouldn't have suggested the third round, but he could have said no. Jack was a man with an iron will. He knew his limits. The fact he'd chosen not to observe them tonight meant she was right. Something was eating at him.

"Your head is going to ache like a son of a bitch tomorrow."

Jack stuffed one of the potato, ham, and cheese croquettes in his mouth before washing it down with another big sip of sangria.

"So, are you going to tell me what's bugging you?"

Jack's head lolled to the side. He put the cup down, reaching out to touch her. The table was small enough he was able to stroke her cheek. It would have been sweet if he hadn't had mashed potato all over it.

"Jack," she prompted when he didn't answer.

He picked up the glass in a toast. "Oh, I'll never tellsh." His words were slurring now.

Mara raised a fine brown brow. "You sure about that?"

"No one's eversh gotten me to talk when I didn't want to." Jack wagged a finger at her, or at least he tried to.

Mara grabbed the roaming digit, settling his hand back down on the table.

"Why are you sad, Jack?" His despair was palpable, and it was starting to depress her as if his feelings were contagious.

His finger went up again, pointing at her nose. "Can't tell *you.*"

Mara pursed her lips, then refilled his cup. *I am going to hell for this.* She was still deciding if she should push it toward him when he pried it out of her hands.

After he saluted her, he drank. His lips were ruby red by this point. When he put down the glass and grinned, he bore a disconcertingly strong resemblance to Ronald McDonald.

"Feel like talking now?"

"No." Jack was almost lying across the table now. "Why are you so pretty?"

"So, it is something to do with me?" *I knew it.* Unexpected pain welled up in her chest, and Mara blinked rapidly to soothe her stinging eyes. Had his stupid apology been an empty gesture?

"Would you rather be working with someone else?" she asked, forcing the question past the lump in her throat.

Jack leaned against her arm. He batted his thick gold lashes. "*Nooo. Don't leave.*"

Mara wanted to strangle him. "Then tell me what's wrong."

Silence.

"Would you rather have Derrick taking point on this?"

Jack made a derisive sound. "Derrick is a bummer."

Mara frowned. "Did you talk to him? About me?"

A snore was her only answer.

Damn it. Getting Jack drunk hadn't been her brightest idea. Groaning aloud, Mara got to her feet, dragging Jack up after her.

She draped his arm around her shoulders and started the long walk to the door.

"Sweetheart, leave this trash in the alley where it belongs and come dance with me," a man called in Spanish.

"Some other time," she said, waving him away.

The return trip to the apartment was hellish, but Mara had no one to blame but herself. And Derrick. It seemed she could blame her cousin, too.

"Y ou told him what?" Mara cried.

"The truth." Derrick scratched his head on the tiny screen. "I told him the truth. You're in a tough spot."

"That's still no reason to tell him about *Malcolm*," she insisted.

Mara hadn't loved the shifter who had served as her father's third in command. She and Malcolm hadn't even been together when he died, but that didn't stop everyone from treating her like his widow after he was gone.

Groaning, Mara passed a hand over her eyes, but she slid it off to double-check Jack's position on the couch. She'd tried to lay him face down so he wouldn't choke if he vomited, but he'd just rolled to the floor. After hauling him across three blocks and up two flights of stairs, she'd given up and left him there.

"Look, this is a good thing. He should know the score. The sooner he accepts it, the better off you will be."

Mara ground her teeth together. Everything Derrick said was sensible. She hadn't wanted to be another notch on Jack's bedpost.

But he's not supposed to be upset about it. Jack was the epitome of a happy-go-lucky lady's man. He played the field, and he won more often than he lost. Where the hell was all this emotion coming from?

"What the fuck am I supposed to do with him now?" She could have throttled her cousin. "His sadness is seeping into my skin. He smells so fucking miserable *I* want to cry. I'm surprised he cares this much."

"Yeah, well..." Derrick looked constipated. It was the expression he always wore whenever he didn't want to talk about something.

"What aren't you telling me?"

"Jack's sort of...maybe....possibly..."

"Derrick," she warned, loading as much warning as she could to her tone.

Now it appeared her cousin was trying to pass a kidney stone. "He likes you. Too much. I think he wants more than a hook up from you. The man is sniffing after a mate."

Mara blinked, trying to match what Derrick was saying with how Jack had behaved.

"It's a kindness," he was saying when she tuned back in. "You know someone like Jack wouldn't fit into our world. He's too much like us. Lower-ranking wolves would want to fight him, but, in this case, it's not a good thing. Even a beta could damage him. Unless you accepted a demotion, that is, and then where would you be?"

I would be in hell. And Jack knew that because Derrick had told him.

Her head started to hurt. This would be the end of it. No more offers to share a glass of wine on the balcony. No more food treats. No more flirting at all.

A small ache developed in the middle of her chest, but she didn't acknowledge it in front of her nosy cousin.

"So, he'll mope for a bit," Derrick finished with a shrug. "But you know humans. He'll get over it. I'm sorry you'll be uncomfortable, but I don't think this mourning period will last too long. Give him a couple of weeks, and he'll be asking for nights off to go pick up girls on La Rambla."

The hell he will.

"What was that look for?"

Mara blinked, the picture of innocence. "What look?"

Derrick narrowed his eyes. "I know that face. Your brother gets the same look when he's about to do something foolish and reckless. Don't do anything stupid. Are you listening, Mara? *Mara?*"

She clicked off the chat window before he could work on another guilt trip.

CHAPTER FOURTEEN

The Michelin restaurant Dubois and Galt had chosen was too crowded and noisy for the long-range sound amplifier in Jack's surveillance truck. Even Mara's superior hearing couldn't pick out Galt or Dubois' voices from the mess coming in through the earphones, so they gave up and waited for the men to finish up.

"We're not going to get anything from out here," Jack complained, setting down the amplifier. "I still can't believe the hostess turned down my bribe."

Neither could Mara since Jack had gifted the hapless woman to his megawatt grin along with the hundred euro note.

Even my knees went weak, and I've seen it before.

"I think you would have been more successful if I hadn't been with you."

There hadn't been a single table open in the restaurant, but had Jack been alone, the woman would have squeezed one in somewhere.

But the restaurant's crowdedness made sneaking in through the back a bad bet.

It wasn't like in the movies where someone could slip in and steal a uniform and pretend to be waitstaff. In a place this small and exclusive, any pretender would be outed immediately, the authorities called. Since the men were escorted to some private room or hidden nook, lip-reading through the window was out.

Jack grumbled something noncommittal under his breath, and Mara sighed.

He hadn't tried to flirt at all tonight.

After he'd woken up, this Jack had made a huge pot of coffee, joked about the size of his hangover, and asked if he had done anything stupid.

"Other than streaking naked down the Champs Elysees?" she'd asked with a perfectly straight face.

"Again?" he replied, tsking in self-chastisement before going to the bathroom to find some aspirin.

That had been the most personal conversation they'd had all day. Since then, Jack had been all business. He still smelled sad, though. And it wasn't getting better. If anything, his melancholia had deepened.

Derrick is right. In a few weeks, it would start to fade. Maybe it would take months if his feelings for her were deeper than she suspected—a year at most. That was a blink of an eye in the grand scheme of things.

"I feel like hacking the electrical system and turning everything off," Jack grumbled, scowling at the restaurant's facade.

"What purpose would that serve?"

He shrugged, his gaze on the restaurant's entrance. "It might force them to choose another place nearby. One where we could get in."

"Except we're supposed to keep me off his radar, which means you'll be going in alone. And we still don't know if he'll remember you or not..."

Jack swiveled in his chair. "It wouldn't work anyway. These turds don't strike me as the type to roll with the punches."

Left with little choice, they waited the men out, snapping pics of Galt and Dubois together at the restaurant's door. They had to split up to follow them back to their respective hotels.

That was when things got a little tense. Jack wanted to follow the newcomer while she trailed Dubois back to his hotel. That was fine with her. Mara wanted to keep Felix in her sights, but no sooner had she gotten up to follow the freaky little fucker than Jack balked, visibly torn at letting her go off on her own.

Standing, Mara tried to draw herself up to her full height. However, the smaller nature of European vans cut her dominance off at the knees, almost literally as she had to bend them to keep from banging her head on the ceiling.

"Are you worried I'm going to claw him to death in some back alley, or are you scared I'm going to get captured and dissected?" she asked, her voice dangerously flat.

Jack hesitated, then smirked. "Nice try. I know neither of those is the right answer."

Mara peeked out the tinted window of the van. "You better decide now. They're getting ready to split up."

Jack sprang up. He looked like a man caught between the devil and the deep blue sea. Outside the window, the men were shaking hands. "Which one do you want?" His tone was carefully neutral.

She narrowed her eyes as Dubois started walking down the Rue de Varenne, weaving through the well-heeled Parisian crowd.

Galt was an unknown quantity, his part in the hunt of her kind not established yet. On the other hand, Dubois had sliced and diced an unknown cat shifter and would have done the same to one of their wolf cubs if Denise Hammond hadn't found him.

She wanted nothing more than to follow *him*...which was exactly why she couldn't.

"I should take Galt," she decided. "I don't trust myself around Felix. If he steps into a dark alley, I may not be able to help myself."

Jack gave her a measuring look. "Sure. Just remember, if Galt ends up being a bigger bastard, I don't have bail money."

Mara rolled her eyes, but Jack reached out and caught her arm. "I'm kidding. I trust you with either of them."

Her chest tightened. Jack was telling the truth. Maybe he did trust her.

She nodded, hiding how much that meant to her. "I'll take Galt," she repeated.

When he nodded in agreement, she hopped out of the van, winding her way through the crowd after her man.

And so it began.

Mara followed Galt around Paris for the better part of a week while Jack was forced to jump on a plane to trail Dubois to Berlin. And then Galt went to Amsterdam for a conference, so Mara did the same.

Both men were globetrotters. They conducted business all over Europe, always in major metropolitan cities. There seemed to be little rhyme or reason to their movements until Jack figured out each city they had visited had a Denon office in it.

Eventually, Galt went back to Paris, where he appeared to be based. He had offices in the fifty-nine-story monolith that was the Montparnasse tower office building. Dubois, on the other hand, appeared to be a perpetual itinerant. He kept moving from city to city, where he preferred to stay in luxury hotels instead of renting an apartment.

With each visit, the network of known associates grew. They had to pull in other pack members to follow the new players, but, so far, none had led them to another research facility.

Jack had argued about the latter. If the Denon corporation was hunting shifters, bringing in more was begging for trouble. But Douglas Maitland had made his position clear—no outside contractors besides Jack. This was the pack's fight, theirs, and any other shifter pack who wanted to join them.

"I understand why," Jack told her over video chat one night. "But I don't like it."

Mara considered his tense handsome face. "You can't shield us all."

"I can try," he said, his lips compressing in a thin line. She didn't lecture him about it because she knew he was thinking of the woman in Barcelona.

The cat's corpse had been identified. A small leopard colony in Aguas Calientes, Mexico, had answered the chief's alert. The woman's name had been Reina Rodriguez, a moderately successful realtor. One day, she had gone to show a listing to a prospective client before dinner one Friday night. She had never come home. Since Reina was divorced with no children, her pack hadn't known she was missing until her secretary reported the disappearance three days later.

"I would still like to add my own people to the tracking effort—I work with a specialist at times, Cassandra. She usually just books my jobs, but she's an excellent hacker and would be a valuable asset."

Mara hesitated "Are you talking about Cass Carter?"

Surprise flickered across his expression. "You know her?"

Oh, dear. "Err...yes. And you don't have to worry about bringing her aboard. She's already on this."

Jack's head tilted, and knowledge flitted his eyes. "She's pack!" he accused.

She sighed, uncomfortable. "I can neither confirm nor deny that."

"You just did." Jack laughed on the screen. He pushed his hair back with both hands. "Damn, if I'd known, I would have asked her to be my back up the Lansing job. I could've used someone with enhanced senses there."

"Oh." Dismayed, she glanced down at her hands. "I guess you haven't met Cass in person."

"No...why?"

Mara vacillated, trying to decide whether to tell him. He must have known her for years, but Cass hadn't shared that she was in a wheelchair with him, something she could have done without letting him know *what* she was. "It's not a secret, but there's a reason she does all her work remotely. But it's not my story to tell, so I'm not going to tell it."

Jack was quiet, but, after a moment, he nodded. "I understand. Don't worry about it."

"Thank you," she said, knowing the curiosity was killing him. "I will, however, get in touch and let her know that we've granted you friend-of-the-pack status."

That would leave it up to Cass whether to open a dialog about her accident.

"What does being a friend of the pack mean?"

"It's different for different people, but, for you, it means information. We don't hold back anything that might impede your investigation. And as long you don't share this information with anyone else, we won't have to kill you."

He chuckled. "Oh, good. The death threats are back. I was starting to miss them."

She shook her head, the corner of her lip twitching. "I don't know why you love being menaced so much. I swear you get off on it."

A flash of teeth worthy of the toothpaste commercial flashed across the monitor, the impact of the grin only slightly dimmed by the fact it was on a screen.

"Only when you're doing it," Jack replied before signing off.

Mara carried that interaction with her for the rest of the afternoon, letting it warm her. Unfortunately, it wasn't enough to withstand the message she received later that day.

Her father, Douglas, passed on a voicemail message from Reina's mother, Carina. After listening to it, Mara went drove out to the nearest boxing gym. When she didn't find what she was searching for, she went to another one until she tracked down another shifter, a Were-bear with over seventy pounds of muscle on her. She challenged him to a fight in the ring—bare-knuckle.

"What do I get if I win?" The bruiser attempted a charming grin.

Mara stripped off her shirt before ducking into the ring. "What do you want?"

The bear licked his chops. "You—all night long."

Mara narrowed her eyes at her opponent. Not only was he heavier, more muscled, and six inches taller, he had a break in his nose. It appeared healed over, which meant it had been broken and rebroken enough times for the shifter's healing ability to give up on it.

This one was a brawler. Not surprising. He was a bear, after all. Mara hated to stereotype a species, but there were four things bear shifters liked to do. Eat, drink, fight, and sleep.

Well, there was one other thing he probably did often—and the bear shifter wanted it as his prize.

Mara moved her head from side to side, cracking it. "You have a deal."

Twenty minutes later, the fight was over. Feeling halfway human again, Mara thanked the bear, who was groaning and bleeding on the mat.

A surprisingly good sport, he managed to lift his thick arm. "I think I love you."

"Sure you do."

She walked out of the gym to the sound of the bear shifter shouting his phone number to her.

When she got back to her hotel, there was a message waiting from her from Derrick.

"I'm on my way to Spain. Meet Jack and me in Barcelona—I have news."

CHAPTER FIFTEEN

Mara stood on the landing in front of the door to Jack's flat, feeling like an idiot. Was that anxiety or anticipation she was feeling? Ugh. When did this get so difficult?

Shaking her head at her stupidity, she opened her backpack, fishing for the key, when the door swung open.

Jack stood on the other side. He was bare-chested, his hair sticking up at one end as if he'd just climbed out of bed. Blinking, she stared at the gold-dusted expanse of skin.

Werewolves were some of the most impressive physical specimens in the world. They weren't shy, either. Nudity was par for the course in any shifter pack. She'd seen enough naked men in her life to fill a small stadium. A good fraction of those weren't even related to her. There was absolutely no reason for her to feel as if her knees were melting.

"Hey, I thought you were Derrick," Jack said, his voice still husky from sleep.

"He's not here yet?"

"No." Jack lifted his watch. "He's not due for another hour. And I was expecting you after him."

"I caught an earlier flight."

They stood there awkwardly until he reached out, pulling her into an unexpected hug. Mara stiffened, but she didn't pull away.

"Please don't take this as any sort of comment on your skills and ability, but I'm glad you're back and in one piece," he whispered into her hair.

There was more melting, but this wasn't in the region of her knees. It was closer to her heart.

Damn it. Jack's warmth seeped in through her light linen shirt. She couldn't decide whether to be annoyed, gratified, or aroused. It may have been a mix of all three, but arousal was starting to win.

He let me go after Galt because he trusted me. And he's willing to let the possibility of us go because he doesn't want to ruin my life. That wasn't something any of her suitors had considered. Their only concern was how she could benefit *them.*

"I did check-in," she said, sounding out of breath.

"I know," he mumbled against her hair. "Are you going to hit me when I let go?"

Giving up, Mara leaned into the embrace, trying not to make it obvious she was inhaling his scent. "I'm strongly considering it."

Jack snickered. "I can tell."

"Good, so long as we're clear."

He released his hold, backing up to let her inside. "Come in."

He turned, walking ahead of her to the living room. Mara followed, wondering how in the world it was that his back was as defined as his front. She wasn't even talking about his ass—which was world-class. Mara was getting turned on by his shoulder blades of all things.

What is wrong with me?

Jack moved around the kitchen, randomly grabbing fruit and bread and piling it on the counter. "Are you hungry?"

"Always." Mara laughed.

He started digging through the fridge. "Do you like eggs?"

Mara waited until he turned around to grab his face and kiss him like there was no tomorrow.

She hadn't planned it. She hadn't thought of it while they were apart the last few weeks. Instead, she simply acted.

Jack dropped the eggs, his arms closing around her like a steel trap. He pulled her against him, taking over the kiss with aggression and just the right amount of tongue.

Aw, hell. Big mistake. She knew it as soon as she touched him. But she couldn't let go. He felt right, like the last puzzle piece sliding into place. It didn't help that he smelled of the ocean and sunshine.

Mara forgot everything, except that she wanted to bottle his scent. They would call it *Summer,* and it would make millions.

His lips firmed. He walked her backward, pushing her against the counter. A crunch filled the air.

They broke apart. Mara looked down, bursting into laughter.

Jack joined her, shaking the egg yolk off his foot. "Okay, so you're going to have to try my signature Spanish Omelet some other time."

Mara raised a brow. "Is that a when-in-Rome kind of thing, or do you make that for all the ladies?"

Jack crossed his arms with a knowing expression. "It's a Denver omelet in the States and a Tahu Telur in Indonesia."

She put her back to the counter, propping an elbow on it. A corner of her mouth curled up. "Sure it is."

Together, they watched egg yolk drip off his foot. "I better hit the shower."

She swept out an arm, giving him leave to depart as if she were royalty.

Grinning, Jack hopped to the hallway, disappearing for a second before he popped his head around the corner. "I don't suppose you want to join me in the shower?"

"Nope."

"Not even to wash all the airplane smell off?"

She shook her head, and he smacked his lips. "Yeah, I didn't think so."

By the time he got out of the shower, Derrick had arrived, and what he had to say changed everything. Mara closed her eyes, flopping back on the plush fabric of Jack's couch. It hurt to breathe.

Eight packs were missing shifters.

Among the missing were cougars, leopards, lynx, an entire African hyena family—even a juvenile bear as of a few weeks ago.

No wolves, however. Her father had sent word out to every wolf pack on the continent, warning them to guard their own after they realized little Oliver had been taken from his human mother, the widow of one of their pack. That was over a year ago, but his warning must have been enough. The wolf packs hadn't lost anyone since.

Mara winced. *We should have made it wider.*

"How many are missing?" Jack asked in a clipped voice after dragging something heavy toward him. "The total?"

Mara twisted her head. The noise had come from his desk. Instead of pulling up his chair to it, he had dragged the heavy table to him.

Derrick glanced down. The legs had made fresh deep gouges in the worn wooden floor, but Jack ignored them. Her cousin raised his brow, and she shrugged.

Her cousin passed a rough hand over his face. "Our current count is twelve, possibly thirteen that we know of. But it's probably a lot more. Some packs are only now reaching out to their extended membership, the ones on the periphery of pack life, so we won't know the actual number for a while, if ever."

"And these are only the ones we can check," Mara said for Jack's edification, sinking deeper into the cushion. "There are plenty of shifters who don't belong to packs at all—a lot of solitary hunter types. They wouldn't be easy prey, but there are plenty of non-predator shifters out there."

Which meant the number could be easily double or triple their current count.

Mara could barely swallow. "Fuck, how long has this been going on?"

No one answered.

And to think I spent the last few years sitting on my ass in Colorado, spoiling for a fight—any fight—and all this time people were disappearing.

Guilt settled on her like an invisible cloak. She felt responsible. Hell, she *was* responsible. This had happened on her watch.

In Connell's absence, which was fairly constant these days thanks to his adventures with Logan, Mara was in charge of security for her father's territory. To most people, that meant their compound in Colorado and the surrounding areas. In reality, it was all of North and most of South America.

But the fight she'd been looking for hadn't come charging to her door. It had snuck in the back like a thief in the night, stealing the vulnerable right out from under their nose.

Jack was so grim she swore the air around him was at least two degrees colder. "When did the first one vanish?" he asked, typing something on his keyboard.

Making a rough sound in his throat, Derrick consulted his notes. He rattled off the name and date, and then the next, repeating the process until they had run down the entire list.

Jack cross-referenced each disappearance's approximate dates with what they knew about Felix Dubois and Anders Galt's movements.

"Did you hack the EU customs and immigration database?" Derrick asked, peering over his shoulder. "And the American one?"

Jack paused to shoot him a look from under his thick lashes. "Don't worry about it," he snapped before resuming his rapid-fire typing.

Recognizing his expression as his focused face, Mara went to put a pot of coffee on.

Half an hour later, Jack stalked into the kitchen. He fished out a bottle of whiskey from under the counter, adding a shot to the mug of coffee she'd handed him. "It's not enough data to come to any conclusions. We need more links in the chain."

"There were no matches? Not even Dubois?"

"No," he answered, sipping the coffee. "Although there are four cases where he or Galt was in the same country. That's as close as I could get, but I'm just getting started."

"Still, it's not exactly a smoking gun is it?" Derrick called from the living room.

Scowling, Jack rolled his eyes. "I don't care how good your hearing is. Get your butt in here so I can bitch to your face," he shouted.

Derrick strolled in, holding out his mug. Jack added the whiskey.

"I know it feels like forever, but the reality is we haven't been on these guys that long," Mara pointed out. She wasn't an experienced investigator, but she knew these things took time. "We just need to keep watching them."

Jack took another large sip of coffee. "How long can you devote to this?"

Mara folded her arms. "As long as it takes."

Derrick crossed his arms. "None of the people you've been tracking have led us to another facility. The one here in Spain is the only one, and they are not active at all. According to Jack's last update, no one but the security staff and the regular assistants have been in. They haven't acquired more shifter bodies. Their research has to be taking place someplace else, another faculty. And I don't get why. Why would Denon set up multiple locations for this shit?"

Mara didn't know the answer either.

Light dawned on Jack's face. He pointed his mug at Derrick. "Unless the others aren't bodies yet."

She straightened. "You think they could still be alive?"

Jack hesitated, as if torn about getting their hopes up. "It's a possibility, for some at least. The Barcelona facility is a former med school, perfect for dissection, but the layout isn't ideal for holding prisoners. The school doesn't have the infrastructure, and importing over a dozen people-sized cages would raise eyebrows, even in the ass-end of Spain, which outer Barcelona is not."

Derrick started pacing again. "If Denon is keeping them alive, we have to act. I know they're not our people, but we have a responsibility. Most of the affected packs are smaller than ours. We're the one with the most resources. We gotta do something before some of those shifters turn into bodies, too."

Jack murmured his agreement.

Mara snapped her fingers. "I'm going to text the red baron again."

Jack scowled. "Again?"

She shrugged, pulling out her phone. "I wrote to him while in Paris. I didn't want the lead to dry up."

Pursing her lips, she began to compose a message.

"That's too flirty," Jack said, pointing at the phone. "Say something blunt like your boss is dying, and you need the information ASAP. Make him text it to you."

Mara rolled her eyes. "I got this." She expanded the note, making a brief joke about jetlag.

"Don't say that either," Jack interrupted, trying to take the phone from her to do it himself. "Guys hate funny women."

"Jack, I will bite you. No—don't look like that," she chastised when he appeared intrigued. "I meant it in a bad way."

"Just give me the phone. I'll text the baron."

Derrick's lip twitched, but he hid his smile behind the coffee mug.

Mara held her phone away from the jealous idiot, hitting send. The *whooshing* sound of a sent text filled the air. Jack growled louder than a wolf whose rabbit got away.

He straightened, adjusting his shirt. "It's never going to work."

Mara put her hands on her hips. "Excuse me, I looked damn good in that dress and the torture shoes. It's going to work."

Jack gave her a condescending smile. "I'm telling you he's not going to text back—"

The chime on her phone sounded, and Mara glanced down. A smug smile spread across her face. The baron had texted back in record time.

Jack nodded once, gracefully conceding defeat. But his voice was a little tight when he said he was going for a run.

Aware her cousin was scrutinizing her, Mara wiped away her smirk.

Derrick shook his head. "Don't think I didn't smell him all over you. What the hell do you think you're doing, Mara?"

"What?" Her face was the picture of innocence.

"You know what," Derrick said, his look reproachful.

"It was one kiss," she protested.

Derrick was skeptical. "Mara, you can't toy with him. He's too far gone. I mean, did you hear him just now? He was so jealous he couldn't form a coherent argument."

Mara pulled the bottle of whiskey over, adding some to her own coffee. "This coming from a man who cut a swath through the entire female population of Colorado and *every* contiguous state."

"Is it because he's human?"

Derrick planted his feet wider, crossed his arms.

"Because I believe a fair percentage of the stadium's worth of past partners you've had were human," she continued.

"This isn't some hook up we're talking about. This is Jack... He's sensitive."

She snorted, holding up a finger. "Are we talking about the same Jack who once went home with not one, not two, but *three* bridesmaids at the friend's wedding he was *officiating*?"

"Mara..."

"No," she interrupted. "Did that happen or not? Because you were the one who told me that story."

"That's different."

Mara threw up her hands. "I hate this! You're not even the same species, but because you both have penises, you take his side. What is that?"

Derrick hung his head with a heavy sigh.

She was pissed now. "*No*. Don't do that. You're *my* family. I have known you since I was born. And yet you are hiding behind the bro code."

He put his hand over his heart. "I am on your side. But he looks at you as if he simultaneously wants to eat you and paint your damn picture," Derrick said. "And that is not Jack. Jack swaggers. There is no attitude around you. I think he was serious when he said he was in love with you."

The world slowed to a crawl. Her voice didn't sound like hers. "When did he say that?"

"It doesn't matter," Derrick was adamant. "He's not the right Jack with you, and it concerns me."

And who the hell is the right Jack?

Mara groaned. "Why can't I get to have fun like the rest of you guys? Fuck, even Salome gets to have a fling occasionally."

"You can't go there because Jack wouldn't be a fling—not for you. For you, he would not be *that* Jack. He almost had a meltdown because you were texting a mark. I've never seen him like this. He's never been jealous over a woman a day in his life. I have an awfully bad feeling— if you give him an inch, I foresee he'll be down on one knee in two months. I bet he's already named all your kids."

"You can't be serious." He was joking, right?

Derrick looked constipated again. "I think I might be. You know what they say about reformed rakes…"

"They make the best husbands?"

His mouth flattened.

"What?" Mara protested. "That *is* what they say."

She closed her eyes. Why couldn't she ever get what she wanted— even for a little while? Was that so much to ask?

Derrick grabbed the bottle of whiskey, adding more to her mug. "I know you. You'll fall for him right back. Then what happens?"

Mara stayed quiet.

"I know it sucks…but you're the chief's daughter. The same rules don't apply to you."

After a long and depressing minute, she pulled the mug toward her, downing it in one go. "Yeah. I know."

CHAPTER SIXTEEN

"You are so beautiful..." Henry stared soulfully into her eyes.

"In that dress," he added hastily, his cheeks reddening.

Mara smiled at Henry Carrington, Baron Ventry, as he sipped the cocktail he'd taken from one of the uniformed waitstaff.

"Thank you," she murmured, her long lashes screening her eyes demurely.

She was acutely aware Jack and Derrick were listening through the microphone in her earring. They were also watching. Tonight's camera was hidden in her necklace.

"And thanks for organizing this," she added with as much diffidence as she could muster. "I can't believe you threw this entire evening together so quickly."

A few flirty texts was all it took for Henry Carrington to invite her to London, even offering to fly her over on his private jet for a casual 'hang' with the 'medical visionaries' he knew from the fundraising circuit.

After what Derrick assured her was the appropriate time, Mara told Carrington to set it up, but she didn't take his jet.

Mara flew into Heathrow on a commercial flight instead of the pack plane, in economy class no less, in case the baron monitored her movements.

When she reached Carrington's penthouse, she discovered his definition of casual bore no semblance to reality.

The apartment was spectacular. On the top floor of a twenty-story building, it had a massive patio facing the huge Ferris wheel, the London Eye, which she'd first seen in postcards in the airport.

The interior was a masterful blend of modern architecture embracing the classical world, with antiques and antiquities liberally sprinkled throughout. Henry had invited over two dozen people, not including the three waiters, a bartender, and a chef who attended the group.

The food was surprisingly good, too. Not as satisfying as a Spanish omelet, but still…

"So, when does your boss get here?" Henry asked after he introduced her around.

He chose to ask at the moment she took a large sip of her champagne. Mara began to cough, choking on her drink. Alarmed, Henry patted her on the back.

"I'm sorry, what did you say?" she asked when she could speak again.

"I wondered when your boss is getting here?" A slight frown creased Henry's brow. "She is coming, isn't she?"

"Of course," she said smoothly, touching his arm reassuringly. "She wouldn't miss it. She's flying in especially for it."

Mara wanted to slam her head against the wall.

I am not as good at this as I thought. Why hadn't she made her fake boss male? Then Derrick could have waltzed in, pretending to be him. Sure, his muscles and tats screamed badass soldier, but she could have made it work.

Her smile brittle, Mara almost swooned in relief when her phone rang inside of her clutch. "Will you excuse me for a moment?" She took out the device and waved it. "This is probably her."

Escaping to the bathroom, Mara plastered herself against the door, clutching her cell to her ear like a lifeline. *"It's fine,"* she hissed into the receiver after checking she was alone. "I'm fine. I can use this call to say my boss's flight got delayed."

Jack's voice was calm and decidedly smug. "Believe it or not, I was ready for this. FYI, her name is Sally Henderson."

"What?"

The dial tone was her only answer.

"Who the *fuck* is Sally Henderson?" Mara asked her angry reflection.

Her phone beeped.

Your boss.

A physical description followed.

"You could have warned me you hired an actress." She was grinding her teeth now.

Her phone beeped again.

Get back out there. ETA three minutes.

Mara braced her arms on the sink. "I will not kill him. I will not kill him."

Beep.

Now it's two minutes...

Mara flipped off her reflection.

Beep.

It's Derrick now. He can't see you anymore.

She wanted to bang on the glass in frustration. "Why not?"

Beep.

You'll see.

A smirking little devil face followed it.

"What now?" she muttered. Mara took a deep breath, counting to ten. She had to do it twice before she was calm enough to rejoin the party.

And then she ran headlong into Felix Dubois.

M ara saw red. In a split second, she'd gone from utterly calm to a near-foaming rage.

With a Herculean effort of will, Mara stepped away from Dubois, hiding her hands behind her back so he couldn't see her claws.

You can do this. Mara was the Colorado Basin's Pack enforcer. She had been trained and taught discipline by her father and brother, the two strongest and scariest sons of bitches on three continents. Mara had too much training to inadvertently unsheathe her claws—not since she was a wild preteen experiencing her first rush of hormones and rage.

She certainly had too much education to take advantage of being in an isolated part of the penthouse to hit this fucker over the head so she could shove his broken corpse out the bathroom window.

He'd go splat so hard. They were high enough for it, but she wasn't going to do that. *See*, she told herself. *I am as cool as a cucumber.*

"I am so sorry," she said after a pause, backing away with a laugh. She patted Dubois on the chest with false joviality. "Are you okay?"

"Yes, yes," Felix Dubois, the mad Mengela, said with a brittle smile. He backed away quickly. Going for the door, he rubbed his chest as if her pats had stung his sensitive baby flesh. *Yeah. There's more where that came from, asshole.*

"Mary."

Mara turned to see Henry coming toward her, his arm outstretched. "Darling, come. Your boss and her other assistant are here."

Darling?

"Other assistant?" she echoed from behind gritted teeth as Dubois escaped into the restroom.

Henry's smile was warm. "John, the social secretary," he explained.

"Oh, of course. The boss never goes anywhere without him." Mara plastered on a smile, trying to appear as if she weren't about to scream her head off.

Slipping her hand into the crook of Henry's arm, she followed him to the living room. Jack was waiting with an elegant blond woman in her early sixties.

She wore Versace. So did Jack. Damn, he looked good in a suit.

"There you are, dear," the woman said, leaning over to exchange Gallic kisses that didn't connect with Mara's cheeks.

'Sally' pressed her hand to Mara's arm, murmuring a quiet thanks for her fictional networking skills. Mara blinked. The woman was tall with patrician features and an inborn elegance that couldn't be taught. It had to be something a person was born with.

And for some reason, Sally wore Jack's scent all over her. *What the...?*

That detail swept Mara's legs out from under her. It took her almost a minute to recover enough to make proper conversation, but she needn't have worried. Sally had everything in hand.

"Henry, dear," the woman was saying. "Why don't you introduce me to him?"

To whom? Mara still hadn't caught up. But they wandered off before she could ask, leaving her alone with Jack.

Mara whirled on him, her glare hot enough to blister. He had added makeup and a thin layer of prosthetic skin to change his appearance ever so subtly. The extra skin made his nose broader, and his skin was also ruddier instead of gold. He looked weird... He was Jack, yet he wasn't, which was wigging her out.

"Don't worry about dropping the ball," he murmured. "'Sally' is more than capable of picking it up and running with it."

"Bite me," Mara said from behind her teeth, forcing herself to keep smiling at Henry.

"Anytime, baby, anytime. Or do you prefer darling?"

"Don't be a douchebag," she warned. "Henry's a good host."

And it was true. He'd taken her by the arm, introducing her fictional boss around with self-effacing aplomb. Occasionally, he would look over at Mara with an earnest *aren't-I-a-good-boy* expression.

"Oh, brother." Jack snorted. "Is he expecting a treat?"

Mara snickered, and he scowled. "Never mind. Don't answer that."

Her levity evaporated as Henry and Sally joined the group where Felix Dubois was holding court. Mara's sensitive hearing could pick up her fictional boss launching into a discussion of London society, comparing it to Paris and Rome, scattering the name of people and restaurants like so many jewels.

She had no idea where Jack had found her, but this 'Sally' really knew her stuff. Her services surely cost an arm and a leg. However, in this case, Mara was willing to pay every cent.

After a few minutes of watching the woman work, Jack made a move to join her.

Mara stopped him with a touch to the arm. "Are you sure he's not going to recognize you?"

She told herself it was because she didn't want a fight on her hands, but if she were honest, it was because she did.

"Only one way to know for sure," Jack drawled before drifting into the mix.

Bracing herself, Mara followed him, waiting for the instant when Dubois glanced up and saw him. But the moment came and went without the moment of recognition and accusation she was dreading.

Equal parts irritated and relieved, Mara hung back, not trusting herself to be that close to their mark. Then Henry broke away, asking a waiter to bring them something sweet to share.

Across the room, Jack's jaw stiffened, clearly annoyed, which mollified her.

She gave their host a brilliant smile, joining him for another drink, while Jack and Sally pumped Dubois for information.

Jack's body flashed hot and cold as Mara stepped out on the balcony with Henry Carrington. She tucked her hair behind her ear, her gaze trained on Carrington's face with that unwavering fixation that usually meant a person was totally into someone.

He took a step toward them.

Sensing danger, Sally put her hand on his arm. "What was that hotel again, the one with the spa I liked?" Though the question was addressed to him, she leaned toward Felix as if he were the only person of significance in the room.

"The Caislean," Jack supplied with a nod, not missing a beat despite the fact he hadn't been listening. His attention was elsewhere.

He settled back, turning slightly so he could keep watching Mara out of the corner of his eye.

"That's right," Sally confirmed with an airy wave. "Wonderful masseurs there. I highly recommend them."

"I've never tried a rub down there," Dubois said. "But the chef at the Caislean Paris makes the best Chateaubriand I've ever had the pleasure of eating."

"I'm sure it's wonderful. Have you tried their Omakase menu at their San Francisco hotel?"

"Sublime, utterly sublime."

Jack put his head down an inch, tuning out the rest of Felix's droning reply as much as he could.

On the balcony, Carrington edged closer to Mara until he was mere inches away from her.

Good lord, he's going to start puckering up next. The crystal glass Jack held made a tiny but ominous snapping sound.

"Jack, be a doll and refill this," Sally said, a warning glint in her eye. She held out her empty glass. He took it gratefully, detouring to the bathroom to splash cold water on his face.

"You are a punk-ass little bitch."

Jack jumped, startled. Derrick snickered in his earpiece. Mara hadn't been able to wear one—the three of them had agreed Henry Carrington would be looking at her too closely.

Ogling is more like it.

"Shut up," Jack snapped, wiping his face. "How's Sally doing?"

"She's a pro. Where did you dig her up?"

Jack adjusted his cuff links. "My father had the good taste to marry her. It didn't stick, but she kept in touch. She has a background in acting and loves this sort of thing. I don't use her much, though."

Most of the jobs he took didn't require this kind of social infiltration. That and he'd never put Sally in any genuinely dangerous situations. He was too fond of her for that. Still, when the stars aligned, he was happy to have her at his back. That and she had a lot of fun doing these jobs.

"Are you through primping?" Derrick asked in his ear. "Because Sally is getting some good stuff in there. I think Dubois lives here in London. He's trying to one-up her on his knowledge of expensive local haunts."

That was interesting. "Sally knows London pretty well. She did a couple of years at the National theater and a shorter run at the Old Vic." Jack straightened, adjusting his tie. "If he can keep up with her on exclusive London spots, it's a good sign he lives here or has in the past."

Let's hope it's current. They needed to find where this asshole lived.

There was a pause as Derrick listened in to the other conversation. "I didn't think he'd be this much of a brown-noser," Derrick said with a disgusted sigh.

"Better that he is," Jack pointed out. Dubois's social-climbing tendencies had given them a way in. "How is Mara doing with the weak-chinned wonder?"

Derrick snickered. "Don't you mean how is the weak-chinned wonder doing with her?"

"Like she'd be impressed with Carrington," he scoffed.

"Yeah, Henry Carrington is only young, wealthy, and handsome with a noble title. What's to like?"

Handsome? Jack wrinkled his nose. Maybe he was a little, in that effete highbrow British way. There were plenty of women who would be into that, but Jack hadn't thought Mara would be one.

She's not, idiot. This was a job for them both, and his jealousy was jeopardizing their job.

"Henry is like a puppy in human form. Do I have to remind you that Mara is a wolf?"

"As if I'd forget," Derrick griped. "Hey—"

There was urgency in his tone. Jack's pulse sped up, and he started to reach for the gun he'd strapped to his ankle. From now on, he wasn't going anywhere unprepared. "What is it?"

"We have confirmation. Sally got Dubois to admit he lives here in London."

Jack resisted the urge to pump his fist in the air. This fish had been slippery, but he hadn't gotten away.

"If he leaves before us, follow him," Jack said. "We need an address."

There was the sound of movement in the background. Derrick was grabbing his gear. "I'm on it."

CHAPTER SEVENTEEN

Derrick was off trailing Dubois. Mara could see his camera feed bobbing up and down through an unfamiliar wealthy neighborhood on the screen of one of Jack's computers in their hotel room.

Her mind should have been on that. Finding Felix's home base was their entire purpose here in London. But she couldn't focus on that now. Not when Jack was saying goodbye to Sally at their rented apartment's door.

The woman had been with them since they left Carrington's penthouse.

Henry had been disappointed to see her go, but it had been for the group when Sally had said their goodbyes. Mara and Jack had stepped behind her, as appropriate for staff departing with their boss.

Now Jack was thanking her. Mara cocked her head in amusement.

What did she just say? Mara wondered as the woman hugged Jack as if she hadn't seen him in a year. *Schmooshies.* Sally called kisses *schmooshies,* and she was plastering a big one to Jack's cheek, which she then proceeded to pinch.

Mara's chuckle was silent, but it shook her whole belly.

Sally must be a relative or close family friend. Well, at least that explained how he got her scent all over him. Well, it made a hell of a lot more sense than Jack being interested in a woman old enough to be his mother.

Wait. Was that it? Mara squinted at the pair. They didn't resemble each other at all, but there was something maternal to their interaction.

Sally took off with an airy wave, and Jack returned to the living room. "Is Sally your mother or an aunt?"

"My former stepmother," Jack corrected.

Ah, yes. That fit. "How long was she married to your father?"

"About two years. But Dad switched out from the diplomatic corps to a job in the capital. Sally found it stifling, so they called it quits. No hard feelings."

"You weren't upset by the divorce?"

He shrugged. "I liked her, but I was old enough when they met that she was never really a mother figure. And I knew for a fact she hated D.C. I did, too, so I opted for boarding school not long after."

He settled down next to her, checking the screen. "How is Derrick doing?"

"Dubois' cab stopped at a building in the Kensington neighborhood."

"It's not another hotel, is it?"

Mara smiled a dangerous predator's grin. "No," she said, letting herself enjoy the sensation.

She was a hunter after all, and they had finally cornered their prey. "It's an apartment building. Derrick is casing the place, narrowing down which unit is his and identifying the security's weak spots."

"Good," Jack sank back into the sofa, putting his hands behind his head and closing his eyes. "We'll break-in at the earliest opportunity and bug the shit out of everything—phone, computers, cars, and coats. Everything. The fucker will have tracking devices in his underpants."

She snorted. "Do you have bugs that small?"

"The best money can buy," he assured her. "Of course, their range is crap, so they don't work unless you're on the same city block, but we could do it."

"A witch's mark would work better."

Jack's head snapped to her face. "What is that?"

"A kind of spell."

His lips parted. "Can werewolves cast spells?"

"Not really," she confessed. "Our magic is different. But we can use them if they've been made for us."

"Really. That's cool." Jack rubbed his chin. "Do you have one?"

She shook her head. "No, but it's pointless now. We're not letting him out of our sight."

"So, if he gets on a plane, we follow?"

"To the ends of the earth." They would bring down the entire Denon network if they had to.

Mara took a deep breath, then exhaled. This war wouldn't be won in a day, and tonight she was here alone in a sumptuous suite with a handsome male whose arousal spiked whenever she was near.

"You were jealous of Henry."

He smiled. "Yup."

She was glad he didn't try to deny it. "That's stupid."

Jack opened his eyes, a watchful stillness creeping over him. "Is it?"

"Of course it is," Mara said. "Henry is a means to an end. I feel guilty about it, abusing his generosity the way I have, but I'd do it again. The pack's security is more important than my feelings."

The irony was Mara believed if she could have shared the truth with Henry, he would likely have volunteered his help. He'd rolled out the red carpet for her without asking for anything in return. He was that kind of man. Okay, now she felt terrible again...

"What's wrong?" His brow creased in concern.

"I may not be wired for this kind of work. I prefer a straight fight to subterfuge and skullduggery."

Jack was incredulous. "This is about Carrington?"

Mara winced.

"You never made Henry any promises," he said. "Carrington threw that party all on his own. He wanted to impress you—and he succeeded. Hell, he impressed me. Getting Felix Dubois properly liquored up and in Sally's sights is a feat. But you don't owe him anything more aside from a little gratitude. You can write him a thank you note or bake him a cheesecake."

Mara giggled, an unfamiliar bubbly feeling in her chest. She recognized it as happiness. Jack was jealous...but, this time, it made her happy. There was a lot wrong with that picture, but she was willing to give him a pass because he hadn't acted on it.

Jack had stayed put, playing his part and letting her do hers. She knew a few wolves who would have given her the same latitude, having enough confidence in her abilities to get the job done. But she was related to almost all of them.

"And just so you know," Jack continued. "For future reference, I don't want you because you're beautiful or because you smell great. I want you because you can kick my ass."

His words sent a flood of warmth through her body while making her want to laugh at the same time. The delivery was so nonchalant.

"Masochist," she murmured, shaking her head and closing her eyes. When she opened them, Jack was reaching for her.

He pulled her toward him, kissing her with hard possessiveness. Blood heating, Mara opened her mouth, letting him in.

In the back of her head, a little voice whispered a warning. This wasn't cracking the lid of Pandora's box—it was busting it open on the floor and dancing around in the debris in her underwear.

But she couldn't help it. Jack tasted indescribably good—possibly better than he looked, and she hadn't thought that was possible.

How had she gotten on Jack's lap? Mara had been sitting next to him a second ago. Yet, now she was straddling him, trying to swallow his face.

Jack made a sound deep in this throat halfway between a growl and purr. He paused, embarrassed. "Sorry, I don't usually make so much noise—"

Mara put both hands on either side of his face. "Shut up." She laughed, kissing him again.

He closed his eyes, giving himself over to the kiss. He was so hungry for her that she could feel the urgency he felt in his every touch.

It was contagious.

She tore at his shirt, but she couldn't get it off because his hands were in the way, trying to undress her.

"Okay, stop," he begged. "Let me."

His hands moved over her back. The warm air hit her skin as he unzipped the bodice of her dress, tugging it down to her waist. He pulled her toward him, his mouth flaming up and down over her neck.

"Ah, God! My eyes! *Stop that.*"

Startled, Mara jerked her head up. Her cousin stood five feet away, covering his eyes as if he'd been burned.

"*Derrick?*" She gaped, her mind still on Jack's hot body. "What are you doing back so soon?"

"I've been gone over an *hour*," Derrick stressed, still covering his eyes. "I need to go back in daylight to get a full bead on the security rotation. Unless you want me to break in while Felix is there."

Mara glanced back at Jack. He was biting his lip. "I, um, I can explain," he began.

"Believe it or not, this requires no explanation." Derrick put his hands on his hips. "What I want is an apology."

Jack scowled. "To you? *No.*" He hugged Mara closer to him. "*Never. I will never be sorry about this.*"

Damn. Mara had never wanted to laugh and cry at the same time.

Jack may have been sitting, but he was standing off against a were-wolf who could eviscerate him. He went blithely where angels feared to tread…and he was doing it for her.

Something broke inside her, and a cold lonely place inside her flooded with warmth

"Derrick, go away," she told him.

Her cousin's face screwed up as if he'd tasted something sour. "At least go into one of the bedrooms." He closed his eyes. "I can't believe I just said that. Your dad is going to kill me."

Derrick covered his ears. "I'm going to bed. Try to remember how sensitive my hearing is."

Mara twisted her neck, watching him stalk out of the room.

When she turned back, Jack watched her intently. "I know we got a little carried away. I, um, I understand if you want to stop now."

Her lips parted. She could feel his arousal, smell it weaved into the air all around her. But he was still giving her an out.

She made a show of thinking about it. The hungry little spark in Jack's eyes started to dim, but he nodded in understanding.

"Here," he said, sitting on his hands. He gave her an artless smile. "To avoid temptation."

Mara climbed off him. He started to follow her up, presumably to take a cold shower, but she pushed him back down. Then she pulled the sides of her wrap dress apart, letting the belt fall to the floor.

Jack's mouth dropped open. He made another sound, this one closer to a whimper.

Mara took his hand, then led him to her bedroom.

Mara had never woken up next to a man before. Having the first one be Jack Buchanan should have been enough for some serious self-recrimination, but she couldn't summon the energy. She was too satisfied.

See, this is what life should be like.

Mara could be like every other wolf in her pack—they had casual affairs all the time. She could do casual. Even if Jack was a bit more serious, he measured by human standards. People didn't go into a relationship thinking this was 'the one'. They would be involved for a time and then it would end, like most human and Were relationships.

They could be happy for the duration. It would be intense but most likely short, like a flash fire. That didn't change the fact they had a defined shelf life.

Jack moved, cuddling closer. Mara froze, doubts flooding her brain.

Okay, *stop.* The key to having a successful affair was not to think about it too hard. *Don't make any plans, no talk of tomorrow. Just live in the moment.*

Except she hadn't done that last night. In between all the impossibly hot sex, they had talked. In fact, she'd spilled her guts. Once she got going, she was unable to stop. But she'd felt so close to him, and he'd been so understanding...

Mara grimaced. *Those are famous last words.*

Jack rolled over, his stupidly long lashes fluttering open. All at once, her misgivings faded away. "Hey," he said, putting an arm behind his back and yawning adorably. "How are you?"

She opened her mouth, but nothing came out. By the Mother, why was this so awkward?

Jack's eyes flared. He sat up, his expression concerned.

"I'm so sorry about that," he said, touching her neck. "I don't know what came over me. I've never bitten anyone before."

Mara slapped a hand to her neck. There was a tender spot under her palm. "What?"

Chagrined, Jack winced. "You don't remember?"

He removed her hand, tracing the marks with his index finger. "I still can't believe I got so carried away. It was, um, during a high point. I didn't realize until I was doing it. But the entire night was so...primal."

He reddened. "I'm an idiot. Sorry. It's not like you weren't there."

Mara groaned and collapsed on the bed, but she was laughing at the same time. *It's okay. It doesn't mean the same thing to humans.*

She was still trying to figure out what to say when Jack's phone beeped. "Oh, it's Sally. She wants to have lunch with you."

"Wait, what?" Mara drew her head back. Why did his stepmother want to see her? "Did you tell her anything? About us?"

Jack pursed his lips. "Well, not exactly. But she knows me pretty well. That and the part where I wanted to kill our host? It kind of gave me away."

Mara chuckled, but there was an underlying anxiety to it. "I didn't realize you two were so close. I didn't even know she existed until yesterday."

Having lunch with her lover's stepmother didn't fit into her image of a casual relationship.

125

"You don't have to go if you don't want to," Jack assured her. "And my relationship with Sally is erratic at best. If we don't run into each other at least once a year, we try to get together. Then we'll paint the town red. It's not unlike a blitzkrieg attack," he said. "We raid the high-end stores, eat at the best restaurants, and catch the latest shows —if she's not performing in them, that is."

And you tell her about your love life?"

"She gets a synopsis," he said. "An abbreviated one."

Mara huffed. "I think the word you meant to use is 'censored'."

The corners of his mouth twitched. "No comment."

He stretched out on the bed. "If you do feel like joining Sally, she won't grill you. She's too laid back for that sort of thing. And she does know the best restaurants."

Mara wanted to say no. Even if his relationship with his step-mother was atypical, getting together with her was a slippery slope. Of course, Mara owed the woman a debt of gratitude. Sally's charm and air of importance had broken down Felix Dubois faster than she ever could have.

"I will think about it."

Someone started pounding on the door hard enough to make it vibrate. "It is six AM," Derrick announced. "If you all are done—please God be done—I am going to start the stakeout. I expect to be relieved in four hours. I would make it six, but I don't want to leave you alone that long."

Groaning, Mara pulled a pillow over her head. But she still heard Derrick muttering under his breath. "Four hours," he repeated. Foot-steps receded, and the front door of the apartment banged shut.

Jack pulled the pillow off her face. "Four is three hours and fifty-nine minutes longer than I thought he'd give us. I don't suppose you'd be interested in making the most of them?"

Mara started laughing. "I can't decide if that is the best or worst proposition I've ever heard."

Jack started nibbling her neck. "*Best*. I can make it the best. Just give me ten of those minutes. You won't regret it."

M ara ate her sandwich in silence. She kept trying to meet Derrick's eyes, but her cousin kept his head down as he worked through a huge pile of eggs and bacon. He'd come back to the hotel suite a few minutes ago, while Jack took over the surveillance, watching the building from a cafe across the street.

"So how many days do you think it will take to establish Dubois' routine?" she asked. "Because I don't think we should wait too long to bug his place and electronics. The bastard likes to fly off at a moment's notice, and we want to bug the things he carries with him."

Her cousin put his fork down, crossing his arms over his wide chest. "Are you seriously going to ignore the fact you bedded Jackson f-ing Buchanan? Didn't you call him the original man ho? And were you the one who compared him to a rutting dog?"

"I compared him to you guys, Connell included, before he met Logan, that is. I called you all dogs."

"Mara."

The warning tone grated on her nerves. She slammed her hand down on the table. "*No.*"

He groaned. "It's a mistake."

She threw up her hands. "I don't care. I should get to make as many mistakes as I want—at least as many as you and my brother do."

Derrick gave her a derisive glance. "I don't think I've ever made one quite this big."

Mara crossed her arms, spitting out one word. "Stacy."

Derrick made a face, raising his finger. "You promised you would never say that name again."

"*Sta-cy,*" Mara enunciated while holding up one finger, then another and another. "Three times. She was a mistake you made *three* times."

He rose, picking up his still-full plate. "I am going to finish this in bed... then I'm going to crash because I could not sleep last night thanks to someone's very loud sex."

127

Derrick left the room, sweeping away as if he had a cape.

"Buy earplugs," she shouted after him, determined to protect a connection that was new but already precious. "Because there's more of that coming."

CHAPTER EIGHTEEN

Felix Dubois was a jogger. It wasn't something he'd indulged in at the various hotels he'd stayed at while abroad, but here in his hometown, he ran every morning for half an hour to forty-five minutes.

On the third day of their surveillance, Jack and Derrick went in, dressed in coveralls with a local broadband company's logo.

Jack had printed up a fake work order to flash at anyone who asked what they were doing there. However, despite being an expensive residence, the older building had no real security to speak of beyond a passcode on the main door. Dressed the way they were, no one they passed batted an eye.

He and Derrick split up, one taking the stairs and the other the elevator so they could plant tiny button surveillance cams in unobtrusive corners. The cameras' resolution was crap, but they would be good enough to recognize Dubois should the man cut off his run prematurely.

The apartment itself had an excellent lock, but Jack was a pro. He put on his gloves, then whipped out his lock-picking set. The door was open less than ten seconds later. They ducked inside before a neighbor down the hall left their apartment and spotted them. Once inside, they had a moment of apprehension when they didn't find a phone or laptop out in the open.

They started searching everywhere—cabinets, bookshelves, under the couch cushions. Jack even checked between the mattress and box spring in the bedroom. After several long minutes, Derrick found the electronics hidden in a locked bottom drawer of the desk.

The computer was password-protected, of course.

Jack set himself up behind the desk, plugging in the thumb drive storing his de-encryption software and setting out his portable hard drive.

"Fucker's paranoid," Derrick remarked as he got to work.

Jack didn't take his eyes off the screen of Felix's computer. "Oh, so you're finally talking to me?"

Derrick had been giving him the silent treatment since this morning, right around the time he caught Jack coming out of Mara's room wearing only a towel.

"I should be beating your head in," Derrick said with a grunt. "You're the reason I'm going to get my ass kicked. Mara is my baby cousin, and this happened on my watch."

Jack didn't stop typing, but he smirked. "Stop being so dramatic. Mara is an adult—"

"Stop right there. Because if you're about to give me the 'we're both consenting adults' talk, I'm going to jump out that window," Derrick said, pointing to the massive bay windows.

Jack snorted. "I don't think those open, but if you keep warning me off Mara, I'll be happy to throw you through one."

Derrick snorted. "You can try, *human*."

Jack typed the next command with extra hard keystrokes. "Is everyone in the pack going to have that much of a problem with Mara dating me? Will the chief be waiting for my ass with a baseball bat or something?"

He was genuinely curious.

"We don't use bats. We have claws," Derrick replied matter-of-factly. "And I wasn't talking about Douglas. I was talking about Connell. Do you remember your dear friend Connell, Mara's big brother? And you are not dating her. You're hooking up. There's a difference."

"Connell is only two minutes older than Mara," Jack scoffed, focusing on cracking the computer's password. "Plus, ten seconds," he added absently.

"*Exactly.* And he's—" Derrick blinked. "Wait. How do you know that?"

Jack made a rumbling sound in his throat. "I *am* trying to focus here. Unless you want us to get caught."

"But how do you know that Connell is older?"

He raised his head to shoot Derick a scornful glance. "Because Mara told me. Now let me crack this sucker before you open your trap again—and keep an eye on that camera feed."

Derrick narrowed his eyes, but he shut up.

Jack typed faster. The password was tricky, but his cracking script was clever. It did the job in a few minutes. Once he had access, he started a high-speed data dump of the computer contents to his portable drive while adding a key-logger program that would masquerade as one of the computer's utility programs. It was set to send the data through an SSL connection whenever the computer accessed the network, so the added payload would be virtually unde-tectable in the background.

Derrick hovered over him like a passive-aggressive mother hen. "So, you two aren't just boning? You...talk?"

"On occasion," he replied sarcastically.

Despite his flippant response, Jack didn't take that for granted. As strong and brilliant as Mara was, she'd spent most of her life in an insular community. Being part of a tight-knit pack looked great from the outside, but Jack was smart enough to recognize that it would be suffocating at times. Once Mara had decided to confide in him, she'd unloaded. And her trust was precious to him.

"Has Mara said you two are in a relationship?"

Good grief, were all werewolves this nosy? "No."

Derrick started hopping and pointing. Jack could tell he was winding up for another tirade, so he held up a hand.

"Before you declare victory, I did hear what you said earlier. I'm not trying to ruin her life. I'm not going to put any pressure on her, but I'm also not going to walk away. As long as she's willing, I'm here until she tells me otherwise.'

"And how long do you think that will be?"

He shrugged. "I don't know. At this moment, though, she is having lunch with my stepmother, so I'll take that as a good sign."

"I thought she was having lunch with Henry Carrington? I was there when he called, and she agreed." Derrick frowned. "To keep the channel open and all that."

The invitation had come earlier. Mara had considered it but, in the end, she'd put him off.

"She postponed the baron," Jack said, not bothering to hide how happy he was at that particular turn of events. "Sally is leaving for New York the day after tomorrow for an off-Broadway thing. The show is supposed to run for a month, two if it goes well, so it was kind of Mara to squeeze her in."

"Oh, so you obligated her to go," Derrick sniffed. "Mara is just being nice."

Done with the computer, Jack closed it and put it back in the drawer. "Can I ask you something?"

Derrick grunted.

"When is the last time Mara did something because she was feeling nice?" Jack started to work on the phone.

His question was answered with blessed silence.

"Is there a hairbrush in the bedroom?" he asked.

"Let me check."

He came back a minute later with an antique silver hairbrush. Fortunately for them, it had a flat handle. Taking out his kit, he applied a small amount of fingerprint dust, finding most of an index finger on the front part of the handle.

Jack lifted the print, sticking the double-sided tape to his own finger and pressing it down on the phone's home button.

"Neat trick," Derrick said. "Remind me not to leave my phone lying around in you."

Jack snickered. "Too late. Cute cupcake shots, by the way."

"*What?*" Derrick sputtered.

"The ones in the gym, where you're flexing," Jack said, downloading his track-and-trace program to the phone's OS. He cloned the whole damn thing, determined to record every conversation Felix the fucker had from here on out.

When he looked up, Derrick studied him, his nose wrinkled. "Are you attracted to me?"

"No."

"Then why the hell did you steal my gym pics? I take those to send to women—single ones."

"I showed them to Mara so we could laugh at you," he replied evenly, turning off the phone and putting it away.

"I hate you so much," Derrick muttered.

Jack leaned over to mock punch him in the jaw. "You know you love me."

"The hell I do. You are my punishment. I just wish I knew what the hell I'd done to deserve you."

The other man was still arguing with him when they hit the street, having made a clean exit.

"Hold up," he said, pushing Derrick to the left, stopping short before he shoved him into traffic.

Behind them, Felix Dubois jogged back into his building. The mark saw neither his nor Derrick's face.

Feeling fairly good about himself, he started for the street. He and Derrick piled into the van they'd parked a few blocks away. Jack let the werewolf drive so he could check his phone.

"Mara should be done with lunch soon. Let's pick her up," he suggested, rattling off the address.

Derrick grunted his assent.

"Have I told you how much I enjoy our talks?"

More guttural noises followed. They sounded suspiciously like swear words, but through the lens of an animal, like human words transformed into growls and barks by the synthesizer he used to play with as a child.

Grinning, Jack tugged off his coverall, revealing his jeans and the blue t-shirt that had instantly become his favorite when Mara complimented the shade, remarking on how closely it matched his eyes.

Mara couldn't believe she was having such a good time. She laughed at one of Sally's outrageous theatre stories as she sipped her Bellini.

Sally was dressed as stylishly as last night in an elegant white silk shirt and grey slacks paired with a cashmere capelet. She had a presence, people watched her, almost as if they believed her to be somebody they should know—an actress or a socialite—and they were trying to figure out if they recognized her.

But despite the elegant shell, she was genuinely nice and surprisingly fun. Sally had dropped the highbrow New York accent, settling into the soft honeyed twang of a proper southern belle. She loved to talk, and her voice was a pleasure to hear.

Mara had expected an inquisition from the moment she sat at the elegant table at the trendy bistro Sally selected near the Borough Market. *Who is Felix Dubois? What was all that business at the baron's penthouse about? How did you meet Jackson? Are you dating? What are your intentions? Do you like kids?*

But Sally had asked none of those things, instead telling her anecdotes about her life, entertaining tales of her fellow actors, and the various jobs she'd done for her stepson, mixing in tantalizing tidbits about Jack's childhood. She even sprinkled in tidbits on the techniques she had employed to get Felix to talk.

Eventually, Mara's curiosity got the better of her. "Sally, why did you ask to have lunch with me? Was it to give me advice on how to break down a suspect without their knowledge?"

Laughing, Sally threw her head back. "No, of course not, sugar," she said, the endearment tripping off her tongue so naturally that Mara didn't even blink. "You need a bit more practice, but I think your instincts are very good. Jack thinks so, too, no matter how he behaved last night."

She leaned forward to put a manicured hand on Mara's arm. "He didn't say anything to upset you after I left last night, did he? If he was critical, I hope you know it didn't have anything to do with you and more to do with him being mad with jealousy. I was tickled pink to see it, just tickled."

Caught off guard, Mara blushed. She couldn't very well say they didn't discuss her performance or his and instead had scorching hot sex all night. "I'm not interested in Henry," she said, deciding it was a safer answer.

"But you are interested in Jack?" It wasn't a question.

Mara flushed, feeling like she was fourteen years old again. "I, uh, it's complicated."

"No doubt it is." This was said with an indulgent smile. Sally waved a languid hand. "After all, this is Jack we're talking about. He's not happy unless he's neck deep in intrigue. It's why we get on so well. I've often said he inherited his love of drama from me, much to his father's dismay. But I haven't seen him ever behave the way he did last night."

Uncertain what to say, Mara sipped her drink to avoid answering.

A spark lit Sally's eye. "I confess this is why I wanted to have lunch with you. Jack doesn't get invested in very many people—male or female. Only his friends from his military days, and a few ex-girl-friends from when he was young."

Mara blinked at the unexpected information.

"Oh, I don't mean there is anything romantic there," Sally said, reading the dismay she tried to hide. "These were purely puppy love and mostly one-sided. But those girls got over him eventually, else he wouldn't have stayed friends with them. They're both married now—one even happily."

She smiled awkwardly. "I wasn't concerned. Jack's past is none of my business."

"Well, of course it is sugar," Sally declared with an airy wave. "He obviously cares deeply for you and vice versa."

Mara was horribly embarrassed. "It's, um, a little soon to say."

135

All the drawbacks her cousin had pointed out to her came crowding back in her mind. Then an image of him at her family's table followed—how he had seemed to fit and been welcomed despite his poor choice to wear cologne.

"I'm not sure what your expectations are…" she began.

Sally waved a hand. "Don't worry about that, sugar. I realize you have a complicated situation on your hands with the baron and that persnickety little man Felix, but as long as Jack is involved, I have faith things will work out. He's good at untangling Gordian knots."

Smiling with genuine warmth, she leaned forward. "Jack has flitted through life in a ramshackle fashion for so long. No deep ties, friend-ships, or relationships of any depth. But I sense this had changed now. I wanted to take this opportunity to make friends with the girl he is very sensibly smitten with—it's no mean feat, I assure you."

Sally raised her Bloody Mary glass in a toast. "I salute you, sugar, and I look forward to getting to know you better."

Fifteen minutes later, Derrick began to parallel parking in what had to be the narrowest spot on the street. Jack was eager to see Mara, and perhaps wish Sally a bon voyage, so he hopped out of the van while it was still moving.

"Catch up when you're done," he shouted back at Derrick, laughing when the Were gave him the finger.

He was thinking of a suitable punishment for Derrick when he spotted Mara at the other end of the block. Regardless of the distance, he would always recognize her. To him, she glowed, standing out like a beacon. On the crowded street, every other woman was colorless as if they were moving in a black-and-white movie while Mara alone was in technicolor.

She stood under the awning of the restaurant, checking something on her phone. Sally was nowhere in sight, but Jack wasn't that sorry to have missed her. He'd call her later. In the meantime, he'd focus on figuring out how to ditch Derrick.

It was too soon for dinner, especially considering Mara had eaten recently. But they could have fun in the meantime. There was lots to see in this area. Plenty of shops. And later, Jack could take her out to a romantic restaurant, just the two of them. They'd get Derrick a doggie bag or something. He'd love that.

Jack was still halfway down the block when Mara turned and saw him. Her entire face transformed, going soft and welcoming. Mara would hate knowing she looked like that when she saw him, which was why he'd never tell her.

She wore a peacock-blue dress with a flared skirt that hit her right above the knees. It was a simple dress that looked stunning on her. He wasn't the only one who noticed. It seemed as if the street had suddenly spawned men. Mara drew their eyes like magnets. One passerby casually turned, saw her, and promptly tripped.

Then she smiled at him, and he forgot everyone else. Jack stopped dead in his tracks, pressing a hand to his chest.

Damn, she knocked the breath out of him. Wondering why he no longer cared how stupid he'd looked, Jack picked up the pace, weaving his way toward her on the crowded street.

She was less than five feet from the restaurant when it happened.

Out the corner of his eye, Jack saw a white van stopping behind her, tires squealing. But he was so focused on Mara he didn't register the popping sound at first, not until Mara stopped and looked down.

Her welcoming smile faded. She paled, all the color leaching from her face. Hand shaking, she touched her stomach. Blood bloomed under her fingertips.

A pain-filled howl rent the air. For a second, he thought it was from him, but his mouth was closed. It must have been Derrick. He was running flat out, but the crowd on the sidewalk panicked. Too many were stampeding in his direction, blocking his way.

Jack's lungs were burning. He was fighting to get to her when another shot popped off. The impact spun Mara around, and she fell to the ground.

Men wearing black balaclavas swarmed around her like insects. They picked her up off the ground, bundling her into the white van at the curb. The door slammed and the vehicle pulled away, the engine roaring full blast.

Jack shoved the last bystander out of his way and jumped, throwing himself bodily at the door. His hands scrabbled for the door handle.

He missed.

His head hit the corner of the van, the impact spinning and knocking him back down to the asphalt. Less than a second later, a hand grabbed him by the collar, hauling him back up. He didn't have to look to know it was Derrick.

Together, they ran after the van, but it blasted past the red traffic lights, narrowly missing a double-decker bus.

Another block and it took a sharp right, disappearing from sight and taking Mara with it.

CHAPTER NINETEEN

Derrick had seen some terrible shit in his day; accidents, soldiers dying on the battlefield—even the betrayal of his pack by one of their own.

None of that compared to the expression on Jack's face after Mara had been shot. Looking into his eyes at that moment was like getting a literal glimpse of hell.

Derrick flinched, forgetting his rage and heartbreak for a moment. Mara was his baby cousin, and he was supposed to be keeping an eye on her.

My watch, he reminded himself. They'd been made. Somewhere along the line, they had fucked up, been spotted, and been identified. He'd dropped the ball, and Mara had paid the price.

They were in their vehicle now, trying to find the van. Jack typed furiously on his laptop, his face paler than any human Derrick had ever seen with the possible exception of a few corpses.

He turned the wheel, taking a sharp right. Horns blared. "Jack, I'm going to need you to snap out of it. We need to find the van."

"Then turn right."

Derrick snapped his head to his friend and back to the road. Jack's voice was scary flat, totally devoid of emotion.

"I hacked into the CCTV network," Jack continued.

Thank fuck. "All right," he turned, gripping the steering wheel tight. "We got this."

But they didn't. By the time they found the van, it was sitting empty in an airfield. Someone had wiped everything down, then thrown bleach all over the back of the van.

A Gulfstream G500 had taken off minutes before. The flight plan was for New York, but the plane disappeared from radar less than an hour after it took off. It never landed.

They'd lost her. Mara was gone.

CHAPTER TWENTY

I'm not dead. That much Mara knew. There was too much pain for this to be the other side.

Jack. Where was Jack? He'd been right in front of her, and now... What the hell was happening? *Fuck*, she'd been shot. It had hurt, too, more than she could have ever imagined.

Okay, no more telling her cousins and brother to man up when they caught a bullet.

Mara had been clawed up in her job as a pack enforcer. She'd always been more skilled and faster than her opponents, so it hadn't been that bad, not with her rapid regeneration. Getting shot, however, was an entire other world of pain.

She tried to open her eyes, but bright sunlight seared her eyelids. Squeezing them shut, she tried to brace herself as she was jostled. The wind whipped across her face, but the movement was too much for her. The pain rose like a wave, and she got swept back under.

The next time she opened her eyes, she was lying on a narrow bed, staring up at a ring of people wearing surgical masks and caps. Then the room jerked, and the people grabbed the bed for support. Someone shouted words she didn't understand.

What the...?

Mara reached up, ripping something off her face—a plastic mask fitted over her mouth. A hand clamped onto her wrist, forcing her hand back down. Then everything went dark again.

The next time she rose to the surface, the world had stopped moving. She was lying in a giant four-poster bed. Mara tried to move her hands, but she couldn't. They were bound.

Eyes watering, she blinked until she could see her restraints. Wide metallic cuffs were wrapped around each wrist. Each had a ring welded to the top, with a thick chain snacking from it. A thick band of padded leather lining each cuff interior protected her skin. She didn't have to look to know that it was bolted to the floor.

Mara tentatively touched the flat of one cuff to the opposite arm.

Fuck. The burn told her whatever metal this was, it had a hell of a lot of silver in it. *Okay, don't do that again.* She was already weak. Burning herself with silver wasn't helping.

And what the fuck am I wearing? The unfamiliar nightgown had a structured bodice and a long, wide skirt of green satin, the same shade as her eyes.

"How?" She tried to rise.

"You're awake," a familiar voice said.

What the fuck? No. Sweat broke out on her brow. This was not happening.

The air thickened to the consistency of molasses. That had to be why it took her almost a fucking calendar year to turn her head.

When she did, her stomach twisted and sank to the floor at the same time.

Henry Carrington, Baron Ventry, beamed at her from the door. He closed it softly behind him, then came inside.

Henry wore one of his thousand-dollar suits, his boyishly handsome face ruddy as if he'd been standing outside in a brisk wind.

Please let him have rescued me. Don't let him be involved.

"What is going on?" Damn, her voice sounded as if a cheese-grater had scraped up her throat.

Henry sat on the side of the bed. He gestured to the chains. "I am so sorry about this—precautions. You understand."

What little hope she had that he wasn't responsible for her condition crumbled into dust.

"No…" Mara shook her head, regretting it instantly when it made the world swim. "I don't understand. Not at all. Please explain what the *fuck* is going on!"

Henry flinched as if she'd hurt his feelings by swearing.

His face was the picture of chagrin. "I understand you're upset, and justifiably so, but there is no need for that kind of language. I admit, the way we brought you here wasn't ideal, but the team wouldn't bend on that, I'm afraid. You're too dangerous to bring in any other way—you see, we have some experience trying to capture your kind."

"My kind?" she echoed. The pit in her stomach nosedived deeper. It went all the way to hell now.

"Werewolves, of course."

Her stomach roiled. He *was* a part of it. Why hadn't she realized that? How could she have been so stupid?

But Henry's gaze radiated an incongruous innocence. Her instinct was to absolve him instantly. What the fuck was wrong with her?

He reached over as if to grab her hand, but he withdrew, thinking better of it. *Smarter than he looks.* She would have broken every finger in his hand.

"It stood to reason there would be a hierarchy of some kind, some sort of organized group of shape-changers," he said. "I knew eventually someone would come around, trying to dig at our organization's efforts. But I was in no way prepared for that person to be a woman like you."

Henry hesitated. "I need you to know I was not on board with them using silver bullets—any bullets. I didn't want you to be hurt, but the few times we dealt with wolves, the sedatives didn't work fast enough. The targets didn't allow themselves to be taken alive, and they usually took one of our men with them. Sometimes more than one."

Good. Mara hoped those fuckers died screaming. But despite the rage that was nearly making her blind, she gentled her voice.

"Henry, you need to speak to someone. If you think werewolves exist, then you have a profoundly serious problem."

He watched her with this weird light in his eyes. "Mara, you were shot twice less than forty-eight hours ago, and you're already exhibiting over a week's worth of healing. That alone is superhuman, but there's more."

"Let me guess." Mara strained against the chain, but the links didn't bend. *Not enough silver.* How ironic and enraging. "Is it that you're insane?"

Henry pulled out a nearby chair, moving it closer to the bed. "You don't have to do that. There is no need to ever lie to me. Because I know what you are—the most special woman in the world."

Mara closed her eyes. He was making her dizzy. "I thought you said I was a werewolf."

"Yes, I recognize the irony of that statement," he said with a laugh. "That's my gift, you see. I can always tell. People like you, shapechangers, have this light, almost like an aura. It used to scare me when I was a child. I would be on the street, and there would be a stranger across the way, a man or a woman, and I would simply *know* they weren't human."

Mara sat stock still. Did he know what he was saying? Did he understand the significance of it?

She watched him, wide-eyed. But Henry's face was open, guileless. There was no glint, no secret knowledge he was holding back.

Henry had no idea what he was.

Mara groaned aloud. *Fucking witches.* Henry was a witch, and he had no clue.

Which may have been why she hadn't realized. Witches stunk of the spell ingredients they used. Black practitioners, in particular, acquired a scent that was unmistakable, hints of wormwood and death.

But Henry's scent was clean. Nothing in it spoke of a lie. He was either the world's best actor and was packing some heavy-duty masking spells, or he'd never cast a spell or a curse in his life.

"It wasn't a particularly useful talent. It didn't protect me, and it certainly didn't provide for me," Henry continued as if she hadn't made a sound. He gestured to the room around her. "And I still had this place to take care of, my ancestral home, crumbling all around me."

"So, you joined forces with Denon for cash. That's great, just great," she bit out. "Do they pay you per body? Any bonuses for children or pregnant women? Or do you take a pay cut when one of the people you *hunt down* loses a limb during capture?"

"No," he said, managing to look penitent. "My involvement is not for anything as crass as money. I joined in to help humanity. So normal people can enjoy some of the benefits you enjoy—your rapid healing, your strength. We know your kind are highly resistant to many human diseases."

Mara was going to be sick, but she kept her voice level. "And how exactly did you discover this supposed immunity?"

He didn't speak. Instead, his answer was a wave of sensation. It washed over her, regret mingled with an earnest desire to please and make amends.

Mara's stomach roiled. "Stop that," she gritted out from behind clenched teeth.

He blinked. "Stop what?"

Un-fucking-believable. Henry was radiating powerful magic, and he didn't even know it.

Werewolves were able to repel many of the spells the practitioners cast, but they weren't immune.

I am the Canus Prime's daughter, for fuck's sake. In werewolf terms, that meant she was at the top of the food chain. She had been trained to shake off direct magical attacks—anything to keep fighting. Spells and curses bounced off her. But this wasn't an assault. Henry's energy was passive. Whatever the hell it was kept screwing with her judgment of him. It was coming from inside of him, a persistent and innate enchantment.

"My agreement with Denon came much later, long after I had made my fortune. It was enough to buy a significant stake in the corporation." Henry said after a pause. "How my peculiar quirk came to their attention is a story for another time. What's important is that it's not some aimless conspiracy. None of the experimental subjects have been intentionally harmed—"

Mara lunged at him, but the chain caught. She came up short. *"You shot me,"* she hissed.

He held up a finger. "But you healed. And yes, we've had some regrettable incidents, some deaths, but you need to know we did everything we could to try to avoid them."

"Sure you did." Mara closed her eyes.

A tentative touch on her hand made her open them. "Mary, I don't want you to worry. I've made arrangements—Felix's people already have everything they need from you."

Mara's blood ran cold. "What does that mean?"

"The physicians took a few samples during your surgery." He waved a hand as if this were incidental. "What's important is that you're not going to be a part of the program."

She blinked. There was a program. *All those missing shifters.* Jack had been right about that, at least. They were alive. Well, some of them were alive...

"Should I thank you for not dissecting me?" Mara lifted the cuff, waving to make the chain rattle. "And for these lovely bracelets you've given me?"

"The restraints are for my protection and yours, of course. We both know if you were free, you would sprout fangs and claws and do your best to kill me. But those feelings of anger and betrayal won't last."

Sighing, Mara closed her eyes. "So, you *are* going to dissect me."

"No, of course not." Henry sat on the bed, that insidiously warm sorcery trying to sneak in under her defenses.

"I meant that the more time you spend with me, the less inclined you'll be to gut me with your claws." His smile was self-deprecating. "It's inevitable. You'll forgive me. Once you do, we'll be able to move past this."

He spoke with such sureness and finality. There was no scent of a lie. Mara had a sinking feeling it was all true

Henry surveyed the room with pride. "This castle has been refurbished from the ramparts to the dungeons. It's been completely restored, surpassing what it was at its height—with all the modern amenities, of course."

"Why are you telling me this?" Mara asked, knowing she wouldn't like the answer.

Henry gestured to the room around him. "Carrington Castle has been waiting for you."

"For me?" Where the hell was he going with this?

He leaned forward a few inches. "I've been looking for someone special for a long time. And then I saw you, and I knew instantly. Not only are you lovely, but you're also strong, graceful, and obviously intelligent. You're perfect..."

Henry said it as if she'd auditioned for a specific role.

"Perfect for what?"

His chocolate eyes took on an excited gleam. "Every castle needs a queen."

Mara couldn't decide if he were serious. "Let me get this straight. I'm going to forget you kidnapped me, shooting me in the process. I'm also going to forget you're part of a band of ghouls killing and dissecting living sentient beings. All that knowledge will go poof, and we will live happily ever after?"

"You won't forget your experiences," he corrected gently. "But you'll accept that everything that happened occurred for a good reason. We just need to spend more time together."

Her throat constricted, lots of puzzle pieces clicking into place. "Because it's a part of your gift. Everyone does what you want, don't they?"

He gave her a hapless shrug. "Not right away, but yes. Sooner or later, they do."

A-ha. Henry's meteoric rise from genteel poverty to major stakeholder in a multinational corporation was no longer a mystery.

For fuck's sake. Why didn't they dissect him?

He rose. You must be starving. I'm going to call down to the kitchens to request they bring up a meal. You must burn a lot of calories in the healing process. We need to build up your strength."

Mara scowled. The most disgusting part may have been that his concern was real.

"You can't force me to stay with you. Not voluntarily. It's never going to work."

Henry's smile was tinged with sadness. "You don't know this, but it will. It always does." He broke off, shaking his head. "You know, I had this fantasy I would explain, and you would see this my way. But I understand why you can't yet. But you will. All I need is time. In a few short days—a week at most—this will be a distant memory, and you and I will be so happy."

With that, he left her alone.

Mara laid back on the bed, laughing so she wouldn't cry. *I am chained to a bed in a castle with a magic man determined to make me his queen.*

"Holy shit," she gasped, the realization hitting her. "It's a fucked-up beauty and the beast."

But which one of them was the beast?

Mara closed her fingers, trying to make a fist. Her grip was still weak, but that wouldn't last. Her strength would return.

Me. It's me. She wouldn't let anyone forget that, least of all herself.

CHAPTER TWENTY-ONE

"*U*pdate," Douglas Maitland said, his voice flat and cold.

Derrick braced himself. "Levi Jessup just arrived. Nathan Hale is scheduled to land in the next hour."

"And the human?"

"Well…"

What the hell was he supposed to say? Mad with grief, Jack went off the reservation. He had disappeared at the airport, telling Derrick to call in their nearest operatives, the ones shadowing Denon's people in Europe. Then he'd melted into a group of people deplaning from a seven-forty-seven. The shifting crowd had masked his scent. Derrick hadn't been able to track him. He'd also had to take a cab back to their rental because Jack took the van.

"Derrick, the human," Douglas interrupted. "Was this his fault? Some sort of double-cross?"

"No," he assured the chief. "Definitely not. Jack is…invested. He wouldn't leave even if we wanted him to go."

To stop him, they might have to kill him.

Douglass grunted in response. "You're on the ground and it's your call, but if you think you need to replace him, I can have someone there later today."

Jack chose that moment to return, kicking the door open hard enough to make it bang against the wall. He was carrying a huge black duffel bag.

The bag was moving.

"Uh."

"Derrick, answer me," Douglas snarled.

Jack dropped the bag on the floor, kicking the door shut behind him.

Derrick put his mouth to the phone, speaking as quickly as he could. "The human is your daughter's mate. He's going to kill everyone between him and Mara, so yeah, we can count on him. Okay, bye!"

The bag started to wail. It sounded like a muffled help.

Wincing, Derrick hung up the phone on Douglas mid-sentence. He swung back to see Levi standing at the bedroom's threshold, his face wet.

The newcomer was gaping at Jack as if he had sprouted horns and a tail. "Who's in the bag?"

Jack looked up, giving them both that flat dead stare he'd worn since they lost Mara.

"Who do you think it is?" he bit out. Grabbing a kitchen knife, Jack picked up the bag, disappearing into the spare bedroom. The door being locked was as loud as a shotgun being cocked in the sudden silence.

Levi gave him a bug-eyed stare. *Wow*, he mouthed. Then he made a face. "Do you seriously believe Jack is Mara's mate?"

Derrick scrubbed his face with a rough hand. "Yup, homicide-Ken is the one."

Levi looked disappointed.

Clearly, Derrick had done something wrong for his last ten lives. The universe decided he had to pay for it now. "Aw, don't tell me—seriously, don't say it."

The other man shrugged. "I was thinking of taking a run at her."

"Stop talking," Derrick begged, wishing he could stop up his ears.

"Don't worry." Levi pointed at the door. "That stone-cold killer vibe Jack has suddenly developed changed my mind."

An ear-splitting scream interrupted them.

Derrick raised his eyebrow. "Wise decision."

"How soundproof is this place?" Levi asked, almost conversationally.

"Good question." Derrick went to close all the windows.

Ten minutes later, Jack opened the door. Behind him, Felix Dubois huddled on the floor, holding himself and weeping.

Derrick couldn't decide if he should be relieved or concerned there was no visible blood.

Levi examined the weeping captive. He'd been read in on who Dubois was, and what the piece of shit was responsible for. So, it said a lot about Jack's truly terrifying ability to break people that Levi appeared sorry for him.

"Scotland," Jack announced. "They took Mara to Scotland."

CHAPTER TWENTY-TWO

Mara lay back on the bed, teeth gritted so she wouldn't snap at the terrified girl giving her a sponge bath.

None of this was Elspeth's fault. That was the girl's name. Elspeth was the lady's maid assigned to serve her. She was somewhere between sixteen and seventeen and worked at the castle full time in the summer.

Elspeth bathed Mara, combed her hair, and dressed her in strapless gowns that fastened at the side so she wouldn't have to release her restraints. Not that she ever would. Elspeth was one of Henry's. Every staff member was his, and it wasn't the normal loyalty one reserved for the man who signed their paychecks. This was different.

Whenever she spoke of her employer, Elspeth's eyes would glaze over, the muscles in her mouth slackening a touch. It was almost as if she were on drugs, or in love. But the girl didn't have a simple crush on her employer. She *worshipped* him.

And it wasn't the first time Mara witnessed that reaction to Henry, she realized. She'd seen hints of it on Felix Dubois during those high society meet and mingles. However, Felix had hidden it better, enough for Mara to ascribe it to that mildly starstruck quality social climbers had for the noble class and famous actors.

Elspeth divvied up her Mara-caring duties with an iron-haired woman named Donalda, who introduced herself as the head house-keeper. She saw both women with roughly equal regularity. There was also the occasional visit by an older man called Angus, who never spoke and seemed to be around to carry heavy things like the old-fashioned washbasins Elspeth used to bathe her.

They were all innocents. Deep down, Mara knew that. Neverthe-less, Mara considered herself the model of restraint for not killing the lot of them.

Days passed. She conserved her strength, focusing on healing. The fact she'd been shot with silver bullets and then chained with silver restraints monumentally screwed with the normal healing process.

Shifters healed at an accelerated rate, about four or five times faster than humans, depending on the wound's size and location. Silver was a bitch, though. Shifters were universally allergic to it. It disrupted something in the magic that infused their bodies. The cells that came in contact with it died. It had to be removed, fast. If it weren't, the damage could be catastrophic.

She didn't know how quickly Henry's people had to pull those silver bullets out of her. She suspected they'd waited until she was on the plane out of London. That might have been fast by human stan-dards, but Mara didn't think it was fast enough. Not with the way her body was stitching itself back together at a snail's pace.

The worst part was that she couldn't shift. Held fast by the silver restraints she was trapped in her human form. Had they been steel, it would have been another matter entirely.

Mara closed her eyes, indulging in a short fantasy of blood and mayhem followed by a quick escape into the surrounding mountains. She could barely see the green rolling hills from her prone position on the bed, but she could scent the breezes that came down, carrying the pollen from the grass and all the wildflowers.

Soon, she promised herself.

In the meantime, she tried another tactic. As a high-ranking alpha wolf, Mara could change parts of her body without going full four-footed. But that was restricted to her claws and, if she tried hard enough, her fangs. The silver cuffs kept her arms and legs human, but perhaps she could try a partial shift on the part of her farthest from the restraints. This happened to be her midriff and stomach, the most damaged part of her body.

Waiting until Elspeth had finished drying and dressing her, she began to meditate.

Mara was, hands-down, the least Zen person of her acquaintance. She'd struggled a lot harder for the control that had come so easily to less dominant wolves. The only thing that had made it easier to deal with was that her twin had been in the same boat as her.

That had never seemed to bother Connell as much as it did her. It wasn't a great mystery why. He was a boy, and she was a girl. Her father was an enlightened man, but the pack's sexist expectations had been ingrained over centuries, probably because female dominants weren't as common.

That wasn't true for all shifters. She didn't know why some shifters echoed the structure of their animal counterparts while others did not. Were Lion and hyena prides and packs were matriarchal, like those in nature. But so were Bears, which as far as she knew didn't have packs in the wild.

In nature, wolves were ruled by the breeding pair. When journeying from one part of their hunting ground to another, they allowed the pace to be set by the oldest, most venerable pack members.

But werewolves were patriarchal.

Maybe Logan, her brother's mate, had been right when she said werewolves followed a meme, anthropologically speaking. People saw a ferocious wolf and they assumed it was male, so when the magic merged with the first receptive human bodies, what it spit out was a male-driven society.

Way to be Zen, Mara. She was never going to achieve a partial shift if she kept dissecting the nature of Were packs.

Closing her eyes, she focused on the wind moving softly over her skin. Changing into a wolf was easy. The shift was instinctive, like breathing. Were cubs changed in the first few months of their lives. It was the form they retreated to when threatened. She could do this. Mara just had to let go.

Long minutes passed. The wind coming in the window dried her skin, then grew moist again the harder she focused. *Relax, relax,* she chanted in her head. It was easier said than done.

And then the image of Jack popped into her head. It was a memory of him in bed next to her. He'd been awake, but it was that drowsy half-conscious state where you didn't want to get out of bed, especially if you weren't alone in it.

In her mind, Jack smiled, his long lashes against his cheeks. He kept his eyes closed as he wrapped his arms around her, pulling her against him.

Fur sprouted below her chest, pressing against the satin of the strapless green dress she wore.

Mara had found her happy place. It was Jack.

She smirked. *Damn it.* He was going to love that.

CHAPTER TWENTY-THREE

Jack squinted against the wind, strapping the night-vision binoculars to his eyes. He hadn't dressed for summer in Scotland, but he didn't feel the nip in the air. His anger kept him plenty warm.

Nestled in a small valley below him was a storybook castle. The building was so pretty it looked as if it were about to vomit out a Disney princess or two. It had circular towers with conical turrets and more spires than you could shake a stick at. Just looking at it pissed him off.

"Report," he whispered into his earpiece.

"Seven guards patrolling the perimeter," Derrick reported from the Southeast.

"I counted eight," Nathan Hale said in a low voice. He was on the west side of the castle, halfway up the highest hill.

Eight fucking guards. "We can expect double that number inside, at least."

Static crackled in his ear. "Are we calling it?" Levi Jessup asked.

"Hell no," he and Derrick said at the same time.

"Just checking," Levi grunted. "I'm ready to rumble."

"Good, because I see a hole," Jack said, checking his IR meter for surveillance cams. There weren't any within range. He hoped his portable signal jammer worked when they got close to the building. "When the shorter guard turns the corner, there's a window—about forty-five seconds. Meet me at my position in seven."

The Werewolves made it to him in four minutes.

The moment the short guard turned the corner, they swept down in a diamond formation with him in the lead, Nathan, and Levi flanking, with Derrick covering their rear. They reached the building, then hugged the wall, sneaking to a terrace with a set of wide double doors. A small hidden camera was trained on the entrance, but Nathan, who must have played basketball as a hobby, jumped up to knock the camera out of its axis, so it pointed straight up instead of at the door.

The darkened interior was spare, without any of the ornate furnishings or antiques the exterior had led him to expect. They moved from room to room on silent feet. Fluid and quiet, they stalked the darkness.

Weapon ready in his hands, Jack and the others fell into an easy rhythm. Few guards patrolled the interior, but they took them down one by one before any could raise the alarm.

They had swept the second bound and gagged man into a convenient closet when a third guard turned the corner.

The man's eyes widened. His lips were parting, hand halfway up to the secret service-style earbud he wore when Jack struck. A swift chop to the throat, and his opponent sagged forward to meet his elbow. He smashed into it, then started to go down. Jack followed it up with a kick that slammed the guy's head into the polished parquet floor.

He picked up the guy—who must have been close to two hundred pounds of muscle and bone—and dropped him in with the second one in the closet.

"This one won't need a gag," he said in a low voice when Derrick caught his eye with a questioning glance.

Derrick continued to stare.

"*What?*" he said, jaw tight.

The Were wrinkled his nose, sniffing. "You fit in a little too well."

Nathan leaned over, taking a deep whiff of the side of Jack's head.

"Why the fuck are you all doing that?" he growled.

"You smell more like Mara now than you did yesterday," Levi told him. "It's weird."

Jack lifted an arm, then stuck his face in his armpit. His deodorant was doing an excellent job, but he didn't catch a trace of Mara over the spring breeze scent.

"We'll shelve that for now," he said, tucking away the detail to analyze and possibly freak out over later. "Time to divide and conquer."

As previously agreed, Levi and Nathan took the second story while he and Derrick swept what was left of the ground floor.

The castle interior had been repurposed, with salons and reading rooms converted to conference rooms and conversational spaces, sort of like a men's club without the charm. There were no signs of true habitation.

It made sense if Denon used this place as a corporate retreat. *I should have taken the upstairs.* Mara might be held in one of the domestic spaces there.

His mind flashed back to the street outside of that London restaurant. Squeezing his eyes shut, he banished the memory of Mara falling to the pavement.

She is here, and she's alive. She had to be.

Shoving down his misgivings, Derrick signaled to him from the doorway of the next room. Jack joined him, narrowing his eyes at the blast of air conditioning. This room of the castle, situated squarely in the middle of the building, had been converted into a modern server room. A dozen free-standing cabinets housed row after row of rack servers. Small LED lights indicated they were working.

Either this was an informational hub for the Denon corporation, or this castle housed more than one major operation, things that required a massive amount of computing power.

His first instinct was to whip out his gear and get to hacking, but he stopped himself. Mara was the priority.

Derrick pushed on past the server room. Jack followed, his eyes and ears open for more guards or other staff.

A few rooms later, the castle abruptly transitioned to a research lab. An entire box filled with vials of colloidal silver rested on a nearby desk. Next to it, long benches filled with glassware and plastic pipette sets competed for space with bottles of reagents and sterilized jars of Eppendorf tubes. Vortexes to mix reagent bottles and tubes sat next to centrifuge machines in the middle of the benches, which had two workspaces on either side. It was designed so a pair of scientists could share the equipment without encroaching on each other's space.

A minus sixty-degree cold storage locker sat next to the bench. Derrick threw it open to find numerous white cardboard boxes. Jack opened one that held miscellaneous slivers of something pink, vacuum packaged, and organized with an arcane numbering system. Along each wall were glass-fronted deli cases filled with bottles of cell culture media and small vials of restriction enzymes that cut DNA at specific sequences, and then ligase enzymes to paste them back together.

This was a lab that specialized in gene splicing.

Jack had a bad feeling about this. His misgiving coalesced into a full-blown stomachache when he grabbed a box in the nearest deli case, then another and another.

Strips of colored tape covered the top:

Subject A telomerase + Rec A, pBR322mod

Subject E Uracil D glycosylase, pDenKalpha

"What the hell does all that gibberish mean?" Derrick was reading over his shoulder.

Jack didn't want to tell him, so he summarized. "Nothing good," he warned. "C'mon. I suspect the rest of subjects A through E are around here somewhere."

A grim light dawned in Derrick's eyes. Gesturing for him to follow, Jack pushed open the door to the adjoining room. Cold blue lights illuminated storage units of glass, which housed multiple bodies wrapped in white plastic bags.

Derrick slid open a case, tugging down the zipper of the bag.

Jack took one look at the body and flinched. It was a young man who couldn't be more than twenty-one or twenty-two.

Like the cougar woman in Spain, the boy had been killed when he was trapped in that hellish-looking mid-transition, his wide-open eyes staring past them into the endless void.

"This is wrong," Derrick breathed, staring down at the monstrosity. He looked horrified. "Our transitions are fast, too fast to get caught in the middle like this."

"Yeah." He'd seen Mara shift. She'd changed into a wolf between one blink and another. After Barcelona, she had told him that if a shifter were killed, it would revert to a human state.

"They're doing something to trigger and freeze this partial shift—maybe it's a drug or a device of some kind."

"What the hell is the point of that?" Derrick grimaced. "If they caught a shifter, they have him. Why the fuck would they do this to him?"

Jack bent closer, considering. The man on the table was splayed open from stem to stern, with pieces missing, but it was far more messily done than the clinical dissection of the body in Barcelona. Ragged cuts were made at regular intervals, and each visible organ had more precise incision marks, round and square punctures where tissue samples had been taken.

"Barcelona was a teaching facility—one focused on learning a shifter's anatomy," he said. "This is where they do the hard science."

"What the hell does that mean?"

"Molecular and cellular biology," Jack explained. "They want to understand how shifters shift and how they heal. From their perspective, it wouldn't be enough to have the DNA. They'd want to know which genes were being turned on and off at the time of the change or when they were healing themselves."

Derrick appeared bewildered.

"Don't you see?" Jack pressed. "That's why they look like this. The scientists found a way to force the shift. I don't know how they did—maybe because they're shifters, they can live through this."

He waved his hand over the open chest cavity. "The heart, the liver, spleen, lungs. Every organ I can see has a little piece cut out of it. They hit them with whatever makes them shift, then cut pieces out of them while they are still alive. They stand over them, tossing the samples in liquid nitrogen to get a snapshot of which genes are on and which aren't. It's how scientists study gene regulation, but Denon is going an extra step. They want to *copy* the genes."

Derrick made a guttural noise in the back of his throat. Holstering his weapon, he rubbed his face. "It all has to burn. Denon's gene-harvesting program ends here."

Wait. Jack grabbed his arm with an unforgiving grip. "*Mara*," he said. "Mara is the priority."

Derrick's jaw tightened. "Even she would tell you that destroying this place, razing it to the ground, is more important."

He stepped back, taking a deep breath. "Or I would if we had the materials. We stay on finding Mara. I'm calling in a second team to destroy this lab and suck every megabyte of information out of those data servers."

Jack relaxed, the rock-hard tension in his shoulder muscles easing. "Agreed."

Nodding, Derrick stepped back to make the call.

Jack counted the bodies in the slab. Three torsos, but enough filled specimen jars to represent at least a dozen more.

Derrick headed for the corner, having decided to text so he wouldn't have to speak aloud when he ordered the second team to move in.

A barely audible scuffing sound made him spin around. A middle-aged woman in a white lab coat stood about ten feet away. He briefly registered her sandy-brown hair and the wrinkles around her eyes and mouth. Her skin was paper white. And she held a gun in a trembling hand.

He heard the pops as if they came from miles away. He looked down, saw the blood blooming on his chest. Whatever these bullets were, they had gone right through his bulletproof vest.

Two slugs. Just like Mara.

Jack fell to his knees as the world began to grow dark. The last thing he saw was a blur—Derrick's huge bulk flying through the air, tackling the woman. She hit the ground at the same time as Jack did.

CHAPTER TWENTY-FOUR

Mara stared down at what the maid and the caretaker had brought her. "You're fucking kidding me, right?"

Elspeth flinched. "I'm sorry, ma'am. It's the master's orders."

Mara pursed her lips, crossing her arms. She'd healed sufficiently to get out of bed days ago. The length of her chains gave her the run of the entire bedroom and bathroom. Mara could even bathe in the massive jacuzzi tub. But she had to do it in shackles.

When she'd gotten out of her bath tonight, she had found a beautiful purple silk gown laid out on the bed, along with a pair of matching kitten heels. The dress was next to a single rose and an engraved invitation to join Henry downstairs in the main dining room.

Then his last gift had arrived. "This particular accessory doesn't go with the gown he chose," she informed the staff, her tone arctic.

Elspeth wrung her hands, glancing anxiously at Angus, who'd wheeled in the ball and chain on a dolly.

Mara shook her head, staring at the thing in disbelief. Made out of stainless steel, the ball was a perfectly polished sphere. Mara could see her reflection in it. It was welded to a chain, a thick cuff with a complicated space-age lock at the other end.

"The master insists you put it on before you come down to dinner tonight," Elspeth explained in a halting voice. "He said the weight was a carefully calibrated deterrent."

"I am not wearing this."

There was a short silence. Then Elspeth cleared her throat. "He said to tell you that if you put it on, you could go anywhere in the castle you like."

Did he now? Mara sat on the bed. *How heavy could it be?*

"Please leave." The servants shot out of the room faster than bullets.

Mara put her face in her hands. She was getting stronger every day, but she still wasn't a hundred percent. So far, she'd only seen Henry and the few servants who'd attended her, but she could sense many others. The walls were too thick for her to make them out in the castle itself beyond the surrounding rooms. But if she focused, Mara could hear many distinct footsteps as she lay in bed. They moved below the window in a regular pattern.

So many heartbeats, so many footsteps—enough for her to know that she'd never be able to fight her way out. Mara would have to sneak away. That meant lulling Henry into a false sense of security.

You may have to seduce him, let him believe his magic was working on her.

Mara closed her eyes. The idea made her skin crawl, but what choice did she have? Even Jack would tell her to suck it up to do whatever was necessary to escape.

If only the idea of touching someone else didn't make her physically ill. *And you know why that is...*

She had just found her mate. That was a fact it would have taken her months to admit under normal circumstances, but trapped here in this hellscape, it was crystal clear. She had no desire to deny it—to deny him because she might never see Jack again.

Enough. Mara couldn't afford to think that way. Her pity party was going to end here and now. She had stumbled into a trap, but she had the strength, intelligence, and training to turn this around on her captor—whatever it took.

Giving the ball and chain another disgusted glance, Mara stripped out of the robe.

R olling the ball down the long flight of stone stairs was a huge mistake. It was heavy enough Mara had to push hard with her foot to get it moving, but once it did, the weight gave it too much momentum. Mara ended up having to run down the stairs, so the idiotic assemblage wouldn't pull her off her feet.

Mara landed on the stone tiles of the ground floor with a clang, the ball spinning forward. She stopped it by planting her feet and bracing herself.

"Fuck this," she muttered, bending to pick the damn thing up. It was like carrying a dumbbell set twenty or so pounds over her normal limit—bearable, but she couldn't carry it for long. That would make walking silently anywhere in the castle a challenge.

Great. Well, it beat being hobbled Misery-style.

Despite having no directions, the dining room wasn't difficult to find. Henry had the staff mark the way with votive candles. She guessed it was supposed to be romantic, but all it tempted her to do was to knock them over. However, arson wasn't on the table. The castle walls and floor were made of thick limestone. Votive candles wouldn't cut it. Mara would need thermite to bring this medieval monstrosity down.

The castle's central dining room was twice as long as it was wide, paneled in dark wood inlaid with recessed squares. Two iron chandeliers were suspended over the massive oak table, but the thick white tapers in them were unlit. Instead, electric lights were distributed along the wall in simple sconces. But the lights in them were dim, another attempt at a romantic atmosphere. Three large candelabras rested on the white tablecloth. Two place settings were laid out at opposite ends of the table. The china was almost paper-thin, with thick crystal goblets for water and wine.

Henry sat at the setting nearest the door. He wore a fine black tuxedo, something custom made.

He looked up. His dark eyes flared, and he jumped to his feet.

"Such good manners," she observed sardonically, dropping the ball on the stone floor with a loud crash. Her expression could have frozen their dinner.

Henry frowned. "I was hoping you would be happier to see me." He cocked his head as if confused.

"Is your magically delicious vibe failing you?"

Her host grimaced. "It's all right," he said, gesturing to his recently vacated seat. "This is my fault—I've had some unavoidable work, but I'm trying to clear my schedule so we can spend more together."

"More time?" she echoed in disbelief.

Henry had come to see her every day of her recovery. He would sit by her bed, reading to her for hours. Occasionally he took phone calls, conducting his business on his sleek cell phone. He didn't seem to care if she were listening or not, so Mara would tune him out, plotting his death in delightfully colorful ways.

Her efforts were effective more than ninety-eight percent of that time, but it was that two percent that gave her pause. Her mind would wander, and she'd lie there, enjoying the sound of his voice. On one occasion, she had parted her lips to ask him to keep going when he'd taken a break from reading, only to catch herself in the nick of time.

But Mara would rather eat dirt than let him know she was worried.

She gestured to his chair. "By all means, keep your seat. I'll take the other one."

Pasting on a false smile, Mara dragged the ball down to the other end of the table, trying to make sure she made the most amount of noise possible. Henry was wincing when she made it to the other end. She sat with a glower, ignoring the sweat beading up on her forehead.

Yes, she still had a way to go in terms of recovery.

To that end, she picked up her fork and dived into a delicate salad. There was no sense in letting the meal going to waste. Judging from the aroma, Henry employed an excellent chef. And it wasn't as if he was adulterating the food. She'd be able to detect most poisons and toxins.

Unless they are magically disguised. Mara paused with the fork halfway to her mouth. *He doesn't have the know-how,* she reminded herself. Plus, from what she knew of him, Henry would consider that the height of rudeness. He prided himself on his manners.

Her host took a deep breath before he took his seat. "I'm pleased to see you up and around," he said, leaning forward.

Her smile turned a touch brittle. "Really?" Her voice was all sugar. "Then how about next time don't gun me down like a dog in the street?"

Henry flinched. "I am truly sorry about that. If I had to do it again, I would do things differently."

She hated the sincerity in his voice. "Sure you would. And thank you for my nifty new anklet. How much did this baby set you back?"

Henry laid his napkin across his lap as two waiters melted out of the woodwork. They whisked away the salad plates, then set down the entree. His was seabass. Hers was steak. Rare steak. "North of two hundred thousand pounds sterling," Henry informed her as the staff departed.

Mara must have betrayed her surprise because he nodded as if to say 'yes, really'.

"It's an incredibly special cuff, you see. State of the art. If you were to shift to your four-legged form, the cuff would instantaneously adjust, making itself smaller to compensate."

She blinked. "All right. Hypothetically speaking, let's say I could turn into a wolf and your charming high-tech cuff shrank to conform to my wolf leg. What would happen if I changed back to human?"

"I wouldn't advise that. The cuff is supposed to readjust, of course. However, live trials have proved it's a bit glitchy."

Mara's nostrils flared. "Fucking fabulous."

Henry set down his fork. "There is no need for that kind of language."

She snorted. *Wow.* Her psycho kidnapper was sensitive.

He picked up his utensil and waved it. "And don't worry. I'm sure you'll only have to wear it for a few more days—a week at the most. Then we'll be able to take it off, and you'll be able to move freely about the castle."

With those words, another wave of magic came out of him, lapping around her. It was like sitting on a sunlit beach at the water's edge while a gentle tide was coming in. The seductive warmth beguiled her senses, a hint of ozone tickling her nose.

Not today, witch.

Mara sneezed, then resumed eating. Henry determinedly launched into a one-sided conversation, telling her all about his day and the ongoing improvements at the castle.

"The major renovations are done, of course, but with a place this old, it's an endless campaign," he was saying.

He made no effort to engage her in the discussion. It was as if he'd learned long ago that his mark's participation was not required.

Mara sighed, studying him while trying to analyze his peculiar talent. How long did it take him to break someone down? Did she have weeks or months?

Another warm surge. Mara put down her fork, nauseated. Probably not years… She'd last a month or two at the most.

Closing her eyes, she reached out for Jack. She pictured his blue eyes and soft lips. *Wow. I'd kill for one of his smug smiles right now—the one that used to make me want to smash his face in.* That was how bad this was. Not that she saw his smiles the same way anymore. She saw Jack through a completely different lens now. It hurt, thinking of how little time she'd had with him.

It was going to be all right. Mara straightened her spine. She'd be seeing Jack and the rest of her family again soon. In the meantime, she would take her newfound mobility, such as it was, to learn everything she could about Carrington Castle.

CHAPTER TWENTY-FIVE

Mara waited until the castle quieted down before picking up her ball and chain and heading for the door.

Goddamn, this thing is heavy. But she was handling the weight a little better than before. Halfway down the hall, she stopped and smirked. This was the strength training session from hell.

No one came out to investigate who was giggling in the hallway.

Either Henry tucked in all the staff at ten sharp, or he had meant it when Elspeth told her she had the run of the castle.

That first night, she explored most of the upper story, including one of the towers on this side of the castle. There were four in all, one in each corner of the rectangular keep walls. She left the other tower alone because she smelled Henry strongly there. Figuring it was his bedroom, Mara gave it a wide berth.

Tonight, she was heading down for a little first-floor recon. At first, it was dull and uninformative. Room after room stuffed with antiques and expensive furnishings. Were the windows normally this wide or had Henry enlarged them during the renovation? She was betting on the latter. Castles from this era had narrow lancet windows, the better to defend the citadel.

She'd covered less than a quarter of the rooms when Mara had to take a break. Dumping the weight on a sturdy padded bench, she rested against it…and promptly slipped. Mara smacked against the wood-paneled wall, jerking when it gave, revealing a yawning black space behind it.

The castle had a basement. Mara straightened, squeezing behind the bench and trying to let her eyes adjust. But there was no light to relieve the pitch-black darkness. The nearby window illuminated only the first few steps of a steep staircase.

She suppressed a groan. *I have to go down there, don't I?* Sometimes recon sucked.

Unfortunately, Mara didn't have a handy flashlight or an atmosphere-appropriate candle to light her way. All she had was a hundred-plus-pound weight that would help her plunge to her death if she lost control of it.

Sighing silently, she picked up the ball and started down the stairs.

It ended up being easier than she thought. The staircase was circular, allowing her to brace herself against the wall as she slid down with her back to it. She did have a bit of trouble halfway down when she encountered a recessed doorway. She almost lost her balance, but she managed to throw herself against the door, righting herself in the nick of time.

The door was locked, of course. She would have tried to pick it, but that wasn't happening in the dark. Vowing to come back with a light she continued down, determined to get to the bottom before she gave up and went back to her room.

You should just pretend to like Henry. He'd probably take the ball and chain off if she made out with him a little.

She tried to picture it. Bile rose in her throat.

Yeah, I'm definitely not there yet.

Mara dragged the ball down another turn, nearly falling on her face when the staircase abruptly ended. *And it's still dark. Yay!*

What Mara wouldn't give to be a bat shifter. Echolocation would be sweet right around now.

I wonder if vampires can echolocate? She was going to have to ask Alec, the only vamp she was on speaking terms with. She knew him through Logan, her brother's mate. He was a scholar, an archeologist, and could walk in daylight, unlike the rest of his kind.

If you ever see him again, that is, instead of moldering in Scotland as a Stepford wife.

Without her sight to reference, Mara began to count her footsteps. Eighty-seven paces from the staircase, she noticed a faint light in the distance. At one hundred and ten, she smelled the other shifters.

Mara wanted to kick herself. *Well, of course, the basement is a dungeon.* She was in a gothic horror novel, after all.

She crept to the edge of the light, moving through a darkened lab full of benches and high-tech diagnostic equipment, cursing the weight in her arms. Mara had managed not to drop the ball on the ground, but lugging it around was a lot of work. Her breathing was faster, which was why she was discovered almost immediately.

"You may as well come out and show your face. It's not like I can rip your guts out from behind this door."

Mara peeked around the corner to see a long, wide hallway lined with arches. A small room lay behind each one. They might have been left open in the past, used to store grain or hay or other castle-y stuff like that. Now each arch was occupied by a space-age looking prison cell. Made out of clear thick plastic and steel, the cells were large cages with clear two-inch-thick plastic doors. Strips of LED lights were embedded at the top and bottom. Only the bottom one was lit, and they were dim, as if in night mode. The prisons must have been assembled inside the basement because they were too large to have come down any set of medieval stairs.

Holding her breath, Mara slowly walked down the hall, holding her ball and counting the occupants in the cells. Thirteen distinct scents, including the cat shifters and the missing hyena family, but only eleven warm bodies here. One of the empty cells smelled of bear, but it hadn't been occupied in some time.

Only one of the shifters was awake. The male cougar was in the cell nearest the door at the opposite end. He leaned against the back wall, his predator's eyes reflecting the low light.

Mara set her ball down in front of his cell and sat on it. The cougar stilled in the shadows. Slowly, he rose and moved forward, sitting cross-legged on the other side of the door.

The prisoner was older than her by decades, black, grizzled, and lean with ropey muscles snaking down his arms and tight curls springing out haphazardly from his head. He nodded

"Well, I guess I may have to reevaluate my plans to gut you," he said, pointing to her ball and chain underneath her silk nightgown—a grey one this time. "Seeing as you have your own issues."

"Yeah, you could say that," Mara rested her chin on her fist, a bizzaro version of Rodin's thinker. "Are you Thomas?"

The old cougar blinked. "Yeah. That's me."

She gave him a wry grin. "Hi. I'm Mara. I'm here to rescue you."

They both had a good chuckle over that.

"How long have you been here?" He looked well-fed, but his hair puffed around his head, unkempt, as if he'd missed more than one haircut.

Thomas rocked forward. "I don't know. I think it's been six months or so, but I can't be sure." He shrugged. "Keeping track of time was never my strong suit."

He cocked his head. "So, you know my name. I take it you been talking to my alpha?"

"Not personally. *My* alpha made the calls."

Thomas squinted at her, taking a deep sniff to identify her scent print. "And how is Douglas Maitland?"

"Well, he's not here, so good, I guess. How'd you know I am one of his?" she asked, leaving out the fact she was his daughter.

Outside of the pack, being a Maitland wasn't a detail she advertised. Her father was one of the world's most powerful clan leaders. A man, or woman, didn't achieve such heights without making enemies, or, in some cases, inheriting them.

Thomas shrugged. "Makes sense, given I'm not really on the best of terms with old Saul—that's my alpha. The only wolf he'd talk to, and be straight with, is Douglas. That and the Canus Primus is the only alpha who would care about other kinds of shifters going missing. How many of yours got taken?"

"One that we know of, but we got him back. We've been on the company ever since."

"The company?" Thomas drew back.

Mara's brow creased. "Yeah, the Denon corporation. The people bankrolling this." She gestured at the cells and the adjoining lab.

"Never heard of them. There's only that pasty white boy."

"Henry Carrington?"

"That's the one. But I guess you know the king of the castle," he said, gesturing to her nightgown. "Does he got you earmarked for the queen spot?"

Her stomach soured. "Something like that."

Mara took a look around them. Some of the other occupants of the cells were awake now, listening, but they weren't interrupting or sounding the alarm. *Lucky thirteen. Now how the hell am I going to get over a dozen shifters out of here on my own?*

"Don't worry about them. They're too far gone to sound the alarm. Not great for conversation, either. But I guess you've been doing some resisting?"

Ah. "So, you're familiar with his brand of magic?"

"Yup." Henry gestured around them. "But he ain't that interested in me. I'm too old. The witch focuses his efforts on the younger and more malleable. I'm kind of surprised you're not..." He trailed off, holding his arm out like a zombie.

"I have no intention of being one of Henry's drooling disciples."

He gave her a skeptical look. "Not sure you have a choice. His Pastiness is...uncanny. He has a way of getting what he wants."

Mara raised her chin. "He's not going to get me. I have a mate, and I'm going to get back to him."

Now his glance was pitying. "That's something, but not sure it's going to help much. His Pastiness is like water on a stone. Sooner than later, he'll wear you down."

He gestured behind her. "Case in point."

Mara twisted to look behind her, almost falling off her ball in the process.

A young man in a black uniform stared down at her, pointing some sort of stun gun at her. Mara cursed under her breath, not because he'd managed to sneak up on her, but because *why*.

The guard was a shifter.

CHAPTER TWENTY-SIX

Mara leaned back in the plush patio chair, surreptitiously smelling the arm of the uniformed servant as he set her plate down for what Henry called an *al fresco* brunch.

Normal human. Henry must save the shapeshifters for guard duty. The one who had escorted her back to her room last night had been one. His scent had been unmistakable. The question was how many more of them and had they all started as captives...or were some of them here willingly?

No. Something told her the men and women patrolling the grounds beyond the castle hadn't come here using their airline miles by choice. And they *were* shifters.

This corner of the Highlands was too windy for her to be able to catch their scents from such a large distance, but she didn't need it for confirmation. They gave themselves away merely by walking. Only shifters moved with that fluid gait halfway between prowling and stalking.

She had no idea where Henry had found the bear shifter who escorted her upstairs last night, the one she'd confused him for a man because of his height. The juvenile couldn't have been more than fifteen or sixteen years old. The boy hadn't been able to tell her where he was from—he couldn't remember.

Mara had tried to engage him as she hauled her ball up the stairs. "What's your name?"

The boy's eyes were unnervingly blank, with that tell-tale glassiness that appeared to be the signature for Henry's influence.

"I'm Josh Ellis," he said after she repeated the question twice.

"How long have you been here, Josh?" she asked, stressing his first name.

A long pause. "I'm not sure. A long time."

Mara tried to ask him more questions, but the poor boy grew agitated and she forced herself to stop.

Thomas had tried to warn her, she realized. But that still hadn't prepared her for the sight of her people going '*Stanford prison experiment*' on their own kind. Sure, they may have been different species than her, but they should have sided with other shifters over a witch, at least under normal circumstances.

And now they're here en masse guarding their captor...

How long did it take Henry to brainwash a shifter? She'd wondered before, but she still had no clue.

Mara picked at her food, doubt making her second guess herself and sniff each morsel before taking a bite. She racked her brain, trying to recall the dates of the known shifter disappearances.

C'mon, you were there when Derrick read them off to Jack. Hearing them once should have been enough for her to remember them. Her visual memory was stronger—that was a wolf thing—but she still had enough mental acuity to recall a string of dates. However, no matter how hard she tried, her mind remained muddled.

That's his magic, isn't it? Mara put her fork down. She had lost her appetite.

Narrowing her eyes at Henry across the table, she listened to him drone on and on about not wandering the basement by herself. It wasn't because she wasn't supposed to go down there, but because her 'deterrent' might unbalance her down the stairs. There was an elevator, but it was coded to certain personnel.

"I would advise you not to go down there again without my escort."

Mara blinked, abruptly tuning back into the conversation.

"You would go down with me?" she asked incredulously. "What? Do you want to show off your occupied dungeons like they're your latest kitchen remodel?"

Henry ignored the distaste twisting her face. "No one in the basement is a prisoner."

Mara's head drew back. He believed that. Henry's ability to pretend everything was peachy keen was sociopathic.

She was about to tell him to explain that to Thomas before deciding better of it. The old cougar had told her that Henry didn't pay him much attention. There was no need to put a spotlight on him.

"I saw the place myself. There are cells. Those people are your captives."

"No, no," he insisted, starting to turn red in the face. "They are my *guests*."

Mara leaned forward in her seat. "Well, having experienced first-hand how you treat your guests," she began, whipping her leg out to drag her ball and chain into view. "I would ask you to call them something else, or at least define what that word means to you because your guests rate anything from a sumptuous bedroom suite to a cell in the dungeon. Is your meaning similar to how airlines refer to their guest? Are they in economy while I rate premium class?"

She picked up her fork, waving it. "I would appreciate some clarification here."

Henry's features tightened. For a long moment, he sat there, gripping his knife tightly. Her father had told her once that she could make anyone lose their temper. She'd been fourteen at the time, and the Canus Primus had been within a hairsbreadth of losing his.

That had happened only a few times in his long history. Legends were weaved around them. She'd almost succeeded in making another one, but her dad had stepped away and had gone for a long run.

Did Henry have that kind of restraint?

She kept one eye on his fisted hand. Even chained to a massive weight, she could still take him. But Henry didn't take the bait.

His smile slid back on his face like oil sliding over the surface of a lake. "You know, I do believe clarification is exactly what you need."

The words were threatening, but the tone was, as always, warm and coaxing.

"Regrettably, I have to make a call first," Henry said, rising. He extended his arm, waving at the table and her still full plate. "But please stay. Enjoy the meal. I'll have Gladys in the kitchen send up a pitcher of mimosas to make it an occasion."

He began to walk away backward. "Get ready. This is going to be great," he said, pointing finger guns at her and clicking his tongue before disappearing.

Mara scowled, almost disappointed things weren't coming to a head.

With Henry gone, her appetite returned. She stuffed her face for three minutes straight before daintily wiping her mouth on a cloth napkin. Then she took advantage of the opportunity to step out to the wrought-iron balcony railing. She stood there for an hour, counting the number and memorizing the pattern of the guard rotation.

Then she went back inside.

The afternoon passed without signs of life. Mara was beginning to think Henry had forgotten about his ever-so-creepy promise when he showed up at her door, full of apologies. He then ignored the weight she dragged after her with as much drama as possible before escorting her to the fingerprint-access-only elevator.

Then the real horror show began.

Henry sat her at a table next to a hovering scientist before heading to one of the cells. He came back holding the hand of a small dark-haired boy, about ten or eleven years old.

"Mara, I'd like to introduce you to my very special friend," he said, looking down the child with a paternal air. "This is David."

The little boy looked up at Henry, his small face suffused with a mixture of joy and awe.

Mara's stomach twisted, gooseflesh crawling along her arms.

"David, my pal, we're going to do another little test for Dr. Stuart."

The boy's expression dimmed a notch.

"It's a little pinprick, I promise."

David's smile returned, and he nodded. "Okay."

Mara gritted her teeth, blinking. The sound of the boy's voice, so young and innocent, was like a knife in the back. And then Henry twisted it by holding David's hand throughout the blood draw, promising to bring him a treat for being such a brave and helpful boy.

It made her sick to her stomach, but she was careful not to let that show on her face. Instead, she gritted her teeth and watched.

After the blood draw was complete, Henry walked the boy back to his cell.

Then he sat across from her as the doctor prepared another syringe.

When the man approached her, she reached out with preternatural speed. She held the doctor's hand with an unyielding grip. "You get that needle anywhere near me, and I bash both your heads in with this ball," she said with a nod to her restraint.

Dr. Stuart didn't so much as twitch. "I can bring the sedatives," he told Henry.

Mara smiled, showing all her teeth. "You touch me, and all you'll get back is a bloody stump."

Belatedly, he blinked, the awareness of the danger he was in penetrating that drugged expression he wore.

Henry laughed, a joyous sound. She braced herself as his magic wrapped around her again, looking for chinks in her armor.

"I don't think that will be necessary. You may go, Dr. Stuart," he said, excusing the man with a gesture worthy of a royal.

"But—"

"If Mara doesn't want to participate in the program at this time, then we will respect her wishes."

The scientist deflated like a balloon, but he nodded with traces of the same slack-jawed reaction the shifter boy and the servants had demonstrated.

"Do they all obey you?" Was that why Denon let him run the show any way he saw fit?

"Eventually," Henry said helpfully. "It depends on how hard I try."

He leaned forward across the table. "See, this is why you are so fascinating to me, Mara. I've never had to work so hard for someone's regard before. Don't get me wrong—it's a dance. There is such a thing as being too loved."

"Of course," she said, light dawning. "You wouldn't want anyone growing obsessed with you."

She could picture it now, an adoring crowd chasing him down and tearing him apart like he was a teenage popstar.

Henry stretched out, taking his hand in hers. His thumb stroked her. "I had to learn early on to hold back, and, more importantly, how to direct my persuasive abilities to a single person or small group. Focus is key."

"Does touch help with that?" she wanted to know.

Henry merely smiled instead of answering. He tried to hold on, but she pulled her hand away with the aid of her superior strength.

He didn't try to recapture it.

Well, there goes plan B. It would have been nice if she could get him to overdo his whammy so the others would turn on him. They could have done the heavy lifting for her.

It's okay. Mara liked plan A. It involved a lot more ass-kicking. But if Henry wanted to share to impress her, she'd hold off long enough to get her questions answered.

"How long has this program been going on?" she asked, indicating the lab around her with a flick of her fingers.

He leaned forward, seemingly pleased by her interest. "A few years."

"And did it precede you?"

"How do you mean?"

She searched for the right words. "Did something like it exist at Denon before your involvement?"

"Yes, as a matter of fact," he said. "A colleague at one of the corporate retreats mentioned it. He thought it would be up my alley. Once I learned the details, I knew I had to be involved."

She filled in the blanks. "And with your persuasive talents, the project became a true success."

"Exactly," he said, slapping his palm down for emphasis. "My predecessor thought he was doing well before I came on board. But the few changelings they managed to capture invariably killed themselves in their cells—if they managed to bring one into the facility alive, that is. However, since I came on board, the attrition rate has dropped to a third of what it once was."

"But being a part of it wasn't enough. You had to be in charge."

He shrugged. "It made sense. Before I came on board, the staff couldn't confirm that the person or animal they tagged was a changeling."

The preferred word was shifter, changeling being a strictly fae term. But although she didn't correct him, the impulse was there.

Careful, Mara, her father's voice said in her head. It was a slippery slope, one she couldn't afford to let herself slide down

"But you can confirm on sight," she said. That was a witch gift. It wasn't universal, but some practitioners were quite skilled at it. Others learned it with practice.

"Yes, just by looking." Henry paused as if he were expecting a pat on the back.

Mara smiled grimly. Her plot to sneak away and come back with the cavalry acquired an excessively big hole. Even if she somehow managed to evacuate every shifter in the castle, Henry would simply find Denon more...

Mara couldn't leave Castle Carrington without killing him.

Failing to take him out would allow him to go to ground. God knew, Denon would protect him to the ends of the earth. His talents were too valuable.

"And what exactly is the stated goal of your work here? To create super-soldiers?"

That was sort of the go-to for corporate America.

"The armed forces *would* pay well for certain troop enhancements

181

—anything to have the edge on the field, but that is just the tip of the iceberg," he said, waving his hands in excitement. "But the applications are so much more varied than that."

He stood, then began to pace. "Your people have higher physical endurance, speed, and strength. That doesn't consider your rapid healing ability and enhanced senses. Think of what it would mean to people suffering from degenerative diseases or cancer. Gene therapy would be revolutionized. We could add years to the human lifespan. It could be extended by decades or more."

"And what makes you think these traits are encoded in our DNA? Because, in case you haven't noticed when we shift to our second form, it happens fast—too fast for genes to react. It's *magic*. And magic can't be harvested," she added, massaging the truth.

Technically, that last wasn't true. But Henry wasn't well-versed enough to know the witch reason for capturing shifters—to suck the magic from them.

The effort inevitably killed the shifter in question. But black witches did it anyway. It didn't matter that shifter magic was inherently incompatible with spellcasting. Shifters possessed a lot of raw magic, which was all the witches cared about. If a witch needed an extra special curse cast—and most spells that required that that kind of power boost were curses—then they killed a shifter or another witch.

Few of these black magic practitioners were strong or skilled enough to neutralize an able-bodied shifter long enough to cast their spells on them. That kept the body count down on both sides. Targeting the young or old and infirm was also a mistake. Most shifters had some kind of family or were part of a pack. And most packs had an eye-for-an-every-body-part *modus vivendi*. Revenge was a way of life.

That was why her own pack's history was so bloody. Internecine war used to be the norm. Now they had stacks of carefully worded and hard-won treaties in place to keep the peace. They had been designed so that a pack fomenting dissent lost their territory and any property and cash reserves held by them. Needless to say, anyone getting any ideas about violating them was swiftly put down.

But most of the packs she knew would unite against an outside threat, like a witch or one of their covens. Only the truly evil or insane proceeded, knowing the shitstorm it would bring. Which was why witches were often cannibals, magically speaking. Sometimes literally, too.

Mara gave herself a little shake. *Deal with the monster in hand and not the one in the bush.*

For a moment, she considered telling Henry the truth. There were plenty of other ways for a witch to get power. She could send him against his kind and hope he ran into trouble. But there were no guarantees that ploy would work. He was smart—smart enough to go after weaker prey. That and he'd still have Denon backing him up.

The worst part might be what he could do with proper training. No, for better or worse, he was her problem.

"Hold up," she said as a thought occurred to her. "Even with your special talents, there is no way Denon would let you run an operation of this size without any oversight."

Even if he got results, corporations had assholes second-guessing people built into their structure. He answered to someone.

He tried to hide it, but Henry's vanity got the better of him. Arrogance bled into his expression.

That was how she knew.

"Unless…unless you've used your gift on the entire Denon board," she said, filling in the blanks.

Yes, that made sense. If his gift worked on humans, and judging by the staff it did, then Henry would have sewed up the board long ago. Being beholden to anyone else would have been unacceptable.

He's like a damn tick we didn't know was there. Now that they'd found him, he was a bloated louse, completely dug in.

She rested her forearms on the table. "Denon doesn't list the identity of its board on any website or business registry. That's why it's registered as an anonymous LLC despite its size and global reach. Denon doesn't want anyone to know who is at the helm. I realize this isn't as uncommon as the public thinks. These high-powered executives know identifying themselves means an increased threat of kidnapping and extortion for themselves and their families."

Henry gave her a bemused smile, sitting down across from her again. "What exactly is it you're asking?"

Mara leaned away from the table. "I'm not asking. I'm *saying* that yesterday I didn't know who Denon's president was, and today I do. Or do you prefer CEO?"

The skin around his mouth tightened.

"Perhaps that's too high up. After all, you're here and not in charge of day-to-day operations. So maybe it's CFO?" she asked. "Nah. It's someone who can't be challenged. My money is on one of the first two..."

Henry considered her in silence. Then he nodded. "I'm impressed. This bodes well for the intelligence of our children."

Blech. "So, I'm right?" she pressed.

Another little smile. "Let's just say that our children will want for nothing. And as you've pointed out, I am gifted. I'm also healthy and reasonably attractive. What more could a woman want in a prospective mate, even a rare and remarkable one such as yourself?"

"Oh, I don't know," Mara demurred. "A *choice*?"

His smile grew brittle. His phone beeped. Scowling, he checked the screen. "I'm afraid I have yet another conference call—a company president's job is never done."

He stood. Two shifter guards stepped out of the shadows—not Joshua Ellia. He was probably off duty. This pair were both older. One was a hyena female, African American, around forty. The other was a male lynx. Henry introduced one as Filina and the other as Pat.

Their faces were eerily blank, more victims of Henry's voodoo.

Well, they'd have to be for the lynx to be so calm standing next to a hyena.

Both shifters were holding large guns they didn't need, not to kill.

"Stay as long as you like," Henry invited. "Visit with David until you're satisfied that he's healthy and happy. These new friends will escort you back upstairs when you're ready."

CHAPTER TWENTY-SEVEN

J ack recovered consciousness with a vengeance. He opened his eyes and sat bolt upright, displacing the electrodes taped to his chest. The move also sent a bolt of pain through him, and he fell back with a strangled scream. The noise was rivaled by the alarm of the heart monitor that had lost contact.

He scowled, blinking. The sickly blue-green walls and plastic-covered furniture slowly came into focus. A hospital room. The question was where? And why?

The report of twin gunshots echoed in his mind. *Oh, yeah.* That was why.

Too many bullets flying in this mess. He'd spent years without getting shot at and now look. Both he and Mara had caught lead.

He pulled his head back, trying to peek down the neck of his hospital gown, but layers of gauze bandages covered the bullets. He could feel them, though, underneath the protective wrappings.

Wherever he was, they had excellent drugs, because his chest didn't hurt nearly as much as it should.

Footsteps pounded, and the door slammed open. "*Jack.*"

Derrick appeared in the opening. He was immediately followed by Levi and Nathan, who tried to enter simultaneously and failed spectacularly. Their wide shoulders wouldn't allow them both through the doorjamb. After a little grappling, Levi shoved Nathan back so he could enter ahead of him.

A petite dark-skinned, dark-haired woman followed the men. She was wearing a lab coat over scrubs. Derrick introduced her as Kiera, the pack medic.

"May I?" She gestured to his gown.

Jack waved her on. She untied the ties of his gown, which appeared to have them down the front, in addition to the one around his neck.

The woman carefully peeled back the bandages.

"Holy shit," Derrick said, checking out his midsection. He slapped the woman on the back. "Kiera, you're a fucking miracle worker."

The newcomer frowned, shaking her head. She started to say something, but Levi and Derrick drowned her out, talking at the same time.

Jack remembered he was in charge of the op. He held up his hand. "Report," he croaked.

"You got shot," Levi volunteered.

"No shit," he sniffed, almost afraid to ask. "What happened after? Did...did you find her?"

Jack held his breath. Had they missed Mara somewhere in that mishmash of rooms? Or had they recovered a body?

Derrick shook his head. "Mara wasn't there."

It was almost a relief after that horror show of a lab.

"We didn't find anyone new after you went down," he continued. "Aside from a few low-level staff, an onsite cook, and the groundskeeper.

"And more guards, of course," Levi said. "But we took care of them."

He seemed to need some kind of acknowledgment, so Jack nodded, suppressing the urge to scratch the new holes on his chest. They looked a lot older than he would have guessed. *Fuck, how long have I been out?*

"It was a setup," Levi volunteered.

Jack's brows drew down. "Believe it or not, I figured that out. Did the scientist talk? The one who shot me?"

He remembered her now—fifties, thin, and shaking like a leaf.

"No."

He growled, which seemed to startle the small medic. He threw her an apologetic glance.

"How many times did she get me?" Jack was furious with himself, but slightly more pissed at his body armor. It was supposed to be the best money could buy, but though it had slowed the bullets, it clearly hadn't stopped them.

"She shot you twice to the abdomen. We thought we were going to lose you. But Douglas had sent Kiera. She was on standby—came in on the flight after us. She saved you."

Kiera opened her mouth again and held up a hand, but Jack was too busy being indignant. "And the scientist didn't even have the decency to talk after shooting me? Doesn't your wolf pack cover basic interrogation techniques?"

"Oh, she tried," Derrick replied, raising his massive shoulders to his ears before flopping into the chair on his right.

"But she didn't know much," Levi added. "She was middle management, in charge of the night shift at the lab. That mostly meant taking care of other people's experiments. But it *is* the main research facility, the place where they try to unlock all our secrets."

"But not where they keep the majority of their captives," Jack guessed.

"No. We don't know why." Derrick leaned forward in the seat. "But it's not all bad news. They didn't just do research there. It's a crossroads for a lot of Denon's business. Remember the server room? We've got our people going over every megabyte of data in those drives."

"Hell, we found a cache of African diamonds and laser engraving equipment there," Levi said, putting his hands in his pockets. "Lots of other shit, too."

Derrick gave him a grim, almost feral, grin. "Felix Dubois sent us to the most fortified facility he knew of in the hopes we'd get our asses handed to us."

"Brilliant," Jack rubbed his face. He couldn't give the werewolves shit on their interrogation skills after all. "He's still on ice, right?"

"Yes," Nathan Hale said, speaking for the first time. "He's secure."

Jack collapsed back on the pillows, replaying his interrogation of Felix Dubois. "I could have sworn he wasn't lying when he said Mara was in Scotland."

"Best we can tell, it's a half-truth. According to the paperwork we found, Denon has a few facilities in the country and across England's border. My guess is Mara is at one of those."

Jack sat up straighter. *Well, hello there, pain, emphasis on the 'hell'.* At least he wasn't on a catheter. He'd been there, done that, and didn't want to do it again.

"Give me a minute or ten," he said after a beat. "I will take another crack."

And this time, Jack would make it clear that if Felix Dubois didn't give them Mara's real location, he would be the one using a catheter —permanently.

Derrick held up a hand. "We will give it a try while you rest, but I'm not sure he's going to crack. It could be that he *can't* tell us."

Jack raised a brow. "How does that work?"

The wolfman shrugged. "Every time we try, his eyes glaze over. It's like his brain goes to La-La Land for a few seconds. Then he blinks, and he hedges. But before he does, he looks as if he's racking his brain for an acceptable answer. Someone of his background should be able to lie with greater ease and look less confused doing it. If I didn't know any better, I'd say he's under a vampire's compulsion or something like it."

There was a long moment of silence. Jack glanced around. No one else batted an eyelash at the term *vampire*.

"Yeah, I'm not touching that," he said, blinking rapidly. "That crazy shit can wait until later. All I care about is getting Mara back."

"You have a few more days of healing before you can get out of bed," Levi pointed out.

"It should be less than that," Kiera interjected. Her voice was small but clear, like a perfectly pitched bell.

"Kiera, honey," Derrick said patronizingly. "I know you're good, but you're not *that* good."

Kiera narrowed her eyes. "I'm not referring to my skill at all," she said in a clipped tone before turning to Jack and softening.

"That's what I was trying to say earlier. I haven't done much to heal you besides slapping on a few bandages. You're recovering very quickly—far faster than any human should. But this accelerated healing has nothing to do with me."

The new girl got blank stares all around. Then Nathan shrugged. "I guess that explains things."

"What?" Jack frowned.

Nathan waved a hand to encompass Jack. "You mentioned Jack smelled of Mara, but it's broader than that. His scent profile is pack now. It has been since I got off the plane in London."

Derrick blinked. Everyone turned to stare. Frowning, Jack lifted an arm to take a surreptitious sniff at his armpit.

"I will concede to a deep need for a shower, but I don't think I reek as bad as you lot yet," he said. Jack took a quick look at Kiera. "Female company excepted. I can't smell you—actually, I sort of can. Strawberry shampoo. Not bad."

This was met with more surprised looks and more silence.

"What is it now?"

"A human wouldn't notice the strawberry. We use special shampoos with very faint scents."

Levi scowled, leaning over and sniffing audibly. He rocked back on his heels. "Well, I'll be damned. I think Nate's onto something."

Derrick got to his feet. "Hold up."

He started pacing, keeping his eyes on Jack. Then he stopped. "Mara," he said.

"Yeah, Mara," Jack repeated, widening his eyes for emphasis. She was the reason they were here. Hell, she was the fucking reason he breathed these days. "We need to find her."

"No, I'm asking if she, um, you know..." Derrick waved his fingers at his neck.

Was he asking if she gave him a hickey? "I don't know actually, but you better not be asking about our love life."

"No! And *ick*." Derrick gave himself a little shake. "Bad enough that I had to hear some it, but we need to know—did she bite you?"

He pointed to the base of his neck. "Around here."

"No." Jack scowled, then his expression cleared. "Oh, wait..."

Levi slapped himself on the forehead. "Unbelievable. How can you forget if someone *bites* you? Do women do it that often to you?"

"Oh, shut up." Jack laughed before clearing his throat. "See...the thing is...well, there was some biting. But it was the other way around."

"Say what?" Levi was confused.

"I might have bitten her," he clarified, feeling a little defensive and *a lot* confused. "It was a heat-of-the-moment kind of thing."

Levi's head drew back. He gave Derrick a hard nudge. "Can it work like that?"

"Can what work?" Jack asked. The two men ignored him.

"I don't know," Derrick said, shrugging. "Do you think it's possible?"

"Beats me, man. That's why I was asking you."

The pair continued to talk to each other as if no one else was in the room. It went on long enough that he appealed to Nathan, widening his eyes

"It's part of the ritual," the quieter man explained. Nathan pointed to the base of his neck. "We claim our mates by biting them here. But I've never heard of it working in reverse."

Kiera nodded, looking excited. "To my knowledge, this would be the first case," she said, ducking her head to avoid eye contact when Nathan turned to her. "Although we would need to do extensive research to know for certain. I can call Douglas to ask—"

A chorus of *no*'s interrupted her.

Kiera's shoulders hunched as if she was trying to draw in on herself. "Why not?"

TOOTH AND NAIL

TOOTH AND NAIL

"Yeah, let's just say I don't think the chief is ready to find out his little girl got claimed by a human," Derrick said, pronouncing that last as if he'd said leper. "Let's wait until we find her and let *her* tell him. No offense, dude," he added.

"No problem," Jack growled. He was no more eager to explain the situation to Douglas than Derrick was, but there was no need for the other man to be a dick about it.

"Are we sure this is some kind of transference?" Kiera was thoughtful. "Jack is healing fast, even by Were standards."

"As fast as Mara would?" Derrick questioned.

"I'm not sure," Kiera hedged, appearing uncertain. "I've never treated her. Only her brother that one time, and there were extenuating circumstances..."

The other men sobered, averting their eyes. The teasing atmosphere disappeared.

Oh. "Was this when Leland died?" To his knowledge, it was the only time Connell had been shot. That he knew of anyway...

"Yeah."

There was a long silence before Derrick cleared his throat. "Kiera has a point—this could still be something else. Are you sure you haven't run into a little old eldritch woman in the woods lately, no blessings from glowing apparitions?"

Jesus. "No."

Derrick passed a hand over his face. "Regardless if you did bite Mara, that's not how mating works. It's the dominant wolf that does the claiming. *She* would have to have done the biting."

"Then how do you explain the accelerated healing? Or the change in his scent?" Nathan asked. "He's clearly pack now."

Derrick dug his heels in. "I'm telling you that it doesn't work this way."

"Are you sure it doesn't?" Nathan seemed contemplative. "What if it's just the most dominant of the pair?"

"But humans aren't on the scale," Derick protested.

"Just because we say they aren't doesn't make it true," Nathan pointed out.

191

"We don't we test his dominance?" Levi suggested. He put his hands on Kiera's shoulders, dragging her closer to the bed. Jack frowned as the woman glanced at him, but then swiftly down.

"Hey!" Levi crowed. "I think Nathan's right. She can't look him in the eye, which makes sense. He meets us on a level playing field, doesn't he?"

"Because he doesn't know any better. And Kiera doesn't look anyone in the eye." Derrick's voice was climbing higher in volume.

He was only a few notches from shouting. Any minute now, the rest of the hospital staff was going to come running in here.

"*Enough*," Nathan snapped, pushing Levi's arms off the woman's shoulders. "Everyone has their place in the pack. You're speaking as if submissives are cowards. They are not. A submissive is a *gift*."

Kiera's mouth dropped open. She twisted to gaze at Nathan with stars in her eyes.

Interesting. Jack leaned back, watching the interplay. It was informative—up until everyone began to argue all at once.

Okay, never mind. Fuck this shit. They didn't have time for this. Mara was waiting for them.

Jack pulled out his IV, then started to peel off the electrode pads that remained stuck to his chest. The heart monitor flatlined. Ignoring the resulting beeping, he swung his legs out of bed and stood, shaking off the wave of dizziness.

The crazy part was, he was able to do it.

Yeah, Kiera and Nathan were definitely onto something. He was a hell of a lot better than he should've been.

"Let's not shoot the gift horse in the mouth," Jack announced once the shifters had quieted down.

He was aiming for a dry tone, but it came out more like a ragged wheeze. Okay, so the effort had taken a lot out of him.

"Not that I'm not grateful for this turn of events," he continued, gesturing to his injuries. "But as far as I'm concerned, this super-healing happened for one reason—to get Mara back, so somebody go and get me that son of a bitch Dubois, and we'll get back to figuring out where she is. It could be anywhere in the fucking world."

192

Derrick shook his head. "I think that's unlikely. We confirmed the plane had enough fuel for a hop here or back to mainland Europe, France, or Belgium if pushed to the tank's reserve limit. But the pack's hackers were able to trace the plane for a bit longer than you did. It headed in this direction long enough that a location outside Scotland isn't likely. She's somewhere close."

Nathan held up a hand. He retreated out of the room, returning with a sheath of papers in his hand and holding them up. "The one good thing about hitting the hub is that it was a repository of information. Our people have been tearing those servers apart, bringing us everything of relevance they found. We have a list of places to start."

He separated a sheet of paper from the pile. "There's at least three on this side of the border and another one south of the border in Northumberland. Three of them even have names. We have Oakmont, Carrington Castle, and Leeds Park."

"Hold up." Jack's breath sped up. "Did you say *Carrington* Castle?"

Nathan glanced down at his list. "Yeah. The owner is—"

"Henry Carrington. That *motherfucker*," Derrick spat. "I can't believe it."

Rage boiled through Jack. He pointed at him, Levi, and Zack. "You three with me. Let's lock and load."

He turned, intending to stalk out of the room. The shifters turned to follow him, but Levi couldn't resist opening his big trap.

"That would have been much more impressive if you weren't wearing a hospital gown with your ass hanging out in the breeze."

"I disagree," Kiera piped up with uncharacteristic bravado. "That is the most impressive part."

193

CHAPTER TWENTY-EIGHT

"Henry fucking Carrington." Derrick's voice was icy as he settled deeper into the pack jet's leather chair. "I did not see that coming."

Jack stuck his head in the aisle, checking on Felix Dubois. The mad scientist was lying on the wide bench near the back, trussed up like a Thanksgiving turkey, nearly catatonic.

He'd been coherent at the start of the trip, then Levi had the bright idea of telling Dubois where they were going.

The news had sent Felix into a panic. Kiera had been forced to sedate him. He wasn't unconscious, but the longer they spent in the air, the less coherent he became.

Maybe he is reacting to an embedded compulsion of some kind. It would explain his reaction. But he was still bound tight, in case he was playing possum, putting on an act and biding his time to escape.

Something told Jack that wasn't the case. Someone of Felix's background would try some other ploy, trying to cooperate to lull them into a false sense of security before looking for the right opportunity to bolt.

Whichever proved true, Kiera would make sure he didn't go anywhere. She was sitting next to him, occasionally monitoring his vitals, in between checking on Jack's injury. This last was almost unnecessary. Jack was nearly totally healed, which Derrick and the others seemed to take as a sign of the strength of his connection to Mara.

Despite what he'd learned about submissive wolves in the last few hours, Kiera didn't appear intimidated by their captive. If anything, she was giving him a look that promised pain and death if he so much as twitched wrong. His gut told him she'd do it, too.

I guess Nathan is right. Submissive does not mean coward.

Not that Kiera would have to guard Dubois alone. More members of the pack were going to meet them on the ground in Aberdeen. Some would stand guard over the bastard, freeing up Kiera in case her medical skills were needed. The rest would join his original team, prepping for an assault on the baron's estate.

Carrington Castle sat on over a thousand acres of Highland terrain, somewhere near Kinveachy. According to their research, the estate had been in the Carrington family for six generations and had been in a bad state of disrepair up until the last decade. That was when the last remaining Carrington heir had developed an unexpected and exceptional flair for making money. Henry experienced a meteoric rise in the world of finance and made buckets of money, more than enough to restore his estate. Though he owned property worldwide and traveled extensively, Henry spent the majority of his time at the Highland estate.

Derrick's phone buzzed. He read his texts before leaning forward. "Check your encrypted email."

Jack whipped out his computer, slumped a little in reaction to what he saw. The pack's hackers had dug up satellite images of Carrington Castle. While their previous target had been an open airy fantasy castle made of gingerbread and frosting, Carrington Castle was squat and ugly. It was also a seemingly impregnable fort.

The entire structure was situated on a rise within a shallow valley surrounded by mountains on three sides. The main building of the castle complex was built against the steepest one, such that it was accessible only from one side. Four circular towers were connected by thick stone walls at least a dozen feet high, possibly more. The castle structure was built between two of these, with a large inner courtyard in the center. The walls themselves looked to be almost four feet thick, maybe more. This monstrosity was surrounded by an outer set of walls with a wide inner bailey about thirty yards away from the thicker internal walls.

"At least there isn't a moat. Your kind aren't great swimmers, right?"

"I can swim," Derrick said indignantly

"But not fast. Your muscles are too dense. You have to expend a lot of energy and effort to get from point A to B. It makes you slow swimmers."

"Did Mara tell you that?"

"No, you jag off." Jack laughed. "There was that trip to Angola we all took, don't you remember? After we were done, we stayed in that warlord's mansion, the one with the Olympic-sized pool. We had relays, and I kicked all your assess—and I'm no Michael Phelps. You all are *slow*."

"It was a lot closer than you remember, you smug a-hole."

"Sure, keep telling yourself that," Jack laughed before sobering. "How old are these pictures?"

"A few weeks, maybe a month. We're working on getting more current ones."

That wasn't good enough. "Better yet, does the pack own any high-altitude drones?'

Derrick considered that. "I don't think so, but we have military contacts. We might be able to get one."

"Make it happen." He spun the laptop over to show Derrick the images. "If this is where they are holding the shifters, Denon won't be relying on the fortifications alone to protect this place. There's going to be resistance and a lot of it. We're going to need up to the minute intel when we go in. Someone has to be watching the ground, giving us live feedback."

Kidnapping and human experimentation were war crimes. Not that Douglas Maitland intended to make that public, but he could still use it if he wanted—*look at this evil corporation trying to mix humans with animals.* Not that he'd ever do that. The security of his people was too important for him to risk. That and there would always be some batshit crazies who believed in werewolves. *Like me.*

Whatever. He'd rather be crazy if it meant getting Mara back.

"Agreed," Derrick said, frowning at the picture. "First, we gather the best recon we can. Storming the castle comes second after we have all the info. I'll notify all our battle-ready wolves to be on standby. After what we found in that lab, Douglas will give us as many people as we need."

Jack rose, then walked over to the sideboard across the aisle from his seat. He poured himself a whiskey. "I don't like it, but we don't have a choice. Thanks to that asshole, we lost the element of surprise," he said, gesturing at Dubois with his thumb.

"We should send someone to Barcelona to take care of the facility."

"If you can spare some bodies, do it. But not at the expense of our rescue mission." Jack rubbed his fingers together before clenching his hand into a fist. "A small team won't cut it anymore. We may have to rely on numbers to overwhelm the stronghold. Let's hope Denon doesn't pull up stakes and run. This needs to end. *Now.*"

CHAPTER TWENTY-NINE

Mara had no idea where Henry was. What had started as a blessing was starting to feel like a curse. As much as she hated being in his presence, subjected to his magic, now all she did was worry about what he was doing in her absence.

She stood at her bedroom window alone, checking the pattern of the guard rotation. Still the beta version, the one she had memorized second. They only had four they rotated between. That wasn't enough variation for true security's sake. Not that this knowledge did her much good.

How did someone sneak out of a fortress guarded by over a dozen guards, at least half of who were brainwashed shifters? Mara had been wracking her brain for a solution to that question for two days now. And she didn't like the only answer she'd come up with.

You don't.

All of her options were bad. There was the bit where she might have to maim herself to get the high-tech wonder that was her ball and chain cuff off. If and when she succeeded, she'd then have to slip past guards with preternatural senses as sharp as her own.

That and she hadn't figured out a genius plan to get the thirteen residents of the dungeon free. If she left without them, Henry would have Denon move them before she could return with help.

So, where did that leave her? *Up shit creek without a paddle* as her brother was fond of saying.

For a long pitiful moment, she wondered where Connell was. Off saving the world was the short answer.

Connell's mate, Logan, was an Elemental, one of the most powerful beings on Earth. She was stronger, faster, and more skilled than the witch Mara faced. Logan had dominion over the air. She could get in and out of any stronghold with a flick of her dainty fingers simply by going non-corporeal. She could do it without thinking, taking to the air currents to go anywhere she wanted on Earth. As long as there was air, Logan could reappear there. Hell, if there wasn't, she could probably bring it with her. She could probably create a pocket of air on the ocean floor if she wanted. Mara had never thought to ask.

The fact Logan hadn't busted into the castle keep, with Connell in tow, was proof that whatever they were doing was more important and necessary for the world's continued existence.

Not that she needed a rescue, Mara assured herself.

In a way, you asked for this. Not too long ago, she'd had to sit out a big battle to make sure their enemies didn't attack them on the home front. That had chafed, bad. She'd been thirsting for a chance to prove herself ever since. Well, here it was.

So back to the beginning. How does someone escape a fortress?

Mara jerked back from the window, caught by a sudden idea. *You don't...*

Thomas raised his bleary eyes when the first guard ran past him. When the second and third followed soon after, shouting at each other, he pressed against the clear plastic door, straining his eyeballs to see down the hallway.

There was a flurry of movement at the far end, near the tables, but he couldn't quite make anything out. It took him a while, but he pieced together the snatches of conversation.

Someone had escaped.

He took a deep sniff. It wasn't one of his neighbors from down here. Every inmate of the dungeon was present and accounted for. It had to be the wolf girl above stairs.

Here's hoping she didn't have to chew her leg off to get out.

All too soon, the noises died away. Thomas cursed the thick castle walls. He couldn't hear a damn thing outside or upstairs.

Heat flared briefly before his blood cooled. No use getting worked up. He wasn't getting out of this cell for love or money.

Unless she makes it. Douglas Maitland trained his wolves well. There was always a chance she would succeed where he had failed.

Nah. It wasn't likely. Not with those shifter zombies patrolling the place. He spared a thought for Joshua Ellis, the teenage bear. The poor kid had tried to resist, he really had. But that had only made His Pastiness mad. Once Carrington had come down to meet Josh for his special one-on-one visits, it had been all over for the boy.

That wolf girl was going to end up the same way, and there wasn't a damn thing he could do about it.

"This place is purgatory," he whispered to no one in particular.

"Really? I thought it was one asshole's pretentious attempt at Camelot."

Startled, he jerked his head up, then gazed up some more.

Mara peeked over the edge of the wide exhaust pipe that ran down the middle of the hallway ceiling.

"Holy shit, you got loose…"

She dropped down from the ceiling, her lightning-fast reflexes catching the ball a split second before it hit the ground. "Or not," he amended.

Mara squinted at the lock on his door. "I'll be right back."

She disappeared, only to return with a set of the scientist's laboratory tools—a scalpel, some tweezers, and a few other fiddly metal things. Picking up a thin metal bar and bending it, she began to work on picking the heavy-duty lock built into the plastic door.

"You can't get the keys from the guard? Two of them have copies to the cells."

Mara didn't raise her head. "I'm kind of trying to avoid those guys at the moment. I've been laying false trails all over the place, including outside both sets of keep walls. I want them to think I've escaped for as long as possible."

Thomas whistled, impressed despite himself. *What a sneaky little wolf.* "How will you stop the shifters from tracking you?"

"Other than sneaking into Henry's power shower every morning?" Mara shrugged. "My father—the chief—taught me how to disguise my scent, how to hide, and how to hunt."

Thomas leaned back as Mara put a metal bar in her mouth, bending forward to work on the lock with another one. "You're Douglas' daughter? One of the twins?"

"I am," she mumbled from behind one of the metal bars she'd fashioned into a lock pick.

A little spark that might have been hope kindled in his gut. There was no way the Colorado Basin Pack would let the Maitland heir rot in here. "Should I bow or something? I didn't know I was in the presence of royalty."

He was only half-joking.

Mara wrinkled her nose. "Please don't." A final bit of fiddling, and she had the door open.

He glanced down at the row of cells. Little David was staring at them from three doors down. Even if he helped, they would never get all the doors open before the guards came back. Guilt twisted his gut, but he swallowed it.

"Are we making a break for it?" He didn't add the alone part, not with the little boy listening.

None of the others would resent them going. They were still under Carrington's spell. But Thomas knew what happened to the inmates here. None of the ghouls who were part of the scientific staff bothered to hide what they were doing. He wasn't sure he'd be able to live with himself if he walked away.

"I think I have a better plan, but I'll tell it to you over there." She gestured to the far end of the room.

Most of the shifters would be able to hear them still, but that was the convenient thing about Carrington's whammy. A person had to give very direct instructions and ask hyper-specific questions to learn what was in their heads.

Mara retreated to the far end of the lab. "First, I need you to help me get this off."

"I thought you said you couldn't remove it. It stopped you shifting or something."

"Not exactly," Mara said. "My would-be fiancée explained that if I shifted, the cuff would adjust instantaneously with the likely possibility it would overcorrect and take the whole foot off."

She extended her leg. "Even if I managed to wedge it and push clear, I might not be fast enough to prevent this possibility. So, my plan is simple. I'll push while you pull. I'm hoping that should be fast enough to keep my foot attached to my body."

"Uh..."

Mara widened her eyes. "Please, Thomas."

"I've been in that cell for..." He shrugged. "I don't remember how long it's been. My reactions aren't what they used to be."

"Would a pep talk help?" she said. Mara was grimacing...or baring her teeth. He couldn't tell.

"I believe in you," she said. "You can do it. You can achieve anything you set your mind—"

Thomas held up a hand. "All right, wiseass. You can stop."

He studied the manacle on her ankle. "How do you want to do this?"

She leaned forward. "Tell me honestly, are you weaker than you used to be?"

Scowling, he shrugged. "Are you thinking what I think you're thinking?"

She waggled her eyebrows. "We will need to find something to protect your hands. This thing has a lot of silver in it."

Now Thomas knew for certain that she was Douglas Maitland's

daughter. The girl had a set of brass balls on her. That or she was just reckless. "All right, kid, it's your show."

They found a stash of latex gloves left behind by the scientist. He and Mara put on two layers. Then she heaved the ball on the table before climbing up after it. He followed, remaining standing and taking hold of her leg when she held it up. Wincing, he took hold of the manacle and braced himself, helping Mara when she swung herself over the table.

She was suspended in the air now, hanging by the manacle he held as high as he could with both hands.

Mara did an upside-down sit up, bending in half so she could place her hands on the silver cuff from the other side.

"You have good core strength," he acknowledged with a grunt. But he couldn't seem to wipe the grimace from his face.

"Okay, we go on three. One, two, *three*."

Thomas yanked up, instinctively turning away as the woman turned into a wolf.

The slim beast twisted away from him, hitting the deck in a tangle of dark green silk—the gown she'd been wearing.

For a second, he froze, worried he was holding a bloody foot. Except the scent profile wasn't of blood. He opened one eye and looked down, confirming a comforting lack of blood.

He looked closer at the cuff. "Hey, I think you could have gotten out of this on your own."

Mara's wolf climbed out of the nest of silk. She looked at the cuff in his hand and yelped. After another flare of blue light, she had a mouth again. "*Son of a bitch.*"

His Pastiness hadn't completely lied. The cuff did shrink—by a couple of centimeters. It was nowhere near small enough to wrap around a wolf's foot snugly, let alone take it off.

"Methinks he lied," Thomas announced.

Mara did not find his newfound humor amusing. "I have been dragging that damn ball up and down this three-story castle for *days*," she snapped.

Thomas was having a really hard time not laughing. He fought it as valiantly as he could, but a strangled little chuckle escape. "That was just you being smart. You were lulling the bastard into a false sense of security."

She glared at him sharper than a stiletto. Damn, he missed his knives.

Eh. She can't afford to kill you. He was her only reliable ally at this point. Thomas allowed himself a small smile. Then he hopped off the table, hauling the ball and chain with him.

Damn, it *was* heavy. How had that tiny little thing carried this around everywhere? "We should hide this somewhere," he suggested.

Mara was still pissed. "Do you know how hard it was taking a bath chained to that thing?" Her eyes were almost luminescent with anger.

What to say to that? "Maybe you should have taken a shower," he suggested gently.

"His Pastiness didn't provide me with one," she grumbled. "The little shit probably didn't think they went with the whole medieval aesthetic."

"That or he thinks showers aren't romantic." He shrugged. "You can't sprinkle rose petals and light candles in the shower. I mean, you *can*, but it doesn't have the same impact."

Mara narrowed her eyes. The hair on the nape of his neck prickled, and he realized with a start that the girl was more dominant than him. Thomas decided it was time for him to shut up.

That lasted about ten seconds after she looked away. "Now what?" he asked. "If what you say is true and there is a big, bad corporation bankrolling His Pastiness, then any minute now, he's going to call them in so they'll move this party to another venue."

"I'm counting on that."

The light dawned. His lips parted. "You want them to mobilize *us*."

"I do," she acknowledged. "Without a suggestion from Henry himself, none of the others will follow me, right?"

She was right. "In a nutshell, peanut."

Her lashes flickered, but she let the endearment slide. "Then having them pack everyone into vehicles is the only way we can get them out."

"What happens if we get separated? Doesn't your plan depend on us being loaded up into the same vehicle?"

"Well, luckily for us, we have two drivers." Her head drew back. "You do know how to drive, don't you?"

He laughed. "Yeah, I do."

"Good."

"Be ready."

"I will."

He hefted the ball up. "So, where shall we stash this?"

She stared at it for another minute, shaking her head and muttering. "Give it to me. I have plans for it."

The corner of his mouth turned up. "Let me guess. Does this plan involve bashing someone's head in with it?"

Mara grinned, and he suddenly realized why Carrington had targeted her. It was the kind of smile that incited males of his species to wade into battle and wage wars against each other.

She took the chain, slinging the ball over her shoulder like it was the latest fashion accessory. "Sorry. No spoilers."

CHAPTER THIRTY

Henry Carrington picked up the priceless antique dagger he used to open letters, flipping it in the air and catching it by the hilt repeatedly as he relayed his instructions to Phillip Tenant. Phil was the CEO he'd handpicked to run Denon so he wouldn't be tied to headquarters all the time. Like Felix Dubois, Acton Jones, and Anders Galt, Phillip was one of the men his talent had made indispensable to Denon.

Of the four, Phillip had been with him the longest. He'd met the man while still in graduate school. Phil had come to give a speech, recruiting for one of the many Fortune Five Hundred companies that liked to raid his university's stash of fresh-faced youths.

Henry had found Phillip particularly susceptible to his brand of charm. He'd made the most of it. After a few years, when Henry was finally where he needed to be, he'd handed the reins to Phillip, confident he had a puppet who could follow orders to the letter.

It required a serious effort to maintain his stable of *yes* men, but the payoff made the investment worthwhile.

Henry was confident Mary would recognize his advantages as a partner soon enough.

Speaking of the love of his life, Henry couldn't help but admire the way she was holding up against him. But as he'd learned early in life, anything worth having required work and sacrifice. And she was worth it. Look at the way she was playing hide and seek with him in his own home.

He'd never told her this, but when Henry had his heart set on someone, he could find them just by thinking about them. That was how he knew Mary was down in the basement, no doubt trying to figure out how to get the other shifters out of his care. Of course, that would never happen, but he admired that she was attempting when she could have tried to escape by herself. Such selflessness. She was perfect in every way.

And if things didn't work out, there was always Project Argent. Henry settled the knife on top of the box holding the prototype firearm and ammunition special cartridges.

It wouldn't come to that, of course. He was too skilled to let things get that far. But it paid to be prepared, nevertheless.

Henry rattled off his final set of instructions, then checked his watch as Phillip began his update. Perhaps he'd surprise Mary by setting up a candlelight dinner for two at her favorite tower, the northeast one where she spent last night spying on his perimeter guards. She'd figure out there was no escape from him soon enough.

"We've had an incursion at the main Dublin facility," Phillip said suddenly in his droning monotone.

Henry sat bolt upright. *"What?"* he shouted. "Why didn't you say so?"

"You said we don't do updates first, we—"

His jaw clenched. "Yes, I know what I said, but a breach like this is a priority, don't you think?"

Phillip sucked in a breath, apologizing profusely, but Henry knew his man would do the same if a similar situation arose again. He'd trained him too well. That particular pathway was burned in now, one of the drawbacks to long-term exposure to him, at least for the malleable.

Well, it seemed his decidedly non-malleable love interest was going to get her wish. He was going to move this party to one of his other properties.

Henry pushed the intercom. "Get me Simms."

Static crackled briefly. "Simms here."

"We have a problem."

CHAPTER THIRTY-ONE

Carrington Castle was butt ugly in real life. Unfortunately, it was also as imposing and impenetrable as it appeared in the pictures.

Armies must have taken one look and decided to besiege someplace else...

Jack leaned back in the hotel's uncomfortable armchair, turning the drone footage over from every perspective, scanning for weaknesses.

He and Derrick were staying at a small inn, about ten clicks from the stronghold. They had arrived in the area last night, followed shortly but the second team. The men arrived in ones, twos, and threes, scattering to all the available hotel and housing options within twenty kilometers of the castle in an effort to stay anonymous.

Derrick leaned forward across the scarred wooden coffee table. "Our third team is inbound. They should be here in less than four hours. Douglas says he'll be here in six. He was held up—he had to wait for the cavalry."

Jack frowned—not at the news that the chief was on his way. That he had expected. It was the other news.

"Is that Connell? Did he finally track him down?" Mara's twin would be beside himself with worry when he found out what had happened to his sister. But Connell had been MIA with his girlfriend for over a month. According to Derrick, that wasn't an unusual occurrence, but Jack still expected Connell to drop out of the sky, foaming at the mouth and roaring for Henry Carrington's head on a pike.

In retrospect, he should have guessed Connell wasn't human years earlier than he had.

"No, it's not Connell." Derrick scratched his head, reaching for a bottle of Glenlivet. Ordinarily, Jack would have chastised him. It was important to stay sharp before an op, but Jack had seen Derrick and the others drink enough to put down a Clydesdale and still kick ass the next day. Now he knew why.

"Then who is coming?"

Derrick shrugged. "I have a few ideas, but I'd be speculating. Best to focus on getting Mara out with the people we can account for."

"Agreed." Movement on the live feed caught his eye. Jack leaned in. Something on the screen made him frown. "Where the hell are we on the choppers?"

The plan had been to drop forces inside both sets of castle walls via helicopter. The interior team would look for Mara and any surviving shifters while those dropped in between the two sets of walls would blast holes in both so the rest could make their escape.

He didn't know what other defenses Denon would have beyond the basic castle fortifications, but Jack expected the team to take heavy fire. This time around, they had some state-of-the-art body armor, brought in by the second team last night. However, things had a way of going wrong in the heat of battle.

"We're ready. The choppers are parked less than a mile away at an abandoned farm," he said. "We just need to wait for the right weather window. I warned you the high winds would be a problem up here."

Damn it. "Then we'll have to breach on foot because we've run out of time."

He spun the tablet to face Derrick. On the screen, uniformed figures moved in the central courtyard, pulling up boxes. Two large vans were being moved from a nondescript building outside the walls that must have served as a garage.

"Fuck," Derrick shouted, jumping to his feet. "They're mobilizing."

CHAPTER THIRTY-TWO

Mara pressed a kitchen towel to her bloody leg and swore, holding her breath as the guard ran past her hiding place, the kitchen pantry.

Only a human. He wouldn't smell the blood. She was safe for the moment. Slumping, Mara scanned the pantry shelves, searching for more supplies to hide her scent.

Her staycation plans had been doing pretty well up until half an hour ago.

Mara had somehow managed to stay out of sight for almost twenty-six hours. She'd ducked, dodged, and laid more false trails than hairs on her head.

She'd covered her natural scent with the handy things she found here in the kitchen. Of these, she'd made good use of the cinnamon. But cinnamon wouldn't cover the scent of blood. *This might call for vinegar...*

With luck, this wasn't a wasted effort. She had tried to make the most of her continued presence in the castle, beginning with stealing a guard's uniform from one of the dryers. Mara hoped that by the time they realized she hadn't left, there would be so many overlapping and confusing scents she'd be able to move freely. That or they would buy her gambit and pack up the captives in a conveniently hijack-able transport.

So far, things had gone better than she could have expected, up until the point where she'd run smack dab into a shifter guard. It was a cat, of course, one that moved with skill.

The fight that followed had been short, hard, and bloody.

The cat was pretty damn good. She didn't know what pack he'd come from, but he'd been around the block. Mara recognized many elements of his fighting style from her time sparring with the pack members who'd served in the military. They had been well-versed in many foreign-born styles in addition to Uncle Sam's techniques. This one fought like them, mixing in *krav maga* and *muay Thai* for flavoring.

But Mara had been trained in all that as well, and more.

He came at her with a practiced strike, kicking and whirling like a dervish. Mara caught his foot, slamming her elbow down on his knee. When he cried out, she expected his buddies to pour into the room, but the thickness of the castle walls was a problem that cut both ways.

The cat recovered long enough to twist, letting himself drop to the floor, only spin on his back like one of the damn Ninja Turtles.

Mara jumped up and landed on him, forcing his head and legs apart with the superior strength of her legs. She followed that with a stomp to the kidneys before finishing him with a punch to the head. Her adversary slumped back onto the floor, unconscious.

That was around the time she noticed his left claw embedded in her high. Her plan to make everyone believe she had escaped went out the window. The blood would give her away.

Scowling at the cat, she bent to pick his pockets.

Ouch. Fuck. Mara lifted her stinging fingers to her lips. The hand-cuffs the guard carried were coated with silver, like her cuff.

She took great pleasure in putting them on him.

Then she cleaned up, using bleach she found under the sink. When she'd heard footsteps, she dragged herself and the guard into the pantry.

Once the coast was clear, she stood and applied the vinegar to the kitchen towel. Wincing, she tied it over the claw marks.

That wouldn't fool anyone for long. Her only hope was to hole up somewhere to watch everyone's reactions and maneuvers.

When in doubt, go for the high ground.

Mara scowled at the unconscious cat. First, she'd have to find a place for her new friend here, perhaps one of the storage trunks she'd seen in the basement, the one at the other end of the lab. She needed to go down to the dungeon to touch base with Thomas, anyway. Luckily, she had discovered another set of stairs from the kitchen to the basement, the nearest room of which functioned as a root cellar.

She had to drag the shifter by the legs. Carrying him would have put too much strain on her wound, making it bleed more. She also took a little too much pleasure in letting his head bang on the wooden stairs.

It took her twice as long as normal to get to the trunk in question, only to find it locked. Swearing under her breath, she grabbed a loose brick from deeper in the basement and broke the lock.

Mara opened the lid, trying not to breathe in case there was a lot of dust. And then she tried not to breathe so she wouldn't scream because the trunk was already occupied.

CHAPTER THIRTY-THREE

The skeleton was small, and it smelled only of dust, not decay. It had been here in the trunk for decades, at least.

She wasn't an expert in anatomy, but it was the body of a child, a male. It had been ten or eleven when it died, and there was something wrong with the leg bones. They curved inward, looking thin and weak. She guessed the child had suffered from a kind of genetic disorder. Whether it was what had caused its death was difficult to say, although the fact the bones were in a trunk pointed to foul play.

Without a better idea, Mara shoved the cat in the trunk anyway, after gently moving the bones aside.

At least now I know where Henry gets his crazy. Evidently, he came from a long line of madmen.

"Sorry for this," she apologized to the breathing half of the pair before closing the lid. Mara placed a small chip of debris in between the lid and body, leaving it slightly ajar so the cat wouldn't suffocate or starve in there if everyone evaced.

Guilt nibbled at her ragged edges. *He will wake up,* she assured herself. The mangy cat would heal himself—with luck not too quickly. Then he'd get himself out of the box, Schrödinger be damned.

Hopefully, the company he found himself in wouldn't permanently scar him. As for the bones, perhaps they would be discovered now. The child had been in there long enough...

Mara leaned forward a touch, trying to get a better view without exposing herself. There wasn't much daylight left before full dark, but her father had taught her twilight and dawn were the most dangerous times. Objects in motion were easier to spot than in full daylight or total darkness.

Two vans were being moved out of the modern garage, the one outside the outer wall. But the drivers parked them closer to the gate, hiding them from view.

That's okay. She didn't need to see to figure out who or what was moving. Mara ducked back down, sitting cross-legged with her back against one of the turret's teeth. She closed her eyes. Yes, those were the van's engines. They'd left them running.

Was this it? Were they getting the shifters out?

Mara cursed the wind. The whistle of it make the subtler noises more difficult to hear, but if she focused, she could sense movement.

A shout rang out. The sound of running feet followed it. But she couldn't say how many pairs it was with the wind picking up and carrying the noise away.

Damn this weather. Scotland was the birthplace of the Maitland family. As a rule, her father and extended family looked at the homeland with nostalgia. She had as well, for most of her youth. But the second she got the chance, Mara was blowing this pop stand, and she wouldn't look back.

Maybe she'd give it another chance in a decade or so, but, until then, she'd vacation in the Bahamas.

With the wind so high, Mara chanced a second look.

Her breath caught. Thomas was down there. He stood behind David, his cuffed hands over the boy's head as he looked around, squinting as if he hadn't seen the sky in years, not months.

But they weren't herding the prisoners to the vans. Not yet. It seemed the scientists were packing up as well. Equipment was being dragged up—boxes and coolers.

Of course. They wouldn't want to leave their precious samples. She would have to be patient. This would take longer than she thought. Eventually, someone would pull their heads out of their butts, and they'd prioritize getting the shifters into the vehicles. She had to get into position.

The good news was she could get to the south-facing tower without going back down into the castle since they were all connected with ramparts. The walls weren't smooth. She might be able to scale her way down with her claws. Hell, she'd jump if she had to. It was a bit high for that, two and a half stories, but she could roll with the punches. Thanks to Jack, she'd experienced hurtling to the ground at high speed recently.

Just wait until they load everyone up. Even with Thomas' help, she couldn't get the shifters on that van. Not unless Henry had already told them to get on. Their host wasn't out here, so they must have been following his last order. She guessed that was to obey Simms and the other guards. Her timing had to be perfect.

In the meantime, Mara was faster and had a lower profile on four feet. She let her lips stretch in anticipations. It had been a while.

"*Stop.* We have incoming."

The shout came from the inner keep walls. More shouts and a few screams followed it.

What now?

Mara grabbed the tower protrusion, getting on her belly to avoid being seen. Grimacing, she poked her head back out, risking a bullet to the skull.

Well, hell.

The walls were being breached. Men clad in all black were scaling them with ropes.

Some guards were pulling out weapons, while others shoved at the prisoners, herding them back to the small entrance that led back down to the dungeons.

Perfect. Just perfect.

She ground her teeth together, snapping her head to check out the people responsible for fucking up her exit plan.

Narrowing her eyes, she focused on the team storming the castle. Mara didn't know whether to laugh or cry. That was her cousin down there. Jack wouldn't be far behind.

The cavalry had arrived. However, their arrival meant the shifters were being herded back to their dungeons.

After she thanked the guys for riding to the rescue, she would have to kill them all.

CHAPTER THIRTY-FOUR

Damn it. Mara had been so close to pulling off her plan. Thomas wanted to ask what the hell had happened, but the zombie nation down here never asked questions. As best he could figure out, the guards had begun to yell something about an intruder. He thought they'd discovered the ruse, but the ruckus had seemed too big for one wolf, even one as talented as Mara Maitland.

Thomas swore under his breath as he was shoved at the top of the stairs. For a second, he felt himself yawing over open space. A centimeter more and he would have pitched forward, taking the kid David and everyone else with him.

Suppressing a growl, he managed—but only just—to catch himself. He was afraid he'd given away the fact that his cuffs weren't fastened, but, fortunately, the guard closest to him was one of his own. Filina, the hyena mother, must have been whammied extra-hard by His Pastiness because she frequently had to be given orders twice and tended to obey them too literally. Details weren't her thing, so even if she had noticed the cuff swinging open, she wouldn't volunteer the information.

That didn't stop her from following Simms lead in herding the others back to their cells. They stuffed them in twos and threes per cell, in too much of a rush to bother separating them.

Simms crammed another three shifters in the nearest cell, closing the door with a slam. His walkie crackled, and someone yelled out a code in an urgent voice.

"Get the rest of these guys back into the cells. I gotta get back out there." Then he turned and ran back up the stairs.

As soon as the coast was clear, Thomas quietly slid the restraints off.

Filina spun, taking hold of his arm. Thomas put his head down, then charged like a bull. He slammed into her chest, driving her against the nearest door.

"Sorry, sorry," he chanted before pulling his leg back and kicking her in the ribs. Bones crunched, and he winced as she let out a strangled scream. "You have no idea how sorry I am," he grunted, pinning her arms behind her back and dragging her toward the nearest cell door.

It was a hell of a lot harder than it should have been. Damn, he had gotten soft. "The ribs will heal before you know it," he said, wincing when Filina struggled to breathe.

"Need some help?"

Thomas jerked, nearly losing his grip on the struggling hyena.

There was a blond human in the black combat fatigues holding a big gun on him with practiced ease.

Another man came up behind him, slapping him on the back. "You really can't help being a jackass. Honestly, I don't know what Mara sees in you."

"*Holy shit.*" Thomas put a hand over his chest. "Are you Mara's people? The Maitlands?"

"That's us," the brunette said.

He slumped against the wall, suddenly tired. "Never thought I would be so happy to see a bunch of wolves."

The blond one grabbed his arm. "Have you seen Mara? Where is she?"

Not waiting for an answer, he started shouting, running up to each cell in turn, checking each prisoner's identity.

"Not the brightest bulb, is he?" Thomas whispered to the other man. This one was taller than him by a good six inches, making the man about six foot three, with a linebacker's shoulders.

"I don't want to call my cousin Mara shallow or anything, but I can't say she chose him for his brain," the man began, making sure he spoke loud enough to be heard. He stuck out his arm, offering to shake. "And you are?"

"Fuck off, Derrick," the blond man snapped, interrupting. "It's not as if I can smell the fact she's not in here."

"No shit?" Thomas's nostrils flared. The blond *was* human. "Wolf girl didn't say her mate was a human."

"She told you she had a mate?" The man practically glowed.

"Yeah."

The blond gave the wolf a smug look.

The one called Derrick shrugged. "There's no accounting for taste. About Mara? Is she around?"

He nodded. "She's loose, hiding in the castle. I'm Thomas. Mara and I have chatted, plotted to escape, and then to bash Carrington's head in together. You know…general bonding-type talks."

"How long have you been here?"

Thomas pointed to his cell across the hall. The wolf named Derrick and the human twisted to look at the sets of hash marks covering it. "I stopped counting after I filled up that wall."

"Oh…" Derrick winced, then clapped him on the back. "Well, no matter. Pack your bags cause we're getting the hell out of Dodge."

"You haven't hurt anyone, have you?" he asked, glancing down at Filina in consternation. He hoped David hadn't seen the man kick his mother.

"Not enough of them yet, but we'll get there." Derrick cracked his knuckles.

In halting terms, Thomas explained about the whammy.

"They're not responsible, at least the shifters aren't. That one started in the cell next to me," he said, pointing to the hyena-were.

"Is that true?" The human squatted in front of her on the thick plastic door.

"She won't answer you." Thomas put his finger up, wiggling it at his head. "He told her only to obey Simms and the other senior guards."

"Carrington did?" Jack spat.

"Yeah. You know about him, right?"

"I know he's a fuckwad," Jack volunteered. "And that he's going to be in a world of hurt when I finally get my hands on him."

"Well, for that, you'll have to get in line behind your girl, but I wouldn't recommend getting too close. Mara has been fighting off his mojo, but look at this other one. It's easy to fall under his spell."

Derrick swore. "So, he has magic?"

"Oh yeah. That fucker is a *bad* witch, but the only saving grace is that he doesn't seem to know it. He thinks he's special. Calls it a gift, not part of his craft. He doesn't do spells. He just *is*, and people fall like dominoes."

Jack's brow creased. "We assumed Carrington was paying the shifter guards we encountered."

"He might be," Thomas shrugged. "I don't fucking know. Money is nothing to him. He can go up to anyone in the street and ask them to transfer their entire life savings to him, and they would do it. Maybe not right away, but soon enough. His Pastiness likes things tied in a neat bow. His castle, his servants. He likes to be seen as a benevolent ruler. He runs the whole fucking show without having to resort to violence or threats. All he had to do is talk to you. At first, you tell him where to stick it, but he keeps going. Then lo and behold, it starts to sound reasonable. Before you know it, you're dancing to his tune, like the fucking pied piper."

"That's fucked up, but now Dubois makes sense," Derrick scratched his head. "And it's not a spell he casts. It's passive?"

"As far as I know, yeah."

"Mara," Jack said hoarsely. He cleared his throat. "Has Mara been, um, dancing?"

"No. Like I said, she's been resisting."

"Why did he take her in the first place?" Derrick asked. "If she's immune, why does he want her? I mean, he gunned her down in the street for fuck's sake."

"Probably *because* she resisted." Jack put his hands on his hips. "He wanted to teach her a lesson."

"Maybe so, but he can spot a shifter. He knew she'd survive. It's more that this king wants a queen, and she's...well, you've seen her."

Thomas hadn't wanted to say it, but somebody had to. He expected an explosion of swears. But Jack grew grim and quiet. His face could have been carved from a glacier.

Oh, yeah. The human could be Mara's mate. Lots of control there.

Derrick got on his comm, then startled rattling off instructions. "Take the shifters alive. I repeat, no kill shots."

He covered the mike, jerking his head at Thomas. "Even the humans are under his influence? There's no sadistic warden you want to get even with?"

It was a fair question. "Even Simms is only doing what Carrington says, but that doesn't mean he and the others won't still shoot at your ass."

Derrick made a sound low in his throat. He got back on the comm. "No kill shots unless you can't avoid it."

"I'm going to go find Mara," the human announced.

"Check the high ground," he said. "Mara was hoping her escape would trigger an evacuation, so she was keeping an eye out for the vans."

"All right." Jack unholstered his weapon. "Signal me if you spot her before I do."

Then he was gone, moving faster and lighter on his feet than any human Thomas had ever seen.

Derrick scowled at the locked doors. "Who has the key?"

"Only Simms and his lieutenant."

The werewolf rolled his big, muscled shoulders. "Then we have to bust them open. Is there anything strong and heavy enough to break these locks?"

Thomas frowned before he remembered, then started laughing. "I have just the thing."

He limped over to the bench near the stairs, fishing out the ball and chain he'd helped Mara remove.

"She is going to have to find something else to beat His Pastiness's head in with. We were going to take turns."

He dragged it over to Derrick, who picked it up with a gloved hand and scowled, smelling the cuff. He swore under his breath.

"Yup," Thomas confirmed.

"Good thing Jack left," The wolf sniffed. "He's already on edge."

Derrick pivoted, winding up like a major league pitcher. He started bashing the lock, and not simply as a means to an end. He hit it like he was working some issues out.

"Therapeutic, isn't it?" Until now, the shifter had seemed totally in control, but he was demolishing these doors like a wrecking ball.

"My cousin got…kidnapped on my watch…and almost got her free will…sucked away," he said in between swings before stopping to face him. "And I didn't realize the fucker was a witch. The chief is going to have my balls."

He resumed swinging. The crashing was enough to wake the dead.

"Why don't I go watch the door?" Thomas suggested, pointing his thumb at the stairs.

Derrick didn't answer. Thomas nodded, backing away slowly.

CHAPTER THIRTY-FIVE

Mara lay back on the roof, fighting to catch her breath. She was bleeding from her side, where her love handles would be if she ate her feelings instead of punching them out.

Her leg wound had started bleeding again, too. Having to fight another shifter and tossing them off the roof had not been part of her grand design, but what was it they said about the best-laid plans?

Here's hoping Pat the flying Were lynx went unnoticed. It was mayhem down in the inner courtyard, so, with luck, that human guard he'd landed on hadn't realized what direction he'd come from.

Mara twisted to lay on her good side, inching closer to watch the action. The newcomers were wearing balaclavas, but she recognized most of them by the way they moved.

That one was Alvarez, and that other bigger one moved like Levi Jessup. She recognized the left hook he'd used to lay out Simms.

Oh, it was a good thing she didn't like the head guard that much because he'd just gotten his face rearranged. She almost couldn't decide which fight to watch.

A tall lean shifter who could only be Nathan Hale landed a roundhouse so beautiful that she had to stop herself from standing up and clapping. And then another black-clad man ran out into the courtyard. He, too, was wearing a mask, but Mara got a glimpse of his eyes before he turned away.

Jack. Oh God. Jack *was* down there. He'd come for her.

Please don't get shot. And please don't shoot one of the zombie'd shifters. Not fatally anyway. Flesh wounds were A-okay with her.

She had to get down there.

Mara crawled away from the edge, getting to her feet when she was sure the occupants of the courtyard no longer had a direct line of sight. She was almost to the stairs when hard hands grabbed her from behind.

"Going somewhere?" Henry asked, pulling her back to his chest.

Mara jerked away, using too much force. She landed on her ass a few feet away from him.

"What the hell are you still doing here? Don't you see what the hell is happening down there?"

Henry shook out his arms, then began to unbutton his blue suit coat theatrically. "I'm touched that you're so concerned about my well-being."

"I don't *fudging* care," Mara burst out.

He kneeled in front of her. "Mara, love, you can't even swear. And you're urging me to leave because you are worried for me."

"And I will leave." Rising, Henry dropped the coat, then began to unbutton his crisp tailored white shirt. "But not without you."

Mara blinked. Her tongue felt thick in her mouth. She shook her head. "No. None of that is happening, certainly not the part where I go anywhere with you. I wouldn't go to the end of the driveway with you."

Henry chuckled, his boyishly handsome face so serene, almost as if a gentle inner light lit him. "I do love that spunk. It's so refreshing. But I'm afraid we no longer have the luxury of time."

Henry continued to unbutton his shirt, pulling the ends of it out of his waistband with a snap. "You'll have to forgive me for rushing this now. I was savoring your defiance, you see. Your kind of strength of will is rare in the world." He paused at the last button, meeting her eyes. "You'll have to take my word for that."

"What in the Sam Hill are you doing?" Mara blinked, giving herself a hard shake. "*Hell*, I meant hell. See, I can still swear. So, what is with the fucking strip show?"

"I told you. We've run out of time." He parted the shirt, took it off, and dropped it to the floor.

"What the…" Mara used her arms and feet to sidle backward.

She couldn't speak. There weren't swear words strong enough to describe the sight.

Henry's arms and torso were perfect—from the pecs up. But his abs and stomach were covered with closed *eyes* and *lips*. His scent changed, the ozone in it spiking so high she could taste it on her tongue. But through it all was the familiar scent of him.

This was why she liked how he smelled. All those pieces of shifter were *alive*, melded with his body. Had they been dead, she would have been repelled, but they weren't. Living, those pieces made him familiar, something she welcomed.

She put a hand over her mouth, her involuntary gag reflex working overtime. Bile rose in her throat. Mara swallowed, forcing it down. "I repeat, what the *fuck*?"

Henry passed his hand over his stomach. The eye right over his belly button popped open, blinking. His hand kept moving.

Not one of the mouths. Please not one of the mouths. If one of those fucking pairs of lips opened and started talking to her, she was going to hurl.

Overwhelmed, she watched the eyes blink, the eyeballs darting back and forth.

"What did you do?" she whispered. "Henry, *what the fuck did you do?*"

His mouth tightened. "Well, it's a long story involving a tragic fire in the west tower. I was pinned under a beam, and I suffered a third-degree burn on my back." He turned, so she could see that the horror show did a complete three-sixty around his torso.

"I had some grafts done ages ago, but some scarring remained. And then my dear friend Felix asked if I wanted to advance the cause, and have an experimental graft provided by one of our guests. He explained the drawbacks. They didn't deter me. You see, I've experienced rejections before. But Mara, neither of us understood the benefits until after the first graft."

But she did understand. Mara *was* going to be sick now. What he'd done should have been impossible.

Stealing a shifter's magic was a violent act. Most witches failed. The spells were intricate, and Weres had to be incapacitated, something few could pull off. But this ignorant witch, aided by the butchers at Denon had stumbled on a way, and he'd done it without any knowledge or study of spell-craft.

Henry had successfully absorbed shifter magic—many shifters. All he'd had to do was cut them up and stitch them to him.

No way should have worked, but here he was in all of his Lovecraftian glory.

"How many?" Her voice was tinny and distant as if she were listening to herself from far away.

Henry didn't answer. He ran one of his fingers over an eye, the one below his sternum, stroking the dense eyelash fringe with his fingertip.

Only children have lashes that thick.

"Never mind." Mara shuddered.

She could figure out how many he'd killed by counting the eyeballs and lips on his corpse.

CHAPTER THIRTY-SIX

J ack ran up the stairs two at a time, his heart working more than it should. He was amped up, operating harder and faster than he ever had, the controls he'd built mission by mission gone, obliterated into dust.

But he didn't care. What the prisoner downstairs had said kept running on a loop. Henry was a witch, and he could make people do whatever he wanted.

Jack tried not to think about the days Mara had been in his power.

Thomas had said she was able to resist, Jack reminded himself. She'd escaped and hid.

But none of those details made him feel any better. The urgency poked and prodded, throwing him off his game. He ran up the steps faster.

M ara tried to get to her feet, but she couldn't get her legs to work. In fact, her entire body wasn't responding.

It felt as if a thick blanket was pressing her down. The weight was warm and filled with sunlight, but the damn thing was heavier than a truck filled with rocks. She couldn't seem to throw it off.

Gritting her teeth, Mara pushed up against it, trying to force it away, but it just flexed and flowed back, responding like a thick viscous liquid.

Mara had once read about an accident that happened over a century ago. A storage container full of molasses had exploded, flooding the North End of Boston. She used to have nightmares about it, imagining she had been one of the victims drowning in that dense, sticky ocean.

This was exactly like that nightmare, only worse. Here the wave was a living force. Henry's magic wasn't trying to crush her. It was trying to invade.

Mara flipped over on her stomach as if that would help. The brief easing of the pressure was probably in her head, but she grasped the straw anyway, taking advantage to suck in a deep breath. She struggled to get to her hands and knees.

Cotton filled her ears and her mouth. She didn't mind that, though. It made Henry harder to hear. Not hard enough, however.

"It is remarkable, the way that you continue to defy me." He laughed. "But you and I both know that you can't keep this up. I'm too powerful. Pieces of you are already unraveling under the strain."

He knelt beside her, sending another wave of energy over her head.

"My friends from Denon have ensured there isn't a soul alive who can resist me. Of course, they didn't know that was what they were helping me achieve with their endless rounds of experimentation. Had they realized, they might have cut their trials short. Now it was too late. None of them can stop me, and neither can you."

Henry reached over to touch her arm. Mara jerked away and he frowned, his lower lip trembling in either anger, hurt, or disappointment.

He was close enough now that she could see a trace of luminescence along the edge of his jawline, along with tiny beads of sweat on his upper lip.

He was straining. She was taxing his strength.

"Free will is an illusion," he continued. "No one gets to choose, not really. Unless we are fortunate enough to be orphaned at an early age, as I was, our lives are determined by our parents and the station we were born in. Then it's whether we went to the right schools or mixed with the right people. Even the people we marry—we meet along those predetermined paths. Choice doesn't factor into the whole thing. Not when you stop to think about it."

He wasn't expecting an answer, which was why she fought to give one. "Is...that...how...you...sleep...at night?" Her own words sounded muffled to her ears.

"I haven't had a nightmare since I was ten years old," Henry confided, stroking the back of her neck. "I sleep like a baby."

Mara didn't doubt that. Sociopaths were rarely troubled by their actions. And, of course, Henry was a special case. He didn't have to dwell on the people he'd wronged because they always came around to his way of thinking. And they did it with a smile.

"Who are these people who've come here?" Henry asked. "The ones who dare to invade this castle I call home? Is it your wolf pack? Are they your relatives?"

The cloying warmth clawed its way down her throat. She fell back down on her knees, the pressure smothering.

"I can tell they're like you, Mara. And only people who care for you enough to try to assault this castle must be close to you, so you may as well tell me the truth. These are your people."

She didn't want to answer, but it slipped out.

"They...are."

His face creased. "You realize I have to punish them, right?"

She snapped her head up, meeting his eyes. "*Please* don't."

"I don't see that I have a choice." Henry's eyes were sad, a wealth of pain and regret reflected in their depths.

Jack. No, she wasn't going to let that happen. Her entire body ached, but she finally managed to push herself to her feet. "They won't understand...about you...about...us."

"*Us?*" Henry's head cocked to the side, the tension easing a fraction.

231

"You can't hurt them," she said. "Because you want them to be your family, too, don't you? Isn't that what you want?"

He blinked "I…I'm not sure. When I saw our future, it was only the two of us."

The weight was gone from her shoulders. Mara had never felt so light, almost giddy.

She stretched, bouncing on the balls of her feet. "I come with baggage…and the future father-in-law from hell unless you treat him right. With—and I cannot stress this enough—*respect*. My father is a very important person."

Henry was intrigued. "How so?"

"Among my people, there isn't anyone higher."

He smiled. "I knew this about you. I could sense it right away. You are as special as I am."

She laughed. "Oh, no. I am *way* more special than you."

Henry's expression dimmed.

"Don't feel bad," she told him, coming close to place a comforting hand on his arm. "After all, you're just a baron. But in my world, my father is a *king*."

"Oh." Henry appeared mollified by that. And why not? A baron was a rather low step in the peerage. But Henry had grown up with the awareness of rank. Nobility and his place in it meant quite a lot to him. That was in his blood.

"Is he here?"

"No. He wouldn't come in person."

"Why not?"

Mara gave him a condescending look. "He's the chief of the Colorado Basin pack and the Canus Primus of the Americas. He rules from afar, like most kings."

She turned, gesturing at the melee in the courtyard. "This is merely a vanguard. The rest will be coming."

For the first time, Henry appeared a bit worried. "We have to leave. We can contact your father later after we reach safety."

She shrugged, unconcerned. "It's a bit late for that. My relatives are the kind to shoot first and ask questions later."

Henry's smile returned, appearing like the sun from behind the clouds. "Mara, that's where your upbringing and mine diverge. I learned early on there is always a diplomatic solution. All I have to do is talk to them. They will understand. I will make them understand..."

His hand snapped out melodramatically before passing over his stomach. One by one, each eye and mouth opened wide. His skin went from mildly luminescent to a bright incandescent yellow.

He was beautiful, almost ethereal... In her mind, Henry's face began to blink in and out, merging with another visage.

Mara's lips parted. "Oh, I get it now."

"What do you understand?" Henry's shoulders hunched at the sound of an explosion. It sounded like a grenade had gone off in the courtyard.

She released a breathy sigh. "That I have to protect my mate."

Henry's features softened with adoration. He opened his arms. "Come to me, my love."

Mara ran to him, seeking his warmth. She wrapped her arms around him, squeezing tight. Wet mouths and open eyeballs pressed against the skin of her forearm and biceps. She extended her claws with a snap, digging them in as deep as she could.

Henry screamed, trying to pry her claws out, but she was physically much stronger than him. "But you said I was your mate!"

Mara dug in deeper, her grip inflexible. "No, I said I had to *protect* my mate," she corrected, twisting her wrist to make him scream. "And that is not you... I almost forgot that for a second. But I do care about you. Never doubt that."

Henry gave her an incredulous look, pain twisting his angelic features. "Then why are you doing this?"

She raised her left hand long enough to rake him across the back, making him scream. Blood and slime dripped from her claws as multiple eyeballs burst under her sharp claws.

"It's simple..." How did he not understand? "I have to save you from yourself."

She wouldn't be doing this if she didn't care. Jack and her family would make him suffer so much more.

Henry continued to squirm, trying to headbutt her, but he did it wrong. The impact stung, but judging from the way he howled, she was sure he'd hurt himself worse.

They stayed locked in their damaging embrace. Henry's light was starting to dim. He barely glowed at all now.

With one last desperate wrench, he pushed away from her, ripping himself out her hold.

Mara stared down at her hands. Big chunks of flesh were stuck to her claws. She stared down at his torn-up body, finally feeling clearheaded.

"You...you will regret this...you...*bitch*," he spat.

Mara wiped her hands on her pants, the tight pinch in her lungs easing. "Yeah, I don't think you have enough juice left to make me feel bad about taking you out."

"Don't need...power."

He lifted a shaky hand, raising a gun straight out of Star Trek. He must have had it stuck in his waistband. She tried to run, but the pops came too fast.

Mara reeled backward. It was like getting simultaneously punched and ripped apart. Fire burned through her.

She clutched at her chest, blood pouring out from behind her pressed fingers. "Not again," she wheezed.

Henry's eyes flared with satisfaction before dimming. The lens of his eyes grew glassy and opaque. The tell-tale shimmer of his magic licked across his skin before dissipating.

She thought it was gone, but it was hard to be sure through the sheen of her tears. What was clear was that his color changed. Henry's skin lost its healthy beige and pink tint, turning a sickly slate grey.

Fuck. Mara fought to take a breath, but it wouldn't come. And she was shivering, too. The only warmth appeared to be in the blood pouring out of her. Her hands were freezing, her fingertips growing more numb by the second.

Not doing the dying part again either.

Mara reached out, trying to grab one of the tower's jutting teeth, intending to call for help. But she misjudged her footing, pitching forward off the edge of the parapet.

Something hard and hot hit her in midair. She twisted. Instead of the ground rushing up to meet her, she was hurtling farther away from the stars.

Distantly, she felt the second impact. Then everything went dark.

CHAPTER THIRTY-SEVEN

J ack cleared the last stair, bursting onto the roof of the tower. Mara stood a mere seven meters away, her clawed hands covering her chest.

For one wild second, he was sure she had gone mad, driven crazy by the dead man at her feet. Jack thought she'd ripped herself up, using her own claws.

But then her hands fell away, and he could see the holes in her black t-shirt.

She stumbled toward the edge, making his heart explode, except it was still pumping so he could run.

Mara had already gone over the edge when he leapt after her. A split second of flight and then he slammed into her back, using his momentum to twist them so he was on the bottom as they hurtled to the courtyard two long stories below them.

They didn't hit the ground. That would have been softer. No, Jack landed on something much harder than that, a rebar-reinforced wall that swore like a sailor.

"*Damn it*, Derrick." The wolf had caught them, but his arms may have hurt Jack's back more than hitting the ground would have.

The werewolf put him and his burden on the ground with uncharacteristic gentleness. "What happened?"

"I think the asshole shot her again."

Tugging the bloody material off her stomach, Jack put his fingers in the bullet hole, using them to rip the shirt apart.

Two large-caliber holes marred Mara's flawless abs, but if that wasn't bad enough, there was something seriously fucked up with them. The skin around them was too inflamed, and thick blue-grey veins radiated from each wound.

Derrick knelt next to him. He picked up Mara's bloody hand. "Fuck!"

"Get the medkit," he shouted.

"On it," Levi called from somewhere behind him.

Derrick looked up, catching the first aid kit in his hand when the other wolf tossed it to him. He swiftly laid out a pair of plastic-wrapped sterilized tweezers and bandage. Then he pressed a pad of gauze to the wound, wiping it to clean the edges.

Jack shook his head. "What the hell are you doing? We have to get her to Kiera."

The medic was supposed to be on standby close to the castle.

"There's not enough time." Derrick's urgency was infectious. "See this veining? This is silver poisoning, and it looks really bad—the worst I've ever seen. The bullets must have been silver, *and* they must be fragmented. We got to get them out."

Jack closed his eyes, holding the howling storm of grief and pain back. *Please God, don't take her.* He almost lost her once. He couldn't do it again.

"I swear if Mara hadn't already killed that son of a bitch—" Jack broke off when Derrick held up the bandage to his nose and swore.

He wiped the pad with a clean piece of gauze, then squinted at the smears. An explosion of swear words followed. "It isn't just the bullet," Derrick was almost crying. "The projectiles were hollow. It looks as if they were filled with some sort of silver suspension as well."

All those bottles of colloidal silver in Dublin were suddenly making sense. *What the fuck, overkill much?*

"There's a saline bottle," Jack said, digging through the bag. "You have to flush the wound out."

Derrick snatched the bottle first, squeezing a hard stream into each hole. Bloody water with metallic specks flowed out.

"What is that shit?" Nathan asked, leaning over Derrick's shoulder.

The other werewolf didn't answer. *"Fuck.* I don't think this is working."

"I smell decay," Nathan piped up.

He snapped his head up to tell him to shut the hell up when Nathan flew to the side, knocked over by a huge black leather bag. Jack clutched Mara to him, wondering if they were about to be attacked again.

"Sorry!" A small Asian woman dressed all in black ran up to them, followed closely by Douglas and another Asian woman wearing a pastel chiffon dress. "It got away from me," she apologized

"Hope. Mai," Derrick sputtered, twisting to stare up at his alpha. "This is the cavalry you were waiting for?"

Jack blinked. "The bag is floating."

The leather apothecary bag next to them was almost as big as a steamer trunk, but it was bobbing in the air as if it were weightless.

Douglas ignored him, kneeling by his daughter. His face was hard, his jaw so tight it was in danger of cracking.

He put his hand over the wounds. Jack didn't know what the hell the alpha was doing, but it felt as if the night had suddenly grown warmer, and then some of the heat began to spin out of him.

After a moment, Douglas rocked back on his heels. "I can't stop it. The silver is in her blood. It's starting to liquefy her organs."

Horrified, Jack tightened his hold on Mara. He turned to the Asian women. They had to be magic, else they wouldn't travel with a floating leather satchel the size of a horse. "Can you get the silver out of her?"

"Silver is one of the metals that can't be affected by magic," Douglas said in a flat tone.

He glared at Jack, gold rolling over his irises. Any minute now,

Douglas would rip Mara out of his arms so he could hold her while she died.

"Well…" Hope's face was a picture of distress.

The one called Mai crossed her arms, planting her feet with her toes out. "There's one spell that might apply. It's complicated and might not work."

Hope touched her arm. "It *could* work."

"Five percent chance," Mai said in a hard voice, but then she turned away and wiped her eyes.

Hope clasped her hands together. "Mai and Mara are close," she explained, crouching next to him.

"Not close enough," Mai said with a snap in her tone. "It will have to be one of them."

Closing her eyes, Hope put her hands over Mara's wounds, echoing Douglas' movement, except hers started to glow with a clear blue light.

"Mai is right," she announced. "We can do this, but one of you must take her injuries and silver into yourself, or she will die. Our spell—a ritual really—it has a greater chance of success if it's someone close to her."

Douglas began to take off his shirt. "I'll do it. I'm the one closest to her."

"Not anymore, you're not. *I'll* do it," Jack said. "And silver is just as poisonous to you as it is to her."

"I am her father and the alpha of our clan," Douglas snarled.

Derrick's head whipped back and forth between the two of them. He froze when they both turned to him as if asking him to decide. "Uh…he has a point, Alpha. Humans are more resistant to silver."

Douglas glared at Derrick as if his subordinate had suggested mutiny. They all began to argue, even the witches.

Jack clutched Mara tighter to him. Everyone had lost their damn mind. "I'm her mate, and I'm human," Jack said, his teeth clenched. "You may not like that, but it's the truth. And the silver won't kill me, but it damn sure will kill you. Stop being a jackass. Let the woman do the spell on me."

Mai nodded approvingly. "This one has sense, unlike you," she told Douglas, giving him a derisive side-eye.

"She is *my* daughter," he repeated.

Hope touched Douglas' arm gently. Her voice was husky but musical at the same time. "If this human is her mate, then this may work, with the added benefit of his being naturally resistant to silver."

"Too much is toxic," Douglas said. "Even for humans."

"But not fatal," she pointed out in that same maddeningly calm tone. "Not in these amounts. His system will be able to handle it."

Douglas pressed his lips together. *"Fine. Do it."*

Mai and Hope guided Jack down on his back, stretching his length out next to Mara so he could hold her hand.

Hope opened her big black bag, pulling out a container of salt and a handful of bottles.

Mai grabbed a satchel that stank of pungent herbs. She started to sprinkle them over their chests while Hope drew a circle around them, adding odd glyphs and runes, marking out the cardinal directions.

"It will be all right. Jack smells like pack," Derrick reassured Douglas. "And he healed too fast for a human after he was shot. If he's got some of Mara's healing ability, then this will work. It's a good plan."

Douglas didn't respond, closing his fist and covering his mouth with it.

The two women finished, drawing back to rest on their knees.

"There is something we forgot to mention," Hope said with a tiny grimace.

"What?" Jack asked.

"This will hurt like a sonofabitch," Mai warned, making a popping sound with her mouth that made it sound like she was chewing gum.

"I don't care. Just do *ittt—*"

Pain slapped him. His body arched up off the ground, jolting as if he'd been hit with defibrillator paddles.

Agony unlike anything he'd ever known racked his body and made him its bitch. It was like an epileptic attack, the muscles in his body spasming wildly, but his mind was still there, aware of everything despite his total loss of control.

I should have requested a belt to bite down on. There was a real danger he'd accidentally chew his own tongue off. But he'd do it again in a heartbeat. They had to get the silver out of Mara before it turned her organs to mush.

"We forgot to mention we must transfer the physical damage of the bullet wounds as well," Mai said, her attractive but slightly dour face softening in sympathy. "Also, we skewed the pain in your direction with that rune over there, to help her damaged system deal with the trauma."

"It's finnee." The pain had receded a touch while she was speaking. Jack had long enough to catch his breath before it rose again, and the spell applied the jumper cables to his nips. *"Betttterrr meee than herrr..."*

Mai clapped her hands together as if dusting them off. "Good."

Jack forced his head to the side, trying to look at Mara. Was she breathing? Her heart hadn't stopped beating. He would know if it had.

The pain hit him again and he gasped, his mouth rounding in surprise. Jack was fairly sure he was bleeding, but he wasn't sure if it was from the transferred bullets holes or if his old ones had opened up.

Was the pain making him have auditory hallucinations, or did Mara just groan? He couldn't be sure because he was starting to lose consciousness.

Right around when his vision began to tunnel, Mai appeared in his rapidly narrowing field of view.

"It's okay," he told her, slurring. "Hit me again."

"Mara is breathing easier. It appears to have worked."

"Are you sure? Cause I can take another jolt," he told her.

"Even the human wolves are damn showoffs," she snickered. "But there is no need, you lovesick fool. We're done."

"All right then," he grunted before letting himself pass out.

CHAPTER THIRTY-EIGHT

"Mara, baby, are you awake?"

Mara groaned weakly, the familiar scents of pine and the ocean breeze fabric softener her family used on the sheets filling her nose.

She was home.

For a second, she wondered how she got there. Was this some hallucination wrought by Henry's magic?

And then she smelled Jack, and she *knew*. Everything was all right.

A warm joy suffused her, making her skin tingle as she stretched under the soft sheets...but she'd be happier with more sleep. Jack would understand. She'd been up for days, or at least it felt that way.

"No," she grumbled good-naturedly after another prod. "Even my blood vessels ache. Wake me up tomorrow."

"Please, kitten," Jack pleaded. "It's been too long since I saw those amazing green eyes looking back at me. Can you open them for me?"

Reluctantly, Mara obeyed...and promptly cracked up. "What the hell happened to you?" she wheezed.

The familiar swear word rolled off her tongue with ease, and some tight spring hidden deep inside her loosened. She snickered again, sharply relieved.

"I would appreciate it if you wouldn't laugh at me," Jack said. "Because it's temporary."

"Why are you *blue?*"

Jack was lying next to her in bed. He wore only a pair of boxer shorts. All the skin above the waistband was a bright shade of silvery blue—somewhere between periwinkle and grey.

"You look like a Smurf." She giggled.

"Trust me, I'm very aware." He leaned back, resting his head on his arm. "As for how, do you remember the part where Henry shot you repeatedly with those hollow-point rounds?"

The image of Henry's broken body flashed in front of her. Shuddering, Mara looked down. Her hands weren't clawed. No trace of blood or tissue remained under her nails. Someone had cleaned her thoroughly.

"Uh, yeah. It's a bit fuzzy, but I recall getting shot. I had no idea the bullets were hollow points."

Jack pulled her to him, kissing her forehead. "The rounds broke open inside you. They were filled with a mix of liquid colloidal and powdered silver. It got into your bloodstream. You were dying."

My old friend—death. She and that bitch needed to have some words, starting with 'come back when I'm a hundred and eighty'...

Her lashes fluttered. "It felt like I was burning up from the inside out."

A shifter could overcome a silver bullet if it didn't hit the heart and someone removed it in time for their preternaturally fast healing to seal the wound. But if what Jack said was true, she'd had liquid *and* powdered silver racing through her bloodstream.

"There would have been no way to remove it," she said, confused. She should be dead.

"There wasn't. Not a surgical way," Jack confirmed. "But there's a magic spell to remove it. Mai called it a transference.

"But the silver needed to go somewhere. Your dad volunteered, of course, but as a human and your mate, I convinced him I should do it." He held up his arms. "I am your mate, by the way. Hope that's not going to be a problem for you."

Mara parted her lips. "I have had some time to come to terms with it."

And happily enough, admitting it didn't make her burst into flames.

He chuckled, nuzzling her. "Good. I thought I was going to have a fight on my hands."

Mara shook her head. "This may be the first time I've ever said this —but I'm kind of done fighting for a while."

"Good." Jack twisted, propping his head upon his folded arm. "So, back to the story of how I got Smurfy. Mai and her sister worked their spell and bing-bang-boom, they successfully transferred all the silver to me.

"This blue is a side effect," he added, holding up his pastel-colored hand. "It's a condition called argyria. It happens when you have too much silver in your body."

She blinked slowly. *Okay, interesting.* "Will it go away? Please say yes."

"Oh, it did," Jack informed her. "The silver from your shots faded pretty quickly. This is from the experiments."

Mara blinked. "Pardon? The what?"

"This is where it gets really weird," Jack warned her. "So, your brother Connell came home with his girl Logan—she's almost as ballsy as you, by the way."

Mara snorted, amused despite herself. She was also deeply gratified that he'd said *almost*. *A mate should find her superior,* she told herself. Even compared to an all-powerful Elemental.

"Connell had been sliced with a silver athame by some high elf because that's shit that happens in this world apparently," Jack said, widening his eyes for emphasis. "The tip had broken off in his arm, but when they went looking for it, the fragment was gone. Logan was worried it was spelled to melt in contact with shifter blood, but Connell seemed fine. Then they spoke to your father, and they figured out the transference spell was still active."

Her head drew back. "It is?"

"Yup." Jack did not seem happy about it. "Connell's silver splinter had disappeared and melted in me, or so Mai hypothesized."

He shrugged. "They figured it was because you two are twins, but they decided to verify."

Jack broke off, smacking his lips. "They had *a lot* of fun figuring this out, first by applying more colloidal silver to a paper cut. Connell feels a little burn, but it dissipates quickly as my body takes it up."

He paused. "And then Derrick had the bright idea to see if it would work on more distant family relationships."

Mara's mouth dropped open. "No!"

"Oh, yes...You don't get this deep a blue with one case of silver poisoning. " Jack waved his arms again. They practically glowed. "I think Sherwin William's calls this particular shade Lobelia. I prefer Pantone's name for it—Air Force blue. That sounds more masculine."

Mara put a hand over her mouth, choking lightly. This straddled the line between hilarious and horrible. "Across how many degrees of separation is the spell active?"

"So far, it's everyone we've checked."

"The *entire* pack?"

"I don't know about that, but we can verify the shifters in the immediate vicinity," he said. "Needless to say, your father loves this new development."

Mara raised a skeptical brow.

"It seems to be consoling him to the fact his future son-in-law is human."

He said it so casually, almost as if he didn't think she would notice. "So now we're getting married?"

Jack grinned. "Well, I'm open to living in sin if that's the werewolf way."

"It's not."

"Then you think we should get married?" He rolled over on his stomach. "Okay, I accept."

Sneaky human. But Mara didn't feel like giving him a hard time about it.

Jack laughed at her expression. "What? You *are* going to marry me," he said, that familiar smug note creeping into his voice.

Mara shrugged. "I don't know. I just spent weeks with a paranormal parasite trying to magic me into being the queen to his king."

Jack's face clouded. "Living in sin it is."

She softened at his downcast expression. "Give me a few weeks and talk to me again."

The clouds disappeared. Jack's normal sunshine smile beamed. It was so captivating that, for a second, she doubted reality.

He smells like Jack. Everything is fine. But her subconscious needed more convincing.

Mara reached out, giving Jack's nipple a hard twist.

"Ow." He laughed and covered the injury with his hand, rubbing it. "What was that for?"

"You were being too charming," she said carefully. "I'm afraid I'm going to react that way for a while whenever you're being too cute."

"*Oh.*" Jack absorbed that philosophically. He shrugged. "Understandable. I will suffer all purple nurples in stoic silence. But try to avoid the family jewels. We want to have children one day."

Mara pressed her lips together. She wasn't sure when exactly it had started, but she *did* love this man, she reminded herself.

"I'm not sure I can think about making babies with a Smurf," she teased. "There has to be a line."

Jack put a blue hand to his heart, pretending to be wounded. "This will clear up in a few weeks, provided everyone stops 'testing' the spell. Personally, I hope that happens soon because I'm pretty sure I'm sunburned now. For a dedicated surfer, it's disgraceful."

He gave his newly pasty legs a forlorn glance.

"I do miss your tan," she admitted.

The golden bronze had covered every inch of his body as if he'd sunbathed nude.

"Don't worry," she said. "No spell lasts forever. My idiot relatives will remember that soon enough." Mainly because she was going to remind them the minute she got out of his bed.

Jack was skeptical. "Yeah, I don't know about that. Your cousins, in particular, seem to be having the time of their lives doing colloidal silver shots."

They were *what*? "All right, that's it," Mara began to sit up. "I'm going to go slap some sense into them."

She'd make sure they wouldn't forget.

"No, don't." Jack put his hand on her chest. "You were right the first time. You need more time to recover. Let me run down and make you an egg and bacon scramble or one of my signature omelets."

"I have to get up," she protested, more dots connecting in her brain.

If she'd been out as long as he said, then a lot could have happened. Mara had to get on top of this. She needed to talk to Derrick to see how much damage had been done.

"There are things you don't know about living here as one of us," she began. "Navigating pack politics is a pain in the ass. We have to show a united front now before some smart ass gets it into his head to challenge you."

"Oh, don't worry, babe." Jack chuckled. "We've burned that bridge already."

"*What?*" Mara sat bolt upright, jostling him and accidentally elbowing him in the gut.

She put a hand on her stomach. Sitting up had stretched the closed bullet hole, the one from London. Since it had been made with silver, it was still there. It didn't hurt, but it itched like crazy.

"It's okay," Jack said, far too nonchalant for comfort. "I got through it fine because it seems I borrow some magic from you. I'm faster, and I heal more quickly than I should. Maybe the rest of the pack, too, at least while the spell is active."

Mara brow creased. She was completely lost.

"It was Derrick's idea," Jack explained. "He decided it would be best to start as we mean to go on. That and they wanted to see if my reflexes were faster since we mated—your father agreed to let us try in a non-lethal challenge."

Her blood ran cold. A non-lethal fight could still do a lot of damage, especially to a human.

"And?" The suspense was killing her.

"They decided Levi should be the one to fight me, since we didn't serve together, and he wouldn't be as inclined to take it easy on me."

That was not good. Levi was brutal in hand-to-hand combat. But except for his blue tint, Jack didn't seem the worse for wear. "Are your reflexes faster?"

"Yes." He grinned. "And not to brag, but I was always better than Levi with a knife. Don't worry. I didn't mess him up too badly. The scar is almost gone. So is mine, by the way, even the bullet wounds."

Jack pointed at four new puckers on his abdomen. "These two are mine from Dublin, from before we found you. This one and this one are yours—part of the transference spell."

He said it in such a cheerful voice Mara wasn't sure she heard him right. "Come again?"

"I caught two slugs while we were searching for you. Here and here," he said, pointing. "And while I heal more rapidly now, I'd like to take a good long break before we test that one cause all this silver might get in the way of the normal healing process."

Mara opened her mouth, but she didn't know what to say. She was out of commission for a couple of days, and the world had turned upside down.

Perhaps a longer rest *was* in order. She lay back down, trying to slow her spinning head.

Jack cuddled against her. "The good news is that your dad isn't as worried about me holding my own or messing with your place in the hierarchy. If anything, I think he's hoping this whole silver repository thing lasts forever. It better not—I miss my tan."

"How is any of that possible?"

Jack was wearing *her* bullet wounds. On top of that, he'd survived a challenge from Levi Jessup. She'd seen Levi in action. That Were was strong, fast, and straight-up dirty in a fight.

"It's a mate thing," Jack said with a shrug. "Or so I've been told."

"Yes, you're my mate," she said slowly. "But it's not official. I haven't claimed you yet."

Jack winced, looking as if he'd been caught with his hand in the cookie jar. "Yeah...about that. Do you remember when I bit you?"

Mara shocked her head. "*No.*"

"Yes."

"But that is not how any of this works," she burst out.

"People keep saying that," Jack snorted softly. "But I think it's how it works now."

Mara collapsed back on the bed. She was right—she needed more time to recover.

"Don't look a gift horse in the mouth," Jack advised. "Especially a magic one."

Suddenly, his eyes lit up. "Oooh. A *magic* one," he said with excitement. Mara put a hand over her eyes. She knew what was coming.

Jack peeled her palm off her face, wide-eyed. "Are Pegasi real?"

Aww... He was so cute that she hated to disappoint him. "I don't think so. Sorry."

"Oh." He was crestfallen, but he wasn't quite ready to give up. "Unicorns?" he asked optimistically.

Mara considered that. There were those horned fae beasts, but they were carnivorous assholes. Thankfully, they tended to stay in Underhill. With luck, Jack would never have occasion to meet one.

"No," she decided.

Jack wrinkled his nose. "Vampires are real but not pegasi or unicorns? That sucks."

Some things couldn't be argued with. Mara patted him on the arm. "I couldn't agree more."

EPILOGUE

Mara stepped out on the porch, lifting her face to the sun. Jack was sleeping off last night's festivities, but being more familiar with pack weddings, she had abstained from the heavy drinking. People had to pace themselves because the party went on for an entire week.

Thomas hailed her from across the clearing. Next to him, the juvenile bear shifter, Joshua Ellis, was putting an old duffel bag in the back of the beat-up pickup truck the pack had bought for Thomas.

She met Thomas near the porch. He and Joshua had been guests of the pack for several months while they recovered from their ordeal, or rather, while Josh did. The bear had made a lot of progress, but he still had a long way to go. The teen remembered everything he had done while under Henry Carrington's influence. He was consumed with guilt and remorse for his actions. Even though he'd never hurt her, he found it difficult to meet her eye.

Almost all the shifters they had rescued were working their way back to health. Filina, the hyena mother, was the worst off, but she showed signs of recovery. Having both her children. David and Jana, and her husband around her was helping.

The humans under Henry's influence were not as fortunate.

Simms, the head guard, and the others under him were more or less fine. Felix Dubois had attempted suicide. Another man, Phillip Tenant, whom Henry had used as a proxy at Denon headquarters, had to be institutionalized.

As far as they knew, Anders Galt was fine, but since the pack's hackers had found evidence of his involvement in the kidnappings, strictly as a middleman, they no longer concerned themselves with him. He was currently in prison for other crimes, the evidence of which had been sent to the FBI by an anonymous source.

The entire Denon corporation was being 'restructured'. A massive SEC investigation was also underway. All their accounts were being audited. Douglas and several other pack alphas were making sure Denon did not survive the investigation.

Carrington Castle and Dublin facility were cleared of all their contents. No trace of the shifter experiments remained. The Barcelona building was razed to the ground, the cat shifter's body returned to her pack. She and Jack had traveled to Aguas Calientes, Mexico for the funeral, the only outsiders who had been invited.

"I thought you were staying for the entire celebration," she said, taking Thomas's hand when he offered it.

"What?" he asked innocently. "I promised I would show you my moves, and I did."

She and Thomas had danced a rather spirited polka, which was his favorite music, after she had shared her first dance as a married woman with her husband and another with her father.

The entire pack had come together to celebrate her bonding to Jack. Some of their relatives had come from as far away as Alaska and Scotland, in addition to the pack members who'd been scattered across the Americas.

It was a testament to Jack's skill and his bravery in her rescue that not a single one made any snide comments about his being human.

Thomas leaned forward. "I was going to stay, but it's too difficult for the kid," he confided with a significant nod at Joshua. "All the extra people in town for your wedding, the noise, and activity—it's all a bit much for him. You understand, right?"

"Of course," she said in a low voice. "But I'm sorry you have to go. I know you were looking forward to it."

Thomas took out a handkerchief, then wiped his brow. "No worries on that score. I had my fill of revelry last night. That was some party. I'm never going to forget the music or that food. I don't think I've ever been to a feast that good."

Mara snickered. "The food had to be extensive, excellent, and plentiful. You've met my relatives."

"I have." He chuckled. "I have to say, you wolves go all out. I wouldn't have thought that given the pack's reputation. You lot are universally painted as grim and badass."

"It's a rep we earned," she confirmed with a nod. "But the pack is in the mood to celebrate—and not only because I'm home and Denon is in its death throes."

Mara looked at the clearing she called home. Above them, high on a ridge, was her brother's house. She and Jack had decided to build one of their own on the opposite side of the clearing so both their homes would look down protectively on the main house.

"Collectively, we've been through a lot in the last year and a half. The pack is eager to blow off some steam and celebrate life," she confided. "Plus, my brother was the last to take a mate. When he bonded with Logan, he didn't have a big celebration—there was no time to plan one before they took off to save the world again."

"Yes, I met Connell and his Elemental mate," Thomas said, his eyes a mix of awe with a healthy dose of fear. He'd tried to hide when he met Logan, but Mara didn't fault him for that. It was a fairly universal and appropriate reaction. "I'm just glad you're around to save the rest of us," he added.

"I had help," she said with a laugh.

"Oh." Thomas patted down his pockets. He withdrew a photo. "I meant to show this to you earlier—it's about the skeleton you found in the trunk."

Mara nodded. They had questioned the other fugitives and house staff to see if anyone had known anything about the poor child, but they'd come up empty.

"I was talking to your people about it, and they had found this at the house."

Mara took the picture. It showed a young boy dressed in tweed, who was seated in a wheelchair. Another boy, this one a little younger, stood next to him. There was a disparity in dress, with the boy standing being dressed more shabbily, but the pair were obviously related.

"It was Henry's brother in the trunk," she said in realization.

"Actually, according to your people, this *is* Henry Carrington," he said, pointing to the boy in the wheelchair. "And he is the boy in the trunk."

Mara's head was starting to hurt. Maybe she should have said no to that third cup of wine last night. "Then who is the other child?"

"One of your wolves said it was Reuben Wilson—the son of one of the maids."

What? "They have to be brothers," she said, examining the photo again. The boys had remarkably similar features, although the one in the chair was thinner and more drawn. But aside from his infirmity and the slight age difference, they could have been twins.

"Your packmate said they were probably half-brothers. In all likelihood, they have the same father—Samuel Carrington, the former baron."

"So, Henry wasn't Henry," she said. "He was Reuben."

"Looks that way," Thomas said. "But it's unclear who did the original Henry in. My money is on Samuel Carrington. He lived to be seventy. He only died a decade or so ago. Long after the boy was put in the trunk."

Mara agreed. He must have known. But did he kill the sick boy to replace him with the healthy one, or did he have his illegitimate son assume his heir's place after the boy passed?

A thorough investigation could answer those questions, but Mara wasn't sure she cared to learn the truth.

"Whether he was Henry or Reuben doesn't matter anymore. He's gone. Our only remaining concern is to fix the mess he made," she said, looking back at Joshua. "The rest is a footnote. We have lives to get back to."

Thomas nodded in approval, tucking the photo back in his pocket. "Well said."

Mara threw an arm around him, walking him to his truck. "You're welcome to come back anytime."

The old cougar smiled. "I may take you up on that. But first, there are some old haunts I'd like to see again. That should take a while…"

"What about the boy?" she asked as Joshua saw them coming. He climbed in the passenger seat after nodding respectfully. "He knows he can come back, too, right?"

"Yeah, course he does. And maybe he will someday, but, for now, he's gonna wander with me, unless we find his people."

The boy's immediate family was gone. That much they knew. But for now, Joshua was content to go with Thomas, rather than applying for entry into the larger bear shifter packs in Alaska or Russia.

Thomas gave her another hug, kissing her on both cheeks. "I'll say goodbye now, but I will check in to update you on the boy and to find out how the others are doing."

He nodded at the porch. "In the meantime, enjoy yourselves. I expect to hear about lots of new adventures the next time I come around."

Mara twisted at the waist to glance back at the main house. Jack was pulling on a t-shirt, the front door closing behind him.

"I should be surprised he's already up and around after your cousins challenged him to that drinking contest, but that particular human can hold his own."

She grinned. "Yes, he can."

Thomas put on a hat. He touched the brim in salute before getting into his truck and driving away.

Mara turned back to the house. Jack met her halfway. It felt symbolic.

He wrapped his arms around her. "Are you okay?" he asked.

She leaned up on her tiptoes to press a kiss to his cheek. "I'm great. The question is, how are you?"

"Mating has its privileges." His grin was devilish. "I'm ready to do it again."

"Good." She laughed as Derrick, Levy, and Nathan appeared at the edge of the clearing. They had just come back from a run. "Because I think you are going to have to."

"Don't worry. I can take anything those guys can dish out," he assured her before his impossibly handsome face sobered. "At least, I can as long as you're with me. Mates are for life, right?"

"Yes." Mara leaned into his embrace, savoring the warmth and touch of his newly restored golden skin against her cheek. "Mates are for life."

The End

ABOUT THE AUTHOR

L.B. Gilbert is another name for USA Today Bestselling Author Lucy Leroux.

L.B. spent years getting degrees from the most prestigious universities in America, including a PhD that she is not using at all. She moved to France for work and found love. She's married now and has a polyglot 5 year old. The family moved back to California a few years ago.

She has always enjoyed reading books as far from her reality as possible but eventually the voices in her head told her to write her own. So far the voices are enjoying them. And judging by the awards, a few other people are as well. You can check out the geeky things she likes on Twitter or Facebook.

If you like a little more steam with your Fire, check out the author's award-winning Lucy Leroux titles, FREE to read on Kindle Unlimited

www.elementalauthor.com
or
www.authorlucyleroux.com

facebook.com/lucythenovelist
twitter.com/lucythenovelist
instagram.com/lucythenovelist

Printed in Great Britain
by Amazon

87694087R00153